Fool Me Twice

LIZZIE MORTON

Bex – For daring me to be different.

Prologue

Britney 18 years old

I quickly open my bag to pull out my lunch. Something feels off as I stare down inside at the contents. I sit and blink, trying to put my finger on what it is, and then it hits me. I've forgotten my gym kit, the same gym kit I need for my next class. *Damn it.* This is the third time I've forgotten it this semester. I'm screwing up left, right, and center. Nobody would blame me, but still ... I need to do some damage control. I'm burning through my free passes, and I can't afford to run out.

I give the measly lunch package in my bag a longing look, not that it deserves it. It consists of a sandwich made with five-day-old bread I had to pick the mold off and half a granola bar I salvaged from the floor, next to where my mom was passed out on the couch. It's the first thing I'll have eaten all day and my stomach groans painfully.

I sigh and close my bag. Food will have to wait.

The woman sitting at the desk in the school office gives me a disdainful look when I explain why I need to leave. *Whatever.* She's the least of my worries and if I stand a chance of getting home and back before next period, I can't mess around.

7

Outside, I pull out my cell and try one last time to get in touch with Ross. It goes straight to voicemail. Helpful ... *not*.

Time is ticking away.

I'd sprint, but my shitty sneakers have no cushioning, and the last time I had to run in them I was hobbling for days. I opt for power walking as fast as I can. I cannot get detention. I have a shift at the diner tonight and the paycheck is the only thing keeping a roof over our heads, and the meals that are few and far between, on the table.

This would all have been easier if Ross had just answered his cellphone. I know he had a couple of free periods and could have run home to grab my stuff, that's if I'd been able to get in touch with him. When I reach our apartment, I unlock the door and rush to my room, grabbing my gym kit off the bed that I stupidly forgot to pack.

I hear a noise. A groan.

I stop in my tracks and listen for a few seconds. Nothing. I must have been hearing things. I'm about to turn and leave, when I hear it again. This time a moan accompanies the groan. It's louder and I know it's not my imagination. The smart thing would be to call out, warn whoever is in the apartment that I'm here. With Mom, you never know who she could have let through the door. But I'm too focused on finding out what is going on.

I should walk away and ignore it, but I don't.

Tiptoeing into the living area, my eyes flicker to the couch where Mom was out cold when I left this morning. She's not there. I walk quietly to her room, a task that should be easy, but proves difficult—each time I lift a foot my shoe sticks to the carpet and I struggle not to fall. The door is ajar, and the noises get louder the closer I get.

8

When I push the door open, I stop.

If my world hadn't fallen apart years ago, this would do it.

Dumbfounded, I watch as Ross, my childhood sweetheart and the only person I thought was left in my life who I could trust, groans while my mom sits on top of him, riding him like she's auditioning for a porn movie.

I clap a hand over my mouth, trying to stifle the gasp that comes out. It's wasted effort on my part, because on the floor are two syringes and a tourniquet. I could make all the noise in the world—they're both too high to care.

I want to look away, but I'm transfixed. It wasn't enough that she fucked up her life, she had to go and destroy the only good thing I had going in mine. Nausea hits when I back away.

I'm done.

I run to my room and shove what little belongings I have left—the ones I haven't already had to sell—into a bag. Without so much as a backward glance, I storm out of the apartment, leaving my pathetic excuse of a life behind.

One

Britney 6 years later

"**B**ritney! Into my office ... now!" Fiona screeches across the room.

Staring at the screen of my laptop, I grimace. *Again?*

I purposefully fly under her radar. All I want is to get on with my job in peace. Despite my best efforts, I keep getting dragged into 'projects' that are anything but peaceful. I've learned the hard way that gossip doesn't appear out of nowhere, and I work for the most raucous gossip magazine in the country. I've worked here for a little over a year and it's safe to say I've hated every minute.

"Be right there," I chime over my shoulder, being careful not to let her see my face.

"Leigh, you too!" she screeches again, as if we're not all squashed together in a room like sardines.

Leigh, at the desk two over from me, sighs. Everyone knows when you get called into Fiona's office, it's bad news ... excuse the pun.

I *hate* this. I worked my ass off to get into college, managed to achieve a scholarship with no support behind me, and this is where I've found myself after years of hard work. If I could be anywhere but here, I

10

would. Unfortunately, I have no choice. Firstly, there's a nice backlog of college fees hanging over me, but they're the least of my worries. When Mom disappeared off the grid not long after I walked out, she still owed a lot of people money. Like *a lot* of money, to the kind of people who don't let debts slide. They couldn't find her, but they found me, thanks to my name being added to our final rental contract when I turned eighteen.

So, now, I work for the devil.

I spend my days chasing celebrities, watching their every move, trying to get the latest scoop. We sell their mistakes and obliterate any hope they might have for a bit of normality. Each time I write an article, I can't shake the feeling that one day this is all going to come back and bite me in the ass. Karma is coming, I just know it.

Saving the piece I've been working on about some lame middle-aged guy sleeping with the nanny, I reluctantly head to Fiona's office to find out what she wants. When I arrive, Leigh is already settled in the only chair available. I'm left standing awkwardly at her side waiting for Fiona to reveal what delightful project she has in store for us next. Twiddling my hands in front of me, my eyes flicker to the wall behind where Fiona is sitting. It's filled with framed covers of some of the magazine's best-selling issues. The issues in which we've done our worst.

"I have a new project for you," Fiona says, as if we're going to be creating a masterpiece, building something great, changing the world. Not destroying someone's life.

Biting on my cheek, it takes everything in me to keep my expression pleasant.

"There's a rumor that the NFL player Becket is having problems with his girlfriend," Fiona continues.

"I hate to break it to you ..." says Leigh, tossing her fiery red hair over her shoulder, "that's not exactly gossip. It's also not surprising considering what a prick he is. And he's boring. He puts the straight in strait-laced."

I remain standing quietly as Fiona narrows her eyes at Leigh. "I'm perfectly aware of that. Which is why you are both here. As I was saying ... there's a rumor circling that he's having issues with his girlfriend and apparently, he is on his way to the city. Someone saw him checking in for a flight to New York from Florida and posted the photo on Instagram. I want you to follow him when he gets here—get whatever scoop you can. This could be big."

Brazenly, Leigh responds, "If we do *whatever it takes*, what do we get in return? I'm assuming this might be a little out of our pay grade?"

Fiona pauses before replying and I wonder if for once, Leigh has pushed her luck too far. "A bonus and a step up the ladder. How does that sound?"

Leigh's mouth drops open. "All for Becket the Bore?"

My eyes dart back and forth between them, I daren't say a word, afraid that if I do, she might change her mind. The worst part about the crap she has us do: the pay isn't worth it. It's still more than I'd get in most other jobs at this level. Even in a city as big as New York, jobs like this are hard to come by. The offer she's put on the table could finally make all this worthwhile, it could be a chance to move away from doing this crap *and* pay off a large chunk of my debts.

Fiona leans back in her seat, looking bored. "It's been a long time since there's been an NFL scandal. The best ones are unexpected. I want us to be the first ones reporting when it comes out and there's only one way to make sure we are ..."

"How can we?" I ask. "It's never a given."

Leigh looks up at me and rolls her eyes. I feel like even more of an idiot, but unlike to her, all this stuff doesn't come naturally to me.

"We make sure we're there when it happens—that we know about it before everyone else," Leigh says.

I still don't quite get what it is they're both suggesting. "You sound so certain. What if there's no dirt to dig up and what if there's no scandal?" I ask.

Leigh and Fiona look at each other with amused expressions.

Fiona replies, "If there's no scandal to be found ... you make one."

***

"I can't believe we're stuck doing her dirty work again," I say bitterly, scrolling through page after page on the internet, familiarizing myself with the life of *The Great Michael Becket*.

Leigh's right, he's as boring as they come. His girlfriend, his stats—perfect. He's a shining star in the NFL as far as his performance is concerned. But it's like someone went through Google and deleted anything that would give him any character or depth. He has no past. The best I can find are articles about him saying the wrong thing or being a hot head on the field.

Basically, when he's not running the perfect play ... he's an asshole.

It's the images that really capture my attention. Page after page, thousands of them. The one thing

13

they all have in common: his eyes. A glimmer of emerald reaching out to me in every single one. But there's something there. Even in the most unclear ones, I can see something is amiss. There's a darkness battling the light in his eyes, and I want to know why.

Leigh spins around in her desk chair. It's late and everyone, including Fiona, has gone home for the day. Now, it's just us left, trying to figure out how we're going to magic up some scoop. I've come up with nothing, I never do, because unlike the redhead next to me, I don't thrive off being deceitful.

"Suck it up," she says. "There's a promotion on the cards and I won't let you mess this up for me." Her expression is cold. She's ruthless and would do anything to move up the career ladder, if you can even call what we're doing a career. An alert flashes on her screen and she turns back quickly to see what it is. She sits quietly reading, then shouts out loud, "Yes!"

"Care to share?" I ask.

"There's a forum we use sometimes when we need a scoop on people." She begins scribbling on a scrap of paper.

"And?"

"And somebody has just responded, saying they have details on Becket. Where he's going to be et cetera."

I stare at her in disbelief as she grabs her bag and stands up.

Before leaving, she looks at me and asks, "What?"

"Never mind the fact you're going to trust a random stranger, but you're going to meet with them too?"

She rolls her eyes, something she does a lot of whenever we work together. "The forum is legit. I use it all the time. This is how we play the game, but you wouldn't know because you never get your hands dirty."

"Huh, I'd say the opposite. So, what's the plan?"

"You wait here. I'll be twenty minutes, max. They're meeting me outside."

She doesn't wait for me to respond or acknowledge that I'm happy to do so, simply bustles out of the office. I now have another person who thinks they can walk all over me. Great.

True to her word she walks back twenty minutes later with a smug look on her face.

"So?"

"So, our source is freakin' amazing! They know everything about him. We don't need to do anything but turn up where he says."

"You're not worried that this person knows Becket's every move?"

She throws her head back and laughs. "No. It makes our jobs easier. Stop overthinking it and just play the game, Britney. We follow him, catch him doing something newsworthy, and it's a job done. Although some interference might be necessary."

My stomach twists. "What do you mean interference?"

She slides open her desk drawer, grabs something, then holds a packet of little white pills in the air.

"What the fuck, Leigh?" I hiss, then smack her hand down in case anyone is lingering in the office who could see and report us. "Are you trying to get us fired?"

"Chill out," she huffs. "It's nothing they haven't seen before. How do you think we get so many good stories?" I watch as she slides the packet back into her drawer.

I shake my head. "What are you talking about? And why are you not putting them in your bag?"

"How do you think we always get the best gossip? Don't tell me you think it's all a coincidence? It's all set up. People here do what needs to be done. And I'm not putting the pills in my bag, because I can't exactly walk on a plane with drugs ..."

"Then where are you going to get them from when we touch down in Jacksonville?"

"Our source." She rolls her eyes again as if she can't believe the questions I'm asking her.

It comes out as almost a squeak when I say, "You're going to take drugs off a stranger?"

"Come on, Britney. Whoever you get drugs from is a stranger. Fact."

"So, we're just going to drug Becket? That's the plan?" I scoff.

"No. Not if we don't have to. Just go with the flow and let's see what happens. If we come up with nothing then we do as Fiona said: we make our own story. And something like this is what's going to help us along."

She waves the packet in front of my face again, taunting me, and I wonder exactly how deep I'm about to sink.

***

"Are you sure your source got it right?" I ask Leigh.

We're standing in the departure area of JFK airport, in the same spot we've been for the past hour, waiting for Becket to show up and check-in for a flight back to Florida. We followed him all day yesterday after Leigh's source informed us he was at Coney Island. Things between him and his girlfriend turned sour, and he stormed off. Thanks to it being packed with people celebrating the Fourth of July we were unable to follow him any further.

We thought we had royally screwed up, until Leigh received a message saying he had checked into a hotel in Manhattan for the night. The same source got in touch earlier today, informing us Becket had booked a flight out of New York. So, here we are. I keep trying to stamp down the feelings of unease that there's someone out there following his every move, even more so than we are. It's creepy as fuck but there's nothing I can do. I need this promotion, this money.

Leigh crosses her arms over her chest and frowns, looking around the crowds trying to spot him. "Stop bitching at me. I'm certain. And before you ask again, my source is reliable."

I grind my teeth, trying not to bite back. If we start arguing, we're going to draw attention to ourselves and we can't screw up again. Images of Leigh pulling out a sachet of white pills flash through my mind. "Did you bring that stuff with you?" My eyes dart around nervously.

She shakes her head. "Seriously, you need to calm down. You look shifty and if you keep it up, we're going to have security on our case."

"Do you blame me for asking?" I whisper. "Two days ago, you were waving drugs in my face. I don't know what to expect with you anymore."

"Yes, but I'm not an idiot. Give me some credit. You know what the plan is. Tease him on the flight, make him want you, then go for a drink together. I'll pick up the supply from the source when we land in Florida, then sneak it to you the first chance we get. You slip it in his drink and the rest is easy."

"The source is now going to be in Florida too. Who the hell is this guy?"

"Honestly, Britney, if you're not up to this then leave it to me, but you're definitely more his type. You scream ball bunny."

I want to slap her. Instead, I narrow my eyes and say, "Its fine, I can do it."

"You're sure? Forget the promotion—if you fuck this up, both our jobs will be on the line."

I nod. "I can do it."

A tall figure in the distance catches my attention. "Is that him?" I ask.

Leigh turns and her face lights up when she sees him. "I told you he'd be here."

With his cap pulled down low, his only recognizable feature is the strands of sandy colored hair peeking free. We don't need to look directly at him. The women passing by as they appreciate his broad frame, and the men trying to not so subtly take photos of one of the best players in the league, tell us what we need to know: it's him.

He turns in our direction and I suck in a sharp breath. Of course, Leigh doesn't miss my reaction to him, she never misses a thing.

"Not hating the job now, are you? There are worse things you could have to do than throw yourself at an NFL player. Just remember, this is work. It's a two-hour flight. Don't go falling for the guy."

"I get it, ok." I shrug her off and stand watching his retreating form as he moves through airport security.

Before we part and make our way to the plane separately, I repeat to myself what the plan involves. She's right, it's easy. Unfortunately, what isn't so easy is getting my heart rate under control as the image of him glancing up from under his ball cap firmly imprints itself in my mind.

18

Two

Britney

You can do this, I tell myself, watching Becket from a distance. He's sitting waiting to board the plane at the departure gate. He doesn't look like the asshole I imagined him to be, he looks hurt, broken. My heart tugs. Get it together, Brit. I bustle forwards, making sure to catch his attention. He looks up in my direction. *Bingo.*

A voice from a speaker overhead announces it's time to board the flight. Becket's gaze breaks and he looks away from me. He probably thinks he won't see me again. Wrong.

Luck was on our side. The flight only had a couple of seats left. Thankfully, none of them were above economy, otherwise, Fiona would have gone berserk over the cost. Whatever it takes unless it costs a lot of money. My seat is conveniently next to Becket's. Coincidence? No. Another prime example of Leigh's skills when it comes to this job, and how far she's willing to take things to get the scoop.

Becket stands, picking up his bag and then gets in line to get on the plane. I walk over and join the line further down, so as not to make it too obvious I'm following him. I take a deep breath, it's game time.

19

"Excuse me. Sorry, sir. Excuse me," I say sweetly as I move along the center aisle.

I can see Becket sitting a few rows up from where I'm standing. The cap on his head is the only discreet part of him—he's well over a head taller than the rest of the people around us. Fleetingly, he looks up and his eyes find mine. Just as quickly he looks away. That's until his luck runs out and I stop at his row.

"Sorry. I need to get to my seat."

"No problem," he drawls out, a smirk on his face.

This is the asshole I expected.

He stands and I move past him to my seat, making sure my body brushes against his as I do. He freezes from the contact and when I look down, the bulge in his pants tells me everything I need to know. Pretending I'm none the wiser to his body's reaction to mine, I go about settling in my seat. He's still standing stock still, staring straight ahead. The bulge in his pants is now in my direct eye line.

Trying to ignore it, I look up at him and say, "Do you want the window seat?"

He shakes his head and looks down at me. His nostrils flare as he snaps, "I'm fine. I don't like the window seat."

Fluttering my eyelashes, I reply, "Everyone loves the window seat ..."

"Not when it involves looking at New York City."

Not quite the answer I was expecting. New York is one of the most exciting cities in the world. What can he hate so much about a city everybody loves? I'm about to ask when I remember I have a job to do.

I raise an eyebrow. "Who shat on your parade?"

Internally I cringe at the words that have just spilled out of my mouth. They're not part of the plan, Brit. I'm meant to be wooing him not pissing him off. It's instinctive. I'm merely reacting to the few words

20

he's shared and his body language, which has alarm bells ringing. He's brash and standoffish, like he couldn't care less about the person sitting next to him. The only person he appears to care about is himself.

He's an asshole basically. Just like the media says.

"Nobody," he sighs.

He's back to looking defeated and my heart flutters. I don't know how to take him. One second, he's hot, the next, he's cold. We've not been together more than a few minutes. The flight is over one hundred and twenty. I'm screwed.

I watch as he sits down slowly, not missing the way he shifts his crotch region away. Unfortunately for him, I've already seen the evidence of his face value attraction to me. He rests his head back against his seat and closes his eyes, very obviously wanting to go to sleep. Sorry Becket, that's not part of the plan. I can't woo you if you're unconscious.

"So ..." I say bright eyed.

He ignores me and blatantly fakes being asleep. Nobody dozes off that fast.

"I know you're awake," I say, unable to hide the smile in my voice.

He opens one eye and looks at me. "Are you always this perky?"

He *did not* just describe me as perky. I bite back a snarky response, trying to remember the point of all this. "I'm not perky, just friendly," I reply. "Are you always this grumpy after a breakup?" The words are out of my mouth before I can stop them.

His other eye flicks open. "I never told you I'd broken up with someone."

Think on your feet, Brit. I roll my eyes, making it appear as though I couldn't care less whether he'd broken up with someone or not. "It's obvious," I say.

"Nobody hates New York that much, not unless someone's made them feel that way. I simply figured out the obvious."

He frowns, before closing his eyes and grumbling, "Whatever."

Another few minutes of back and forth, not very chatty, chit chat pass by before I try and push for more information.

"So, you did break up with someone," I say, after he almost bites my head off informing me, he's had the worst twenty-four hours of his life. A little dramatic if you ask me.

"That's none of your business."

My instant reaction is to narrow my eyes, but then remembering what the plan is, I plaster on the sweetest smile I can manage. We hold eye contact for a few seconds and my heart feels like it's about to burst out of my chest. When it becomes unbearable, we both look away.

"I'm Britney." It's the first genuine thing I've said since we met.

Of course, this is what sets him off. "How fitting," he says.

I frown. "What's that supposed to mean?"

He shrugs. "Well, you know ..."

He is not about to go there. He can't be that much of an ass, surely. "No, I'm afraid I don't," I reply, shaking my head.

"It's fitting you'd be named after a crazy-ass celeb. Psycho comes to mind."

Do not lose your cool, I tell myself. I never expected the articles about his unlikeable personality to be true. Well, if that's the way he wants to play it, then I'll give him a reason to think I'm crazy. It's like flicking on a light switch and tears begin to well in my eyes.

"Excuse me?" I make sure my voice comes out strangled, as if I'm in physical pain by the comment he's made. "You think I'm a psycho?" I throw in an extra snivel just for good measure.

That's all it takes for him to start backtracking. "Maybe not *psycho* per se, but you're definitely some level of crazy."

So much for an apology. He really is a douche. I need time to rethink my plan, so rather than responding, I ignore him and turn to look out the window. I silently say goodbye to New York as the ground below disappears.

***

We're being thrown around in our seats and all I can think is that I'm too young to die. Turbulence, that's what the Captain informed us this was. Yeah, right. What a nice way of putting it, when really, we're plummeting to Earth, about to cross over to the other side. I'm paralyzed by fear, which is the only thing stopping me from getting down on my knees, making the sign of the cross and praying to God. Becket meanwhile is drowning his sorrows in the vast amount of Scotch he ordered earlier.

"Here," he says, passing me one of the last two remaining glasses.

I catch his eye in the dim emergency lighting, and suddenly it's like I'm stuck in a trance. Each time we make eye contact it gets worse. It feels like the world stops. Not a bad thing when for us, it most likely is about to come to an end, it's a welcome distraction.

He places the glass in my hand, breaking the moment.

Quietly, I reply, "Thanks." I'm not thankful. I despise Scotch. Especially the smell. But I'm not about to open that can of worms. Right now, it's irrelevant.

I raise the glass to my lips, about to down another drink of the thing I hate the most, when Becket places a hand on my wrist. I look at him confused as the plane rumbles, watching as he raises his own glass in the air.

"To the end," he toasts.

Talk about morbid. I knock the drink back at the same time he does.

"I broke up with my girlfriend of four years."

I nearly choke on the drink.

The plane drops a few feet, and my stomach goes with it. I close my eyes and grip the seat so hard I'm surprised my nails don't pull away from my skin. What I don't expect is for Becket to carry on talking. Of course, in the moment we're about to die, he chooses to become almost likeable, as he relays the events of the day before his breakup with Abby. He's totally unaware of the fact that I'm here and witnessing it all with my own two eyes.

The plane lurches again.

"Shit!" I squeak, squeezing my eyes shut as tight as I can. I don't want to see the end.

"I'm not the perfect athlete everyone thinks I am."

I open one eye and look at him side-on.

"I once did drugs."

He's telling me his secrets as a distraction. He's handing over everything I need to ruin his future on a plate. Ironically, I don't need any of this now—the disastrous plane ride is going to do the job for me.

He carries on speaking for a while, and I sit and listen. Focusing on his voice, instead of our impending doom.

When he stops speaking, I take a deep breath and reveal a secret of my own. "I hate my job."

He chuckles. "Who doesn't hate their job?"

I stare straight ahead, not wanting to look at him when I say, "No seriously, I detest it. It's the worst job I could have chosen. I have to do things I hate, but I have no choice." Like screwing you over, even though I have a strong suspicion you're not the asshole everyone thinks you are.

"I was charged with assault as a kid."

My head whips around and I'm drawn into emerald eyes. He's told me a couple of his secrets but this—it's the kind of thing that could blow up his NFL career. This is exactly the kind of thing Fiona wanted me to get. Dirt. The question is, can I do it? Can I screw him over? Especially when he's looking at me in such a way that I'm ready to tell him the real reason why I'm on this plane.

I don't know what to do or say, but I have to do something. I'm too close to the end to mess all this up.

"I'm a virgin!"

Becket stares at me dumbfounded. With excellent timing the plane plunges downwards and I'm at serious risk of puking everywhere. We're going to die.

The next thing I know, Becket's lips are on mine, hot and urgent. This time I'm frozen for completely different reasons; forgetting where we are, what's happening, who I am. He pulls away, but I remain still with my eyes closed, wanting to stay in whatever brief moment of bliss that was, away from reality.

The plane dips again and people scream all around us. I'm not scared any more though, because Becket is back kissing away the fear. The guy, I'm meant to be tearing apart, is holding me together.

The minutes pass and I allow him to keep kissing me. I don't feel calmer, quite the opposite; he's sparked a fire that burnt out years ago. We're so absorbed in one another, we don't even notice that the turbulence we were sure was going to result in the plane crashing, has come to an end. The emergency lights go out and the cabin is illuminated once more. We slowly pull away from each other and Becket looks away, assessing what is going on further down the cabin.

Overhead the speaker crackles and the Captain informs us again of what's happened, just in case we hadn't been aware. I block everything out, staring straight ahead at the seat in front of me, trying to make sense of what I'm feeling. I look at him out of the corner of my eye, drinking in each part of his solid frame. This was exactly what wasn't meant to happen. This wasn't part of the plan.

I've screwed up and now I have to screw him over.

I don't know if I can do it.

The way he's continuing to be so nice doesn't help. I feel like I'm sitting next to a completely different person and it's unsettling. I like this nice side of him, and I can't. He shouldn't be around me. I'm no good for him.

Becket pulls an odd face when I say, "Listen ..."

I'm ready for walking away from this whole ridiculous scenario. I never wanted to be a part of this to begin with. Us parting ways is for the best.

He holds up his hands before I can say anything else. "No hard feelings. We were caught up in the moment. Let's leave it at that," his voice lacks confidence, but I hear what I want to, because I need to.

I can't let my mind believe otherwise.

I swallow over the lump in my throat at the same time relief washes over me. I feel put out at the thought the kiss may not have meant as much to him, but at the same time I'm relieved he's given me an out. He's made it easy for me not to do this.

My gaze flickers down the plane and I see Leigh looking back at us from her seat. She looks as frazzled as I feel. It serves her right for putting us in this position. She stares directly at me, eyes narrowed. She's not going to let me get away with leaving things like this. She's the reminder I need. If we do this and it works, I can pay off my debts, put my past behind me and untie myself from her and Fiona. From my mom. I might finally feel like I'm free. That's why, even though every part of me is screaming for me not to, telling me that it's wrong to do this, I plaster on a smile. When I turn back to Becket, he's looking at me like I'm crazy again. I don't blame him. With my rapid change in moods, I can't keep up with myself.

"What are you doing when we land?" I ask.

He frowns and answers, "After that ... I need a strong drink, or ten. So, I'll be heading straight to a bar. You?"

Once again, he's making this all too easy. "Maybe I could join you?" Say no, Becket.

But he doesn't. Even though I want him to. After some persistence on my part, he backs down and agrees to go for a drink with me.

It's the worst decision he'll ever make.

Three

Britney

The cab screeches to a halt right outside the bar that Becket reeled off to the driver. Quickly looking out the window, I can see Leigh in the distance, with a tall figure in a hooded black jacket. I can't make them out as they have their back to me, but I don't need to see them clearly to know they're The Source. They should have been done by now. I watch as Becket pulls out a wad of cash at the same time Leigh starts to walk along the sidewalk. She needs a few more seconds for the transition to work, so I put up some resistance about splitting the cab fare.

When Becket refuses and Leigh gets closer, I back down and say, "Fine. First round is on me."

We step out of the cab and Becket moves around to the trunk. At the exact moment, his attention is focused on popping it open and retrieving our luggage, Leigh sweeps past me, slipping a small sachet into my palm. The transition is seamless, and she carries on walking, no doubt in the direction of the private hire car she booked. Becket's none the wiser to what has just happened, of what is going to happen to him. He also doesn't notice when I order

28

the drinks and slip a pill into one of his when the bartender is distracted serving someone else.

And now … we're here.

I've been standing, staring in the mirror for a few minutes, wondering if I have it in me to follow through with what I'm about to do. My grip on the situation is loosening, and as it does, the potential for things to go wrong increases. I read somewhere once that you should never have regrets. Everything happens for a reason. Everything you do and feel should have a purpose. But I have regrets and one of them goes by the name of Michael Becket.

I'm pulled quickly from my thoughts, flinching when the door to the restroom flies open and slams against the wall so hard that I'm surprised the tiles don't crack.

"What do you think you're doing?" I exclaim, spinning around from the washbasin.

There he is, all six-foot four inches, with his sandy blond hair and striking green eyes, filling the doorway, swaying slightly on his feet. "You."

He's an asshole through and through. I knew this from the start. But there's something about him, something more. He's the NFL player everybody loves to hate. But tonight, on the plane ride from New York to Florida, something happened that changed how I thought about him. When we thought our lives were coming to an end, he let me in and showed me more. He showed me there's more to The Great Becket than meets the eye and that I shouldn't judge this book by its cover. It's a shame that those secrets he divulged, the ones that made me feel differently about him, are what I have to use against him.

He stalks in, not bothering to lock the door behind him or check if there's anyone else in the room. It's so typically him. The few hours of knowing him have been a rollercoaster. I've jumped between disliking everything about him, to wanting to rip his clothes off and do things I've never wanted to do with anyone else.

Before my brain has time to catch up with what's happening, he's in front of me, grabbing at my waist and pulling me towards him. My head tells me to stop, walk away and leave this night behind before the chaos begins. I still have time to back out, but my body has other ideas and I'm putty in his hands. I ignore the part of my brain telling me to resist. Shut it off and kiss him back. If I'm going down, I may as well enjoy myself.

I'm probably the most inexperienced woman Becket's ever been with, but when I'm flush against him and can feel his body responding to mine, I swallow down the nerves bubbling near the surface. It's clear from his body's reaction that he wants me as much as I want him.

I want to remind him that I'm a virgin. The secret I revealed, the only real part of me I let him see. Tonight has been full of slip ups, one after another. I'm left feeling confused and frustrated. It's no wonder when Becket kisses like he does. Sparks fire through every part of my body each time he touches me.

My cell vibrates in the back pocket of my jeans, bringing me back down to earth, almost. Play the game—you didn't come here to lose your V-card to some superstar NFL player. Stick to the plan. I repeat it all over and over, but it's getting harder to hear my own thoughts. Scrap that, I'm not even trying to hear them, because I simply don't want to.

His focus begins to waiver, but his hands continue roaming, even though their movement isn't as fluid. They find their way to my ass, lifting me up onto the countertop. I respond the way I know he wants, wrapping my legs around his waist, encouraging him to continue and lose himself in the moment. The force behind his kisses lessens and I know it won't be much longer. The sleepy stage should come next, and it should be progressive. That's what Leigh told me. But when his kisses stop abruptly and he face plants my chest, I know something isn't right.

"Damn it," I say to myself because Becket is now out cold.

I'm stuck on the countertop of a washbasin, in a public restroom, with one of the biggest NFL players in the country pressed against my chest, with no idea how I'm going to move him. For some this might be a dream come true, all you need to do is look at him to understand why. He's a ball-playing God who looks like he's crafted from the Greek variety. For me, this is a logistical nightmare.

My cell vibrates again, reminding me I'm stuck when I should already be making my way out of the bar. Lifting one butt cheek, I manage to maneuver myself in such a way that I'm able to slip my cell from my pocket. Quickly looking at the screen, I see two messages from Leigh, who is waiting for me in a car close by. I don't bother reading the messages she's sent. Instead, I pull up her caller ID, hit the green call button and place it on loudspeaker.

It rings three times, before she answers, "Is it done?"

"We may have hit a slight snag," I reply awkwardly.

"Why do you sound so weird?"

"Come into the bar. I'm in the restroom."

With excellent timing Becket lets out a loud groan.

"Wait … was that Becket? Why can't you just come out? Is it done?" she asks again.

31

I grind my teeth trying not to lose my patience. Pretty soon someone is going to come in and find me in here with Becket's face glued to my chest. I'll have to come up with a completely unbelievable explanation to what is going on.

"Just come quickly. We don't have time for this," I say.

She grumbles that she should have done this herself and then something to do with hating working with rookies. She then hangs up.

Waiting, I try my best to stay still, so we don't end up tumbling to the floor. Creating a media shit storm is one thing, injuring him when his body is no doubt insured for millions is another.

A deep snore fills the silence of the room. His drool trickling down my chest in between my breasts and heading south nearly tips me over the edge. "You've got to be kidding me. Gross," I mumble.

There's a hesitant knock on the restroom door. I know it's Leigh, but if she's trying to act inconspicuous, she's doing a crappy job. Why would anyone knock on the door of a public restroom?

It feels ridiculous, but I shout, "Come in."

The door opens slowly, and I let out a sigh of relief as fiery red hair bobs through. I never thought I'd be so relieved to see *her*. We rarely see eye to eye, we're not a good fit, but seeing her is a relief, nonetheless. "This is ... different." She smirks. "So which part of the plan was this?"

I roll my eyes at her sarcasm. "I did exactly what we planned. Maybe you should have done it yourself."

She moves in closer, then leans down and her eyes roam over his lifeless form narrowing to slits. She bites at her lower lip and tilts her head to one side. "How much did you give him?" she asks.

"Everything you gave me. Like you said to."

Her eyebrows pinch together. "Something isn't right."

"No shit." If I didn't have Becket glued to me, I'd throw my hands over my head and yell.

"He's supposed to be sleepy, not out cold ..."

"I'm going to point out the obvious here: maybe you shouldn't have trusted a random source to supply you with drugs," I say through clenched teeth.

She rolls her eyes and waves me off. "Maybe he's just reacted to it badly. Some people do."

"Or it's been tampered with. Are you even certain about what we've given him?"

"Shh!" she hisses, as if somebody hearing us is our biggest worry, not that we've monumentally screwed up.

"We could kill the guy." My heart is racing for completely different reasons to five minutes ago. My breaths are shallow and I'm afraid I won't be able to maintain this barely-calm state much longer. I need to get out from under him. I need to get out of here. My stomach twists into a tight knot.

She shrugs. "Potentially, but he's a big guy. No doubt whatever we've given him won't do too much damage."

I stare at her in disbelief. "If that's the case then why is he out cold? And by the way, I'm pretty uncomfortable here. It would be great if we could try and move him soon."

She throws her head back and laughs. "You've seen the size of him, right? How are we supposed to move him?"

"You should have thought about that when you trusted a stranger to help drug someone," I snipe back.

"Yeah, yeah. Stop bitching." She spins around, observing our surroundings, as if it's likely she'll be able to find something that will be able to help ... in a public restroom.

"We need to get him out of here before anyone else comes in. I don't fancy going to jail for drugging an NFL player. I don't know why I even agreed to this. There's getting a story and then there's this," I mutter the last part under my breath.

It wasn't quiet enough, and she snaps back, "You need to chill. You wanna be a big shot reporter? Sometimes you gotta do things you don't like to work your way up the ladder. This is just one of those steps. No one said it was going to be easy or that you would like what you have to do to get to the top."

She might be pissing me off, but I know what she's saying is true. "You've made your point. Can we just try and get him out of here?" I look down at the giant football-playing lump slumped against me, to reinforce who I'm referring to, as if it could be anyone else.

"Fine. Wait here."

"Where are you going?"

"To create a diversion. There's no way we're getting *that* out of here without being noticed. Lucky for us the bar is getting busy. Give me five."

She walks out and I remain stuck on the washbasin with Becket. The minutes pass by and I try my hardest to ignore the smell of his hair and aftershave that, even in this ridiculous scenario, are doing funny things to my insides.

My head flies up when I hear a large crash from outside the door and then shouting. A lot of shouting.

Leigh stalks back in with a look of determination, and says, "We're gonna have to drag him. Between the two of us we might manage to get him out of here.

The initial hit of the drugs shouldn't last too long. When he starts to come round, we can get on with the plan."

The plan. The way she says it, makes it sound so carefree and easy, not like we're about to screw over this guy we barely know for our own gain. Everyone says Becket's the asshole but maybe we're worse.

I signal for Leigh to help move him back to break the connection. The more space there is between us, the better. She somehow manages to pull his hulk-like frame away from mine, supporting his weight while I quickly jump down from the countertop. Without missing a beat, I assist her with supporting him, before she loses her balance under his weight. We both let out a deep breath when we're lodged under his armpits, and the risk of him hitting the deck is gone.

When we reach the door, before stepping out, Leigh asks, "Ready?"

It's a simple question, but my mind reads more into it. I'm not. I'm not ready for the way the rest of the night is about to unfold. I nod even though I don't want to and she swings the restroom door open. My jaw drops when my eyes adjust to the sight in front of us in the dimly-lit bar.

Leigh started a goddamn brawl.

People charge at each other, glasses smash. The noise is almost deafening.

"What did you do?" I exclaim, frozen on the spot.

"Created a distraction. Come on, move." She walks forward, dragging me and Becket with her.

It's not surprising we make it out unnoticed, even with Becket slumped over us, his head lolling from side to side, the bar has turned into a sideshow and we're the least of the bartenders' worries.

Ten minutes and a lot of huffing and puffing later, we manage to get Becket settled in the back of the hire car. I slide into the front passenger seat, clicking my belt in place. "Where to now?" I ask.

"Georgia," Leigh replies, not expanding further.

I frown and look at her. "We're going to a different state. Why?"

She shrugs like it's no big deal. "He's a big shot here. The plan won't work because wherever we go, his die-hard fans will come to his rescue. They could have done it in there. We need to be somewhere people don't care."

"The whole world knows who he is. Jumping state isn't going to make the attention any less."

"No," she agrees starting the car, "but they're less likely to come to his rescue. Quite the opposite. They'd throw him under the bus if the opportunity arose." She pulls out onto the road and drives into the night.

What she's saying makes sense, but I don't want it to. We were only meant to gain some inside scoop. Little did I know Leigh had every intention of decimating his career.

***

Hours later, one shit show after another, all of which we caught on video on our cells, I stand in the distance watching as Becket slurs his words to a beautiful brunette. A brunette who looks just like his ex-girlfriend back in New York—Abby West.

"Are you ok?" asks Leigh, as she walks up beside me after disappearing for a while to meet with 'The Source'.

I'm furious that she would trust this random stranger again after what they've already done to Becket. When I take in her face, I realize it doesn't

36

matter. She doesn't need to trust them because she simply doesn't care. She's ruthless, especially when it comes to bettering her career, even if it's at the expense of someone else's. The only reason I haven't deserted her is so I can keep an eye on Becket and make sure he doesn't end up in even more trouble.

I continue watching him flirt with the brunette and say, "I'm fine ... Well, as fine as one can be considering the shit we've put this guy through.'

"We're not done yet." She smirks.

I turn to her, eyes narrowed. "How much more can there be? We've got enough coverage for the magazine."

She shakes her head. "We agreed to do whatever it takes. We need to finish *big*."

I close my eyes and let out a deep sigh. "What's the plan?"

She smirks again but this time there's a glint in her eye that can only be described as evil. I listen horrified as she rattles off what the next part of the night entails.

"I can't do this." I hold up my hands and start walking backwards, away from him. I'm out—there's no way I'm taking part in the rest, it's too much.

"You're already in too deep. What would be the point in backing out now?" Leigh asks.

I know she has a point. If I give up now, everything we did will be on my conscience and for nothing. She nods in Becket's direction and we watch as he leans in and begins kissing the brunette.

"Looks like he's already forgotten all about you."

She's trying to play on my insecurities, and I have to bite back the response that he won't just forget me, he'll forget everything. She's right though, I'm in too deep and Becket isn't an idiot. Eventually he will piece everything together and all paths lead back to me. At least if I follow this through to the end, there's a glimmer of hope that I can leave my past behind.

It's only later as I sit in the car, watching the feed on the monitor of the camera we've set up in his motel room, watching as he pounds into another woman, that jealousy threatens to consume me. Everything I felt on the plane and in the restroom was real.

"Do we know who she is?" I ask Leigh. I don't know why I need to know her name, it doesn't change anything.

Leigh doesn't even question why I want to know before replying, "Yeah her name's Lola Fisher."

"Right. Whatever." I look blankly out the window and decide if we're going to sit here like we are, I might as well jot some notes down. I look through my bag, but there's nothing there. "Have you seen my notebook?"

Leigh doesn't bother turning to look at me. "What notebook?"

"You know, the one I use to jot everything down. I can't find it …"

"I don't know what you think I do all day, but my time isn't spent keeping tabs on you and your things. Check again."

I look, but the book in which I wrote down all of Becket's secrets during our drive to Georgia, his name clearly tagged beside them, is gone.

It may not be long until Becket's secrets aren't secret anymore.

***

Britney 6 weeks later

I didn't sign up for this.

Standing at the kitchenette in my less-than sub-standard living space, I pour a large glass of wine, down it in one gulp, then fill it again, exhaling loudly. This wasn't meant to happen. It's all too much.

When Fiona dragged me into her office, never did I imagine this is where we would end up. Videos are all over YouTube of Becket pissing off a rooftop into a pool, grinding against a stop sign, stripping in the middle of a club to the *YMCA*. Of course, they went viral, it was like watching a real-life version of *The Hangover*, and even I'll admit they were a little bit funny. What wasn't funny, however, was that it didn't end there.

I groan and bring my wine glass to my lips, taking another large drink as I turn on the television, praying the noise will stop my mind from going over and over all the headlines: *Drug fiend, Cheat, Heartbroken Wreck*. Just a few that have taken over the tabloids in the past few days, and of course, *Michael Becket Assault Case*. It was Leigh, it had to have been. I never would have taken things this far; I never wanted to do any of this to begin with.

My phone vibrates across the shabby counter. I could ignore it and wait for my takeout to reheat in the microwave. One more day and it will be inedible. I sigh. I've gone longer without food. When my phone vibrates again, I admit defeat, abandon the takeout and head to the couch with my wine and phone in hand. I read the texts:

Jess: *How are you doing?*
Jess: *Have you thought anymore about the offer?*

The offer. Another job, away from Fiona and Leigh. One I've been ready to snap Jess' hand off for, but I can't. I have to keep an eye on what they're up to, for Becket. There's more to come, I know it. I've seen them speaking together in hushed voices, in Fiona's office when they think I'm distracted, but I'm never distracted. I'm always watching, waiting.

Me: *I'm still thinking about it.*

The voice of the news anchor fills the small room, "Breaking news just in—"

Choosing to ignore it, I read Jess' reply:

Jess: *The position is going to be filled soon. You need to make a decision.*

I'm about to reply, my fingers hovering above my phone's screen, when the sounds of a woman moaning and flesh slapping together reach my ears. Fuck, what have they done? I look up to find the distorted image of the video Leigh and I made, at the same moment I hear Becket cry out, "Yeah, baby, just like that. You know how I like it. So good."

Shit, shit, shit.

I don't know what to do. I freeze, staring at the screen, eyes wide with horror. *They* did this, not me. But I still had a part to play. It's the last time though, because now I have an out, and they've burnt through every reason I had to stay.

Me: *Set me up an interview. I need a new job.*

Four

Becket 18 months later

Hobbling towards the locker room, there's only one thing on my mind: escaping the heat. It's as relentless as the practices that break me each day. It's all part of the job. We turn up, give it our all, fall apart, then put ourselves back together again. It's the part no one sees. What we do during games is a performance; no one cares about the rehearsals.

Once showered and feeling more human, I make my way to Coach's office and knock on the door. My heart pounds. The last time I was here alone, talking about something unrelated to my performance on the field, was when I decided to dance on the wild side for one night only. It took months to lock that shit down. The NFL have been riding my ass since. The only thing that's helped to weather the storm is that luck is on my side. I have raw talent, the kind you don't often find, the kind that can't be taught. It's a gem and they know better than to let me go, even with my now not so gleaming record.

"Come in," Coach bellows.

I take a deep breath before opening the door and stepping inside.

"Take a seat, Son." When I pause, he chuckles from where he's sitting behind his desk. "If I remember rightly, you're the one who asked for this meeting. So why are you acting like I ordered you in here for an ass whooping?"

"Old habit," I shrug, then slowly lower myself into the seat opposite him, trying not to flinch at the pain searing through my muscles.

He looks me straight in the eye. "What can I do for you?"

I give it to him straight. "I want to do the article."

He leans back in his chair and clasps his hands together, looking for a sign that I might be joking. It's been months of us going back and forth, him trying to convince me it would benefit my career and me refusing. I don't think he ever imagined I would change my mind. The idea was presented to him by Shauna, my PR rep. The pair of them helped save me when it felt like my world was falling apart. They said the article was a chance to put the final nail in the coffin from that night. The night I met Britney and she tied me into a media circus. It might help to make me look pretty and less like a prick to the world, but there's so much more lurking in the shadows. It doesn't matter how deep you bury secrets, if someone digs far enough, there will always be bones to find.

Coach's eyebrows shoot up. "You're sure? You know it's *her* magazine running it."

"Exactly. That's the point."

I'm agreeing to do it, but not for the reasons he would like. This isn't about me, it's about *her*. He most likely knows I have a hidden agenda. Nothing gets by him and he means it when he calls me *son*. He's the closest thing I've got to a family besides the team. Sometimes I think he knows me better than I know myself.

"It will be great publicity," his words don't fit the frown on his face. "They're a national magazine and if you play your cards right and let people get to know the *real you*, the article could help put the past where it belongs. The board will love it."

I hold up a hand stopping him in his tracks. He knows better than anyone why I don't want the world knowing who I really am. He's the only one who knows the truth. Well, him and Shauna. They had to know what they were dealing with, so they could manage it appropriately, also known as burying shit six feet under.

"Let's not go that far. My private life is just that. Mine. Maybe I can be on my best behavior, put on a bit of a show?"

He doesn't back down. "The article is named *The real Michael Becket*. That means if you're going to do this and follow it through, then you will have to show the world who you really are."

I nod my agreement, to pacify him, he might know me well, but he doesn't know the true inner workings of my mind. "Fine," I reply.

The twinkle in his eye lets me know he's bought it and is happy with my response. Not for long, however, because if we're doing this, we're doing it on my terms. "On one condition ..."

He sighs. "Go on."

"I want *her* to do it."

"Who?"

We both know who I'm talking about. "Do you really need to ask that question?"

"What if she won't?" he asks, as if I haven't already thought it through.

I'm not an idiot. I know being in the same state as me would be pushing it, let alone the same room. But

I know what I need to do to get her here. "We force her hand."

He rubs a hand over his face, suddenly looking tired. "This could all go very wrong."

"Or it could all go very right. There's only one way we will find out ..."

***

Britney

It's true what they say, New York is a city that never sleeps. My skin glistens orange, as the morning light rolls through the windows of my apartment gym. My feet pound against the treadmill as I take in the sights of the city. The road is a checkerboard of yellow and black vehicles, all fighting to get somewhere fast, but getting nowhere at all. People hustle down the sidewalks, half of them already starting their workday with their heads buried in their phones. The city is as awake as I am, and it's only six AM. The gym became my passion when everything else felt very much out of my control and the endorphins became my tool to chase away the demons.

When I first moved to New York, I thought I'd found the answer to all my problems. It was a chance for a fresh start. People come here to remake themselves. What they don't tell people is what that change entails. The City provides the same deceitful mask it wears itself—merely hiding who you really are.

The treadmill bleeps and the belt slows, my signal to move on to the weights area. Hopping off, I pick up my towel and wipe the sweat from my face, my muscles already starting to ache with exhaustion. I don't normally fit so much into my sessions, but

44

today I have the urge to chase those extra endorphins.

When the session ends, I leave and make my way up a floor, back to my apartment where I go about my normal morning routine. It still feels alien, being here, knowing that I've moved on with my life and put the shit of the past eighteen months behind me, but as people say, these things take time.

Walking into Allure Magazine, there's a spring in my step. Something feels different. It's not just the change in temperature as we come out of another brutal New York winter, the kind that makes you want to hide away and hibernate until it's done. It's something else. The sky is lighter and more inviting. It makes me feel hopeful. Change is coming.

I pray that it's the good kind.

Settling down at my desk, I hum while waiting for my laptop to fire up. My inbox is full of updates on celebrities, the sports world, the latest make-up craze, DIY tips, home reno. You name it, my inbox is full of it, because the national magazine I now work for covers basically everything. It's nothing like the gossip magazine I worked for when I first moved to New York for which I was made to set up Becket.

"You're spritely today," Jess says in a sing-song, pausing at my desk, before heading to her office—the giant corner office with one of the most amazing views of Manhattan.

I smile to myself. "I have a good feeling about today."

"Careful, you don't want to jinx it," she warns with a wink.

"Right," I chuckle.

When she throws her poker-straight, jet-black hair over one shoulder and continues walking, I focus my attention back on the mammoth amounts of work I have waiting.

The morning passes quickly, as most do. It isn't until I receive an email, from Jess, close to lunchtime, that anything feels out of the ordinary. We tend to catch up on anything work-related in casual meetings over lunch or dinner. The rest of the time she drops by my desk. Naturally, this feels off. She rarely gives a scheduled time for a meeting and never schedules them in her office. Not with me that is.

I reply, agreeing to the time and finish up as many tasks as possible. The current article I'm working on is a piece about the band Six Seconds to Barcelona and the release of their latest album. We have exclusive coverage, so it needs to be perfect. It's hard to focus when my mind keeps wandering, going over all the possibilities of why Jess would want me in an 'official' meeting.

When it's time, I make my way into her office. It's a dream: Sleek, white and organized to perfection—a stark contrast to her actual character. The only part that screams Jess is the chaos of Manhattan, seen through the floor-to-ceiling windows. At work she's a vulture, like so many in her position, but outside her life is in shambles. Maybe that's why she works all hours, to maintain control of something in her life.

I sit down opposite her at the huge desk, notepad in hand, ready to jot down anything needed. Her face is full of excitement, which is unusual. Most of the time she sports a poker face, claiming it makes the world take her more seriously. Whatever news she's about to give, it's big. Big enough to have her visibly buzzing.

Straight away, she confirms my thoughts. "I have something big ..."

"I gathered by the way you're fidgeting in your seat."

"It's like really, really big." She shuffles again.

I've never seen her this unsettled by something work-related. In fact, not by anything. She's always so cool and collected. Some call her the Ice Queen, especially the guys she dates.

I mock her a little, knowing she can take it. "Like *super* big?"

"You do know I can fire you right?" She points at herself dramatically. "Boss, remember?"

I reply sweetly, "But you wouldn't do that. Who would help with all the jobs you hate if you got rid of me?"

"True ..."

I look around for any sign of why I'm here. I come up with nothing. Unable to hide my impatience I ask, "Are you going to tell me what's going on or keep me waiting?"

"I can't tell you yet. We're waiting on someone." She looks over my shoulder, into the office. "They're running late, but let me tell you, this is going to be one of our biggest pieces this year. It's been in the making a while because we couldn't get him to agree."

My ears prick at the word *him*. It's not often our main articles are male orientated. Our focus tends to be centered around women empowering women. "Are you sure you can't give me a clue while we're waiting?"

"No need." She nods at the door and stands, brushing imaginary crumbs off her skirt. "He's here."

"He?" My stomach lurches as I turn in my seat to face where Jess is looking.

An older man walks into her office. He's the old kind of handsome. How I'd imagine George Clooney to be if I ever got to meet him. I clock him in his early fifties, the lines of grey in his buzz cut a telltale sign. One thing he's got that Clooney doesn't: he's stacked. The kind of stacked only someone in sports can achieve. He has a physique built for performance not just for show. His eyes crinkle at the sides when he smiles at us. I'm too focused on the fact this guy isn't from New York to return it. No resident of New York has a tan like his at this time of year. Who the hell is this guy?

Still standing, Jess walks around her desk, holding out a hand, ready to shake his. She smiles like she's known him for years. I've seen her pull this trick before. She uses it with all the important stories, which means whatever this guy is here for, it's big. "Hank, it's so great to see you. I'm glad you could make it all the way here." Pulling out the big guns she throws in a couple of air kisses, then they both look in my direction.

I have to keep up appearances, so I stand from my seat to shake Hank's hand, even though there's a little voice in my head telling me to be on guard.

Jess continues the introduction, "Britney, this is Hank Langford."

She doesn't expand further and I'm still none the wiser to who he actually is—his name means nothing to me.

Trying to shake off the feelings of unease, I plaster on the best fake smile I can and say, "It's great to meet you." Sitting back down, I wait for the two of them to do the same, wondering when Jess is going to confirm who Hank is.

"So, Britney. This is Hank Langford."

I look at him and smile again, trying to hide my irritation that Jess is taking so long to cut to the chase.

"Hank, this is Britney Shaw."

Is she actually being serious? I can't stand this.

Finally, Hank speaks, "It's great to meet you, Britney. I've heard a lot about you."

My mouth parts and my palms begin to sweat. How does he know me? Jess seems totally unphased, so I tell myself to chill out. If she's not concerned there's no reason I should be.

The moment of calm passes when Jess expands, "Hank is the coach of the Jacksonville Jaguars."

Fuck. My mind begins racing at a million miles an hour. It could be a coincidence but deep down I know it's not. This isn't down to chance, he's here for a reason.

"Wow." I beam, trying to feign confidence. "What an honor. They're like a big deal in the footballing world?" I want to get up and run, but I can't. Nobody here knows the connection I have to Becket. I doubt that's the case for Hank Langford.

He nods. "I like to think so." His overall expression is warm, but his eyes are not, as he stares at me, unblinking. He wants me to cower.

I do the next best thing and divert my eyes away, looking back to Jess, waiting for her to move the conversation forward. I hope I'm wrong. I hope he's not here for the reason I think he is.

The giant blond mistake in my past.

Jess clears her throat. "I'll cut to the chase. We're running an article on Michael Becket."

Damn it! She's confirmed exactly what I feared. All I can do now is pray it doesn't get worse.

"Hank's here to provide more information, so I'll hand things over to him." She sits back in her chair looking elated, completely unaware I'm about to be well and truly fucked over. I can feel it.

Nothing good can come from anything linked to Becket because I did nothing good to him.

49

With a glint in his eye, Coach Langford says, "As Jess mentioned, your magazine is running an article on my player, Becket."

"R—right," I stammer.

"There has been some reluctance on our end. Basically, he didn't want to do it."

Oh, thank God. Relief floods through me and it's all I can do to stop myself from jumping for joy. "That's a shame," I reply. "It would have been great to have him featured."

He smirks. "*Didn't*. Past tense. He's finally agreed to do the article, but he has some terms."

My glimmer of hope slips away as quickly as it appeared.

"He wants you to write it."

I think I'm going to puke. Clutching at straws, I say, "Great. So, what will it be? A telephone interview? Email? Video call—"

"No," Jess cuts me off. "Michael has just been shortlisted for a huge award with Sports Elite Magazine, for Sports Personality of The Year. This isn't a little article, it's big." There she goes again with her favorite word of the day, *big*. "We're going to title it, *The real Michael Becket*. We want to capture the side of him no one sees. Gain some insight into his life, besides being a football player."

"Ok." I try to swallow down the lump in my throat, knowing she's not done.

"We want you to spend a few weeks with him, so you can really get to know him as a player."

"Surely that's not necessary? What about all my other projects?" I have one shot to convince them we don't need to spend any more time together than needed and this is it. "I can get to know him just as easily by phone or email."

"Don't worry about your other projects," says Jess. "Thanks to good old technology you can work from anywhere." She's humoring me, but the look on her face, is telling me to back down and shut up.

Coach Langford watches us in amusement, then chips in, "He wants you. Only you."

"What? He personally requested me?" I know I'm stating the obvious, but my brain has turned to mush.

"He did. He won't do the article without you. Which is why I'm here. To get you to agree. He needs this." For the first time since stepping into Jess' office, he looks at me earnestly, genuinely needing my help.

Even though I know the answer, better than the two people in front of me could ever imagine, I ask, "Why me?"

Coach Langford narrows his eyes and the brief glimmer of solidarity between us disappears. "You know why."

That's the thing about team sports, they're a team, a family. If I agree to this, I'll be walking into one seriously pissed-off family. I hurt one of their own and they're going to make me pay.

Jess looks bewildered. "Is there something going on here I don't know about? Coach?"

"Britney and Becket have … shall we call it history?" Coach Langford smiles.

I nod, unable to do much else.

"What sort of history?" asks Jess, looking even more confused.

She's trying to figure out why I wouldn't tell her I have a connection to one of the most famous NFL players in the world. Famous for all the wrong reasons, all because of me.

"I'll let Britney answer that one."

I'd rather the ground swallowed me up than answer. Unfortunately, I'm an adult who has to face up to the consequences of the decisions I made. There was only so long I could run away from what I did and pretend like I didn't have a part to play. I shake my head, letting Jess know that now isn't the time to go into details. "I'll tell you later." Letting out a resigned sigh, I look back to Coach Langford. "If I do this, when do I start?"

"We were thinking the first week of April," answers Jess, even though it wasn't her I was asking.

My eyes widen in shock. I thought I would have more time to prepare. "But that's only a week away?"

Coach Langford jumps in, "We want the article to run before next season, the sooner the better. This is a big deal for Becket. Plus, I've no doubt this whole process will be rocky to begin with."

Jess doesn't say a word. She may be responsible for me and running the show in the magazine, but she knows who's calling the shots in this crazy situation we've found ourselves in.

"Fine," I try to hold back the bite in my tone. "Are we done here?" I don't need to know the minor details, that's Jess' job. I've got a lot of work to wrap up, especially if I'm going to Florida for who knows how long.

Jess nods that it's fine for me to leave and I refuse to say anything to either of them as I stand up and start to walk away. I don't care what impression I'm giving Coach Langford. He already knows my worst.

I'm almost at the door when he clears his throat. "Britney ..."

I pause but don't look back. "Yes?"

"I don't know what happened, or why, but I'm a firm believer that everyone deserves a second chance.

Don't see this as a job, see it as a chance to make amends."

I go to leave but hesitate, deciding to make one last attempt to back out. "What if I don't want to make amends? What if I refuse to do it?"

"Then Becket will sue you for defamation."

I hear Jess gasp and my shoulders slump in defeat as I quietly leave her office. Trying to make amends is only as good as the other person wanting to forgive and I'm almost certain Becket is going to be anything but forgiving.

Five

Britney

The day felt like a new beginning but quickly became a disaster, and I'm now linked to Becket in the most unavoidable way. I feel guilty for what happened, but it doesn't change the fact he's an asshole. I know it, he knows it and the world knows it. If it looks like a duck, swims like a duck and quacks like a duck, then it's probably a duck. An article isn't going to change who Becket is.

"Are you going to tell me what that was all about?" asks Jess with a drink in hand.

I put my head in my hands and groan. "You're going to hate me when I tell you. I don't know if I can."

"I could never hate you." She places a hand on my shoulder giving a reassuring squeeze.

I look up and see her earnest expression. I've done some shitty stuff in the past, she knows some of my murky history, but she's my best friend over everything. She would never judge me for it. I let out a deep breath. "You're at least going to think less of me."

"Everyone has a past, Brit. Nobody's perfect."

"I know that, but this is something else." I look down at my drink, feeling hopeless. Today, even a lethal cocktail can't fix things.

"No matter what it is, we're best friends, remember. Through thick and thin." She holds a hand up for me to return our signature fist bump.

I can't help the laugh that escapes. We clicked the moment we met. You could say it was love at first sight, and in a city where I knew no one, I was glad Jess was the first friend I made. We support each other in what I learned at an early age is a dog-eat-dog world.

"Promise you won't hate me?" I ask.

"You're my best friend. I might tell you if you've been a bitch or done something I don't agree with, but it doesn't mean I won't still love you."

"Ok ..." I take a deep breath, preparing myself to tell the story and relive it in the process.

"Come on. It's like ripping off a band-aid. You've just got to do it."

If only she knew how much more painful it was going to be. Just as I think I might have worked up the courage to start speaking, I lose my nerve, pick up my drink and take a large swig. Numbing my senses will make the whole thing easier. "It was last year. Remember the magazine I worked at before Allure offered me a position?"

She waves me off, getting annoyed with what she seems to think are irrelevant details. "Yes, yes. I remember all that. Come on less of the boring stuff. Can we get to the juicy bits, please?"

There's no way I'm going to be able to placate her with minor details any longer so, I do what she says and jump right in. "I fucked over Michael Becket."

She sits, contemplating what I've said. "Fucked over or fucked? Like shebang?"

I frown. "You know there's no possibility of it being shebang. No, I fucked him over. Well and truly."

"He's one of the most successful NFL players of the decade. How on earth did you, little Britney, fuck him over?" She looks at me with intrigue rather than the horror I expected. But she doesn't know the full story yet.

"Remember the media scandal he was part of ..."

"The one where he was almost kicked out of the league because he decided to dabble in a porn career?" It sounds even more awful when she says it out loud.

"It was because of me."

Jess snorts into her drink. "Yeah, right. Come on tell me the real reason. You guys totally had sex, didn't you?"

"Firstly, no, we did not have sex. You know I'm a virgin. I'm being serious. I hate myself every day for it, even though he is an idiot. I set it up. Well, with another girl named Leigh, but I haven't seen her since."

"How?" She looks bemused.

I don't blame her. I would be skeptical if I were in her shoes, wondering how someone like myself could screw over someone like Michael Becket.

"It was an assignment at my last job. There was word that his relationship was on the rocks—"

"How is it possible anyone would have known that?" she interrupts. "He's like the most private guy ever. At least he was before everything came out."

I frown at her for interrupting me. "As I was saying ... The gossip column I was working for had eyes and ears everywhere. They had a source that knew everything and that was that. It seemed harmless, but then they upped the stakes."

56

"Why? What did they do?" She leans in eagerly.

"It was an unwritten rule in the office, that if you didn't follow through on a job, you found yourself unemployed shortly after."

It's clear she still doesn't get it when she says, "So what? You spied on him? This is the media world. Things like that are expected."

I wish what she was saying was true and it was that simple. "No, I didn't spy on him. I set him up."

I spend the next half hour reliving every moment, hating myself more and more as I tell Jess every sordid detail.

"Do you hate me?" I ask once I've finished my retelling.

Jess is sitting with her mouth hanging open. She hesitates before replying, "I could never hate you, Brit. Am I shocked? A little."

"I'm sorry." My eyes burn at the thought I've disappointed my friend. Having someone know I was responsible makes everything we did to him seem so much worse.

She signals to a server to bring another round of drinks. "It's not me you should be apologizing to."

"I know. I'm saying sorry because you have to associate with someone who did such a shitty thing."

"I've said it before, and I'll say it again: people make mistakes, Brit. I know you had your reasons. Honestly, I didn't know you had it in you."

"Neither did I," I admit. "Once the night started, I lost all control of the outcome."

"I get it, I do. But you can't change the past. You know that better than anyone."

I throw my hands up in the air. "What do I do then? Forcing us together like this is a disaster waiting to happen."

"It's going to be hard, and I don't think he's going to make your life easy. Try and see this as a chance to rectify what you did. He might even forgive you."

She has lost the plot. "That's never gonna happen."

"But he kissed you and you said there were sparks. If you both felt the connection, he might eventually be able to see past what you did."

I understand what she's saying, but I don't think it matters whether there was a spark, or a full-blown fire between us. Nothing can make up for how I hurt him and almost ruined his future. "You really think he'd want anything to do with me after what I put him through? You're living in a dream."

"Stranger things have happened." She takes a long sip of her drink and waits for me to go on another of my rants.

"True, but I think I'm the worst thing that's happened to him. He wasn't wrong when he lumped me into the crazy category. I bet he regrets the day he met me."

"That might be so, but you're not the same person he met on that plane. You and I both know that. You also can't fake chemistry, and if it was there, like you say it was, maybe there's a chance for the two of you."

I want to be optimistic, but what I did to Becket was another level of deceit and I can't forgive myself for it. I'm not certain about much, but I am certain the next few weeks are going to be worse than the almost plane crash that tied us together.

***

Becket

The practices while Coach has been gone haven't been any easier. Today his assistant pushed us harder than ever. He always goes the extra mile when he fills in, as if he has something to prove, that he can run with the big dogs. The pain serves a purpose though and helps to keep the nerves of Coach returning from New York at bay.

We're halfway through running drills on the field when I see him standing at the sidelines. All I get when he sees me is a nod. It's 'the nod.' The one he saves for when he means business. Whatever business he has to share, I'm praying it's in my favor. I have to wait until practice is finished, and I'm cleaned up—he won't speak to me otherwise.

Like I did a few days ago, I pause before knocking on his door. I've been here more times in the past eighteen months than I have in my whole footballing career and each time it's because of something related to *her*.

"Come in," his voice sounds normal, gruff.

Before opening the door, I pause, my hand on the handle, and take a deep breath. I have a feeling things are about to change. Exhaling, I shake my head, telling myself to get it together. Inside, I can't even sit down, there are too many emotions coursing through my body. Combined with post-practice adrenaline, I'm a jittery mess.

Coach doesn't look up. His attention remains focused on the papers in his hands. "It's done."

I blink. Well, that was easy. Just to make sure I've heard him right, I ask, "You're sure she's going to come?"

"Positive. The magazine rang on the drive from the airport to confirm. They've already booked flights and accommodation. If she knows what's good for her, it's a done deal."

"Good." I don't know how to react. For the past eighteen months, my focus has been on getting my career back on track, and one other thing: what it would be like to bring down Britney Shaw—if that's even her real name. I'll bring her down like she tried to do to me. She failed. I won't.

Coach interrupts my train of thought, "She seems nice. Are you sure it was her?"

She fooled me and I've no doubt she's capable of fooling other people. Even a battle-axe like Coach. "I'm certain," I say, frowning.

He finally looks up and stares me in the eyes. "Maybe there's a reason she did it?"

"She fucking drugged me! Made a sex tape among many other videos she posted online. And if that weren't enough, she told my secrets to the world. Exactly what justifiable reason could there be?" My voice grows louder with each word—that's what talking about her does, it brings out the worst in me.

He lets out a huff. "All I'm saying is that the person you described seems out of character to the woman I met."

"It was her. There's no question about it. She's the one who screwed me over." It's pissing me off that he's even questioning this. He's seen the CCTV footage we managed to get hold of from that night. She's in every single shot, hovering in the background, watching. It doesn't take a genius to put it all together.

"Ok." He focuses his attention back on the paperwork in his hands.

"That's it?"

"You're a stubborn ass when you want to be. Nothing I say is going to change your mind. Just go easy on her."

"Like she did to me?" I scowl like a fourth-grader.

Placing the paperwork down on his desk, Coach looks back up at me and sighs. "I get it, you're pissed. I am too. What she did was wrong. All I'm saying is maybe you should hear her out and see if there was a reason behind it all. Sometimes people do things for unexpected reasons. She might regret what she did, but you won't know if you don't give her a chance."

I can't listen to this. Shaking my head, I turn around and go to leave his office. I stop right before stepping through the doorway. Over the years, he's taught me better than this. He's taught me never to leave a conversation unresolved. Looking back over my shoulder, I say, "She's had months to find me to apologize. She didn't find it difficult the first time. What happens next, she did to herself."

Six

Britney

Since the day I met Becket, I've avoided airplanes at all costs. A near-death experience will do that to you. Now, here I am, about to make the same trip, retracing my footsteps from that day. This time, Becket won't be beside me if anything goes wrong.

Standing in line, I bounce from one foot to the other, staring at the plane through the windows. It's not just a fear of flying. It's a fear of him. Fear of facing up to the poor choices I made that night. I seriously doubt Becket is going to be happy to see me again, but he's the one forcing my hand and making it impossible for me not to go.

"Miss?" The flight attendant standing at the boarding desk catches my attention and I realize it's my turn to show my ticket.

Awkward and blushing, I throw an apologetic glance over my shoulder to the passengers waiting in line behind me. "Sorry," I say quietly, then show the e-ticket on my cell before boarding the plane.

Looking at the empty seat beside me, I can't decide how I feel that it won't be Becket sitting next to me. My mind wanders, full of unanswered questions:

does he still hate New York as much as he said he did that day? I'll be lucky if I get any answers after what I did to him. Hell, I'll be lucky if he gives me enough information to come up with an article.

A couple of minutes later, a businesswoman bustles down the center aisle. She throws her bag in the locker overhead, completely ignoring me when I smile at her as she sits down. Typical of someone from the city, she sits typing furiously on her cellphone, totally unaware of everyone and everything around her.

My palms turn clammy when the flight attendants start their safety checks, and an overwhelming urge to bolt off the plane hits me. Trying to get rid of some of the nervous energy building, I wriggle in my seat and in doing so, accidentally knock the elbow of the woman sitting next to me. I cringe. "Sorry, I'm a nervous flyer."

All I get in return is a dirty look before she turns her attention back to her cell. Her focus remains on the object in her hand until it becomes mandatory to switch it off. The engine rumbles to life and the plane moves slowly towards the runway. There's no backing out now.

Attempting to escape reality, I close my eyes. Rather than being provided with a sense of relief, I'm faced with images of Becket ... as always.

***

I make it through the flight with my sanity intact, although it was hit and miss when we went through a patch of turbulence. The "whoop" I gave when the plane touched down had Miss Serious next to me cracking out her best sour face, probably wondering how she wound up next to a crazy person. I should

63

give her Becket's number; they'd have a lot in common.

The irony is, after spending the past couple of hours wishing I wasn't on the plane, as I walk through Jacksonville International, I wish I was back on it. After collecting my bags, I walk to where the cabs are parked, waiting. Of course, there's no line. I'd give anything for there to be a line. I'd happily wait hours. I need more time before I see him. I can't even avoid him by checking in at the hotel. It's on my itinerary to head straight to the TIAA Bank Field—the open-air stadium where the Jacksonville Jaguars are training. I don't know much about football, but I know the stadiums, and everything associated with the NFL are huge. This is going to be intimidation at its finest.

"Nervous?" asks the cab driver, looking at me through his rearview mirror.

I don't need to ask what gave it away, my bottom lip is practically raw from biting down on it so much. I've tried everything to distract myself from the apprehension building, but even taking in my surroundings as the cab flies along the highway doesn't help. "You could say that," I reply, nervously smiling back at him through the mirror.

He chuckles. "I would be too if I were heading to *The Bank*. Must be something mighty important you're going for. Not many people get to go in during training season."

"It's pretty important," I say vaguely. He's prying, I can spot it a mile off. After all it was part of my previous job description. Trying to steer the conversation in a different direction I ask, "How long until we get there?"

"A few minutes." He looks at me again in the rearview. His eyes are friendly. Maybe I should cut him some slack. "Excited?"

64

"No, but I have no choice."

The driver's friendly expression turns to a frown. That wasn't the answer he was expecting. He doesn't say another word for the rest of the journey.

I jump out of the cab once I've paid, retrieving my luggage from the trunk. I can't decide whether it was my decision to wear a black, tailored pantsuit, the Florida heat, or nerves that has me sweating. I begin walking forwards awkwardly, struggling to maneuver my suitcase, along with my laptop case and tote bag over one shoulder. I just about get into a rhythm when a figure crashes into me from the side. Fumbling my laptop case, the tote bag is sacrificed and tumbles to the ground. Papers slide out, scattering along the floor before blowing around in the warm breeze. Clambering around, I expect to at least hear an apology, but I get nothing. Looking up from where I'm crouched on the ground, I find no one, until I turn my head and, in the distance, see a black, hooded jacket darting away. Asshole. They could at least have helped me pick up some of the papers.

I manage to quickly get together all the papers, almost certain none escaped, and shove them back into my bag. I'll have to deal with that mess later. I look up at *The Bank*, as the cab driver called it, and swallow nervously.

Ten minutes pass. My feet remain rooted to the spot. I'm about to finally work up the courage to move when my cellphone pings from in my tote. When I eventually find it, Jess' name is on the screen and I smile to myself. She's the perfect excuse to stall.

Jess: *You've got this.*
Me: *I really don't.*
Jess: *Are you there yet?*

65

Me: *I'm standing outside.*

Jess: *What are you doing standing outside? Get yourself in there!*

Me: *I'm not ready.*

Jess: *And you never will be because it's going to be shit.*

Me: *Are you trying to fill me with confidence? Because you're doing a terrible job.*

Jess: *Just keeping it real.*

Me: *I'm going to start ignoring you now.*

Jess: *Put on your big-girl pants and get in there. You got yourself into this mess now it's time to get yourself out. Plus, you're on the payroll, you have no choice.*

Me: *We're on opposite sides of the country. I can do whatever I like.*

Jess: *Wrong. I have Coach Langford saved to my cell and he's informed me you're late. So, get moving.*

Everyone is adamant I do this, and I haven't felt this out of control in a long time. It's unsettling. If I run, it's game over. Becket will make sure of it. I've come so far, but he's threatening to undo everything.

I stand looking up at the glass doors to the stadium. I have to face him. I'm not a bad person, not like he most likely thinks I am. If I were a bad person then I wouldn't feel any remorse.

But I do.

Every. Single. Day.

A throat clears behind me. "Are you going to stand there all day?"

I spin around to find Coach Langford towering above me. Sheepishly, I say, "Just getting my bearings."

"You've been standing here for over ten minutes. That's more than enough time. Follow me."

Panic sets in as Coach Langford walks away towards the doors in front of us, while my feet stay firmly planted.

He looks back over his shoulder with one brow raised. "Are you coming?"

"Erm ... yeah. I was just gathering myself." Gathering myself? This couldn't get any more awkward.

Finally, my feet move, and I follow him, pausing just inside the doors. What I see doesn't fit the preconceptions I had of the NFL—it's more like a swanky VIP club, not the high school drama I pictured in my head. Huge glass windows create a barrier from the outside world, and the sunlight pouring through bounces up from the marble floor and reflects off the stark-white walls. I expected mud and sweat; red plastic seats smeared with ketchup and mustard; the smell of stale beer. Instead, there's leather and lots of white.

So ... this is the big league.

We move away from the main entrance and start walking along a corridor when Coach Langford attempts to make small talk.

"How was your flight?"

"It was fine."

"I assume it was better than the last one you took here."

Warily, I reply, "I guess you could say that. Where are we going?"

"Practice," he grunts. "We're almost there. The team is out on the field."

Butterflies take flight in my stomach. This is it. Our paths are finally going to cross again and there's nothing I can do about it. I'd hoped our reunion might be private. Alas no. There will be me, him, and his footballing family.

I'm going to be outnumbered.

I hold my breath when we stop in front of a large metal door, which I assume leads out onto the field. Coach opens the door and light floods in. Raising a hand to my brow to shelter my eyes, I squint as they readjust after being in the dimly lit corridor. My mouth drops open. The stadium stretches out in front of us, reaching over two hundred feet into the sky, providing a shelter from the rest of the world. We're in a football bubble. An exceptionally large football bubble. As dusk chases away the remainder of the daylight in the sky, the arena lights blare down even brighter. It's blinding and surreal.

"Shaw," Coach barks. "I don't know how many times I'm gonna have to tell you to follow me." He's enjoying watching the fear take over my face. "If you were on the team, you'd be running laps by now."

"Sorry," I mutter. If this is Coach's attitude towards me, who knows what Becket has in store for this whole farce.

"I won't say it again," he shouts over his shoulder, stalking across the field in the direction of his players.

Reluctantly, I scurry behind, struggling to keep up with his large strides. It takes two of mine to match just one of his. Each step I take, my heels sink down into the ground, slowing my pace even further. My choice of attire couldn't have been less suitable if I'd tried.

Time slows when I stop in front of the large group of hulking men, putting their bodies through their paces. To some, this would be heaven, watching men kitted out, muscles rippling, but this is my version of hell. My presence goes unnoticed, and the team carries on, their uniforms and helmets shielding who

68

they really are. This was part of the homework I didn't complete—learning which jersey number belongs to which player. Major faux pas on my part because now I don't have a clue who is who. I wouldn't know if Becket was here or not. I hope he's not.

I wait for him to seek me out, twiddling my hands together. It's a relief when Coach walks back over to me. He's the only person who seems to care even slightly that I'm here.

"What happens now?" I ask uncertainly.

"You're the reporter, you tell me." His attitude is beginning to piss me off, not that I would let it show when I'm surrounded by his loyal followers.

"I've never done an article like this before," I admit, stumbling over my words. An error on my part because you should never show the enemy your weakness, easier said than done when under pressure. "I don't know what I'm doing."

"I suppose your forte is ruining people's careers rather than bettering them."

"Careful Coach, you're showing your true colors," I snap back, losing my temper. I never expected animosity from someone so high in the ranks and it's throwing me off.

"Nice to see you're still a bitch," says a shrill voice from behind.

A chill runs down my spine at the same time my cheeks flush. My dilemma is over. Becket has singled me out, proving he's the one calling the shots. Now, I get to witness firsthand where his reputation for being the biggest asshole in the NFL has come from. Meanwhile, Coach Langford stands smirking clearly not going to call his player out for his offensive language to the team's guest.

I turn around slowly, expecting to see his face, but his helmet is still in place. "Becket ... Hi." I hold my hand out as a peace offering. Stupid idea, I cringe. Even stupider, I say, "Britney Shaw."

He throws his head back, laughing. "I know *exactly* who you are, Brit."

My fight or flight response kicks in, warning me to get away from this situation.

"I know who you are in the same way you knew who I was when we boarded that plane."

At some point during our short exchange, the rest of the team stopped running drills. Now, they're standing behind him with their arms folded against their broad chests. I'm surrounded by a crowd of giants, all of which hate me for what I did to their teammate. This was my own doing. I deserve this. I need to let Becket play his games and hurt me, because I hurt him. Even if he never admits it, I know I did.

"I—I—" Can't think of anything to say. This is mortifying.

Becket and his team stay surrounding me. "What's wrong, Brit? Cat got your tongue?"

This is going worse than I predicted and I struggle to swallow over the lump in my throat. I only know it's him because of the two green eyes, glowering at me through the cage of his helmet, and his gruff voice, giving only one thing away: he despises me. But I'm not that person anymore. I promised myself eighteen months ago I'd stop allowing people to use me for their own gain and I haven't looked back since. There's no shame in admitting to myself I need to regroup.

"I have to go," I croak. Even with my heels sinking into the ground and my suitcase dragging along the grass behind me, I leave the stadium quicker than I walked in. It takes everything in me to fight the urge to keep walking straight onto the next plane out of Jacksonville. I'm out of my depth, but no matter what, I cannot run.

***

Becket

Britney's almost out of the stadium when I take my helmet off and drop it on the grass. Instinct told me to keep it on as a barrier, protecting me from the devil in disguise, but she's on my turf now and I'm determined to keep the upper hand as long as possible.

The moment she stepped out on the field my eyes found her, not that I'd ever let her know. She's like something out of *Game of Thrones* with her long, white-blonde hair and icy-blue eyes. She's the last person I want to think about, but the only person I can. I screwed up when we met on the plane; I never should have let her in. Walls are built to keep people out and I've been paying for my little slip-up for months.

Now, my mask—Becket—is firmly in place.

"That went well ..." says my teammate and best friend, Brad, walking up beside me.

Together we watch as she bolts through the same door that she came out of just a few minutes ago.

"It went exactly how it was supposed to." I bend down to pick up my helmet as Coach calls the whole team in together.

"What if she leaves?"

"She won't," I sound more confident than I feel. If I were her, I'd be on the next plane out of Jacksonville.

71

We reach the rest of the team, but Brad's not finished and says, "You don't know that. She looked like this was the last place she wanted to be."

I shrug. "That's what guilt does to you."

"If she feels guilt, then maybe she's not as bad as you thought?"

"What do you mean?" I turn to him, confused, not caring if Coach will have our asses for speaking out of turn.

"Feeling guilty shows that she has a conscience. After the way you described her and everything that happened, I thought she'd have no regrets over what she did."

I frown and look over at Coach, replying under my breath, "It doesn't change anything. She still set me up." I don't want to believe there might be some truth in what he's saying. It would mean I've spent months focused on the wrong thing, driven to the wrong outcome. It would mean everything I've come to believe about her has been wrong.

Brad runs a hand over his face and lets out a harsh breath. "She seemed scared." He doesn't get it because he wasn't the one, she screwed over.

"Good," I reply, "she should be."

Seven

Britney

I'm having the best sleep I've managed since Coach Langford set foot in the New York office, when my alarm wakes me. Coming around, I remember that I didn't set an alarm. My cell continues chiming incessantly. A quick glance at the windows, where the curtains are slightly ajar, confirms it's still dark out. It's either really late or really early. My cell continues being intrusive. When I look at it, I see I was right: I didn't set an alarm. Jess' name flashes on the screen as an incoming call, and my eyes catch the time: it's four AM.

"What?" I bark down the line. "Don't try and use the excuse of a time difference because there isn't one."

I can hear the smirk in her voice when she says, "You're nice and grumpy this morning."

"Do you blame me? It's four AM." I'm an early riser, but this is ridiculous. It's like she's never heard of a little thing called beauty sleep. Then I remember, she doesn't need it—she's beautiful enough. She works around the clock until her body gives up, recharges, then starts the whole process again. She's an animal. Some call it driven, but I think she's trying to fill a big hole of loneliness.

"Up and at 'em. You have somewhere to be, and that article isn't going to write itself. We haven't paid for you to go to Jacksonville and sleep." Her chipper tone isn't improving my mood.

"You must know something I don't. What happens at four AM that's so important, besides sleeping?"

"The Jaguars' practice that's what."

Damn it. I make a last ditched attempt to stay in the comfort of my bed, "At this time? How come you know this, and I don't?"

"Becket rang yesterday to confirm and asked that you be there."

Of course, he did. "Did he not think to get in touch with me himself?" It's going to be impossible to do the article if he keeps me out of the loop and goes through Jess whenever there's a need for us to communicate.

"Remember what Coach Langford said, it will take time for the dust to settle. For now, play the game."

Slowly exhaling, I climb out of bed with my cell balanced between the crook of my neck and my ear. "I can't play the game if I don't know the rules. Oh, and it would have been nice if you'd rung and let me know the plan yesterday so I could prepare. Why didn't you?"

"For that exact reason. You don't need to prepare. All you need to do is make notes about anything of interest. I knew if I rang and told you, you'd get yourself all worked up and then come up with a reason to back out. That can't happen. This article could be big for the magazine and for him. You will not mess this up."

I roll my eyes. She's speaking to me like I don't already know what's on the line. Placing a cup on the little ledge of the coffee machine stationed at one side of the room, I insert one of the coffee pods and press the button, watching as it flashes green. Steam billows out and I inhale the aroma of coffee now filling the room. For this, caffeine is needed. "Yeah, yeah." I dismiss her with a fake yawn. "So, I just turn up and hang around?"

"And make notes, don't forget the notes," Jess offers unhelpfully.

"Like I could forget the notes." I smile to myself for the first time since arriving in Jacksonville. She might be annoying at times, but she knows in her own way how to brighten my mood. Even at four AM. "When do I need to be there by?"

"Four forty-five."

I pause, bring my cell away from my ear and check the time. "That's less than an hour! How am I supposed to get ready in time?"

"Brit, you look gorgeous no matter what you do, just have a quick shower and go. It's their early gym session. They won't even pay you any attention."

"Becket staring daggers at me and wishing I were dead is classed as attention, J."

"Give it time. Brit, this is a good thing. At least he's letting you be around him."

I resign, there's no way I'm getting out of this, no matter how hard I try. "Wish me luck?"

"You don't need it."

I wish I felt as positive as she sounds.

We hang up and I quickly get ready, doing exactly as Jess said, hopping straight in the shower and making little effort with my appearance. Who looks pristine before it's even 5 AM anyway? The last thing I want is Becket to think I'm trying to impress him.

Once I look a little more presentable, I pick out some gym gear. I want to blend in, not stick out like a sore thumb in my usual professional attire. Finally, I scoop my long, platinum-blonde hair up into a messy bun and order an Uber with the app on my phone before I have chance to change my mind. The app alerts me that the driver is a few minutes away, so I quickly grab my things off the bed and go to leave, stopping abruptly when I almost trip over a huge bunch of flowers on the floor right outside my door.

Leaning forwards, I glance up and down the corridor, but there's no one around. I pick up the huge bunch of white lilies and open the small, white envelope with a note inside. I read the handwritten message:

It's time to play a game.

Becket. He's messing with me. My cell bleeps again, it's an alert telling me the driver is right outside. I don't have time to over-analyze things, so I quickly set the flowers down on my dresser and bustle out of the room.

The location of the training session is different from yesterday, it's a private practice facility about a ten-minute drive from my hotel. When I've given my name and he's double-checked my details on the system, the security guard at the door lets me in and quickly rattles off directions to the gym where the team will be training.

Stepping foot inside the huge room, I pause. Instead of being greeted by the sound of weights slamming, the whirring of cardio machines and the sight of the whole team working out, there is nothing. Total silence, and not a soul in sight. I walk around, not quite sure what I expect to find. It's not like the team will be hiding, they're giants. I'm alone, with no clue what is going on.

I'm about to pull out my cell to ring Jess and see if she made a mistake, when it vibrates. On the screen is an unknown caller ID with a new message.

I open it, frowning when I read:

Fooled you once. My point.

Becket. I should have known it wouldn't be this easy getting him to co-operate. It's official: the games have begun.

***

There was no point going back to the hotel. The security guard confirmed a two-hour wait until the team's actual practice began, and as I was already at the gym, with nothing else to do, I seized the opportunity to get in a workout, pounding away some of my nerves on the treadmill.

Glancing at the digital clock on the wall, it's close to the start of the team's training session. The last thing I want is to piss anyone off by leaving puddles of sweat for them to maneuver around, so I make quick work of cleaning up after myself before anyone arrives. When members of the team begin filtering into the room, the sun has risen, and the room is flooded by natural light instead of the artificial glare I've been subjected to for the past two hours. Like Jess predicted, no one pays me any attention. I sit on a bench next to one of the water stations located at the side of the room, trying to be as inconspicuous as the only female in a room full of males can be. My pulse elevates each time the door to the room opens and another member of the team enters. After ten minutes, I realize this is part of the game.

Becket is being purposefully late to keep me on edge. Asshole. I wonder if he will turn up at all.

The door opens again, and my breath catches in my throat. It's one thing seeing him in his training uniform, kitted out in all the pads and gear. It's another seeing him in a pair of gym shorts and a skintight workout T-shirt—they leave nothing to the imagination, hugging every muscle, emphasizing where the strength and power he uses on the field comes from. If he wasn't such an ass, I'd almost think he looked adorable with his sandy-blond hair all ruffled and his face still groggy with sleep. I freeze when his eyes zero in on mine. He holds my gaze. I couldn't look away if I wanted to. I'm stuck in a Becket-induced trance. I thought I'd buried them, the memories of his lips on mine and how much I enjoyed it, apparently not deep enough. My stomach twists at the fleeting thought of what it would feel like to have him devour my mouth again.

He walks over and stops, his toes a couple of inches from my own, towering over me. It's painful how far back I have to tilt my head to get a clear view of his face, but I refuse to let him intimidate me. If he wants to play this game, he can throw his worst at me. There's nothing he can do that will shock me, not with my past.

His eyes narrow when they focus on the clothes I'm wearing. "Planning on joining us?"

"No. I've already finished my session thanks to my early start," I keep my voice cheery and smile sweetly. Tou-fucking-che Becket.

"You train?" he asks, as if I'm part of some club.

"If by *train,* you mean exercise to keep healthy ... then yes, I do."

He looks over his shoulder to the bikes where one of his teammates is sitting, leaning against the handlebars, watching us intently. He looks back down and says, "Right. Well, I've got my own session

78

to do. You can shadow it if you want? I know you like to watch me working up a sweat—you'll be in your element."

I don't miss the sex tape reference and roll my eyes. "That one's getting a bit old, isn't it? I have better things to do with my time than watch you and your pals compete over who can lift the heaviest lump of metal."

He blinks in surprise at my snappy response, a sharp contrast to the meek version he witnessed yesterday on the field. "If you aren't going to watch me train, what exactly are you planning on doing?"

"I could do with a shower ..." I reply, gesturing down at my gym bag, internally high-fiving myself for thinking ahead and packing spare clothes and toiletries.

He nods. "There are female changing rooms out the door and left along the corridor."

"Great." I jump to my feet quickly, forcing him to take a step back. Grabbing my bag from the floor, I make sure to bend extra-low, ensuring he gets the full view of my cleavage. I'm pretty certain I hear him groan. One point to me. I add an extra bounce to my step and sway my spandex-clad hips as I leave the gym, knowing it will piss him off. Especially after the cleavage show.

Expecting the best that the NFL can offer, it's disappointing when I'm transported back to high school as I step inside the female changing rooms. I wish I was back in my hotel room where I could enjoy a long, hot, and most importantly, private shower. They could have at least forked out for thicker material, I think to myself when I've stripped off and stepped under the shower. The sheer material surrounding me does little to hide how naked I am. I can't deny the water feels amazing as it hits my skin, easing my already achy muscles. Lost in my thoughts, I startle when cold air hits me from behind.

Spinning around, I yelp.

Becket is standing there, staring at me like I'm some sort of sideshow.

I try to cover my body with my hands and arms, but it's pointless. No one has seen my body like this—no one that matters at least. I've been saving it for the right person and I'm furious he's taken the moment from me without a care in the world, out of spite. With what little self-respect I have left, I storm past him, to the bench where I left my towel. Wrapping it around my body, I try to cover as much skin as possible, failing miserably, because the towel I picked up in my haste before leaving the hotel room, is a hand towel. Of course. I want to slap away the smirk on his face, but I don't because it's what he wants—a reaction.

"What's wrong, Brit?"

"You know what's wrong," I say, failing to keep the venom from my voice.

"You know what they say, all's fair in love and war."

"Prick," I mutter.

He ignores my comment and narrows his emerald eyes. "You did the same to me. At least you haven't got the whole country ogling your assets while you pound into someone."

I snap back, "Yes, but you weren't a virgin."

I wait for him to come back with some kind of scathing response but he doesn't. "You're a virgin? That was true?"

He doesn't believe me. I don't really blame him as it's an unusual scenario for someone my age.

"Yes. Not everything that night was an act." I begin rummaging through my bag, searching for my clean

80

clothes, when I feel him move in close behind. I shudder, anticipating what he's going to do next. "What are you doing?" I whisper.

His proximity mixed with the remaining droplets of water on my skin cause goosebumps to cover my body.

"I'm returning the favor after that little performance in the gym. You might be innocent, but you're also a tease." He leans his head down to my shoulder. His lips are so close to touching my skin it takes everything inside me not to fall back into him. He lets out a throaty chuckle. I hate that he knows exactly how he's affecting me. "Be careful, Brit. You can't win the game if you don't know the rules ..."

***

Becket

Small, yet strong hands trail up and down my body.

I let out a loud groan. "That's it, right there, baby."

"Seriously man, we've already spoken about this," scolds Brad.

I can tell from the strain in his voice he's biting back a moan himself.

"You can't sweet-talk the physios. You've already been told. If Coach hears you again, you're in trouble."

"But they're just so good ... Ow!" I yelp as the physio working on my back presses down particularly hard on a painful knot.

Brad snickers. "And that's what you get for being an ass."

"Stop your bitching. Are we done here?" I ask, lifting my head and looking to the physios for a response.

They both nod and leave the room, giving us our privacy so we can get back into our clothes.

"Well, that didn't end as enjoyably as I would have liked. Thanks for that."

Brad holds up his hands. "That was all you."

"Whatever," I grumble.

"Let's talk about Britney."

I finish buttoning up my pants. "There's nothing to talk about."

"Bullshit."

"Leave it, man," I say, shaking my head.

He's having none of it. "Has anyone ever told you it's good to talk? Even guys. You never spoke to anyone about Abby—it all got brushed to the side after the media fallout and then you stuck your head in the sand and focused on football as you do with everyth—"

"Because that's all that matters. Look where focusing my attention on football has gotten me: right to the top. I managed to reverse everything Britney did to me." I take a deep breath, trying to control my temper.

"That's all well and good, but for some unknown reason, you've requested she fly all the way from New York to do the article. Could you not have just done it by email or over the phone like most normal people?"

"No." I bend over and pick up my bag, getting ready to leave.

"Why not?"

I groan. This is the part about having people get closer I don't like. They push, they want to know more, and he can't know more. No one can. Luckily, I never had this issue with Abby, even though we were together four years. She had her own secrets, so didn't pry into mine. Don't ask, don't tell was the foundation our relationship was built on. "Because then she wouldn't be here and I wouldn't be able to mess with her, the way she messed with me."

"Is that what you really want? To hurt her? Come on, Becket, you're not that guy, I know you."

I start walking towards the door, muttering, "You don't know me, no one does. You don't know what you're talking about."

He picks up his bag ready to follow behind. "I do and that's why you're pissed."

"Seriously, can we leave it? I'm not in the mood to talk about all of this."

"You never are, that's the problem. Speaking of problems ... how is the article going ... and where is she? I haven't seen her for a couple of days. I thought she was meant to be following your every move?"

"I don't know." I shrug, that's the truth. I've not seen Britney since she stormed out of the changing rooms after the stint I pulled. I don't blame her. I'd be pissed too. I am pissed. I'm merely following in her footsteps, making her feel how I felt after everything she did.

"You best figure things out between the two of you. She's here to do a job, which she can't if you won't let her. The article is important for your career, so I suggest you get your act together." Apparently having had enough, Brad barges past me as he leaves the room.

He's right. I know he's right. I've managed to fight back, reverse the damage she did to my career after that night. We're going to have to learn to be around each other, whether I like it or not. The article is my final chance to put that night behind me and solidify my place once more as the NFL's golden player. Easier said than done when you don't know if you're ready to forgive and forget.

Eight

Britney

F estive movies in spring. That's how I've spent my time over the past couple of days. One long, continuous Netflix binge. Cool? No. Productive? Also no. It's served as a distraction though, stopping my mind from reliving the moments with Becket in the changing rooms. Naked. I'm not sure if it's because I'm angry, embarrassed or, whether a part of me I'll never admit to anyone, is a little bit turned on. Just thinking about it for a couple of seconds has my cheeks flushed.

A ping fills the room, coming from my cell on the hotel dresser, where I left it a couple of hours ago. I try to ignore it, but it pings again, and then again in quick succession.

I'm at the best part of the movie, and grumble as I climb out of bed and head in the direction of the offending object, which is bleeping, again. The screen is filled with multiple messages from Jess. She knows my silence means I'm engaged in some sort of pity party.

Jess: *Update on the article please. –Your Boss.*
Jess: *I hope you're not watching Netflix ... again.*

84

Jess: *Seriously. I need to know how the article is going. We're funding this little holiday you know.*
Jess: *I hate you right now.*
Jess: *Do I need to pull the boss card again? I'm about to lose my shit. The powers that be want updates, which means I want updates. Why am I not getting any updates?*
Jess: *You're dead to me.*

I roll my eyes at how dramatic she's being and reply before she can get herself anymore worked up.

Me: *I'm here, don't get your panties in a twist.*
Jess: *You remember this is a work thread, right?*
Me: *Please reread the "you're dead to me" comment. HR would have a field day.*
Jess: *Point taken. Update please.*
Me: *There's nothing to update. I haven't seen him.*
Jess: *And that would be why? How are you supposed to write about someone's day-to-day life if you're not with them?*
Me: *He purposely walked in on me in the shower naked ...*
Jess: *Shit.*
Me: *Exactly.*
Jess: *What did you do?*
Me: *Apart from almost cry? I stormed out and haven't seen him since. I don't know how we're going to work together, he's impossible. I'm supposed to be finding reasons to convince the world he's not an asshole. How can I do that if I'm not convinced myself?*
Jess: *Correction: He's impossibly hot. Could this all be one giant mound of sexual tension?*

85

Me: *I thought sexual tension was between people who liked each other? We don't. You know that saying "time heals," that's not the case for Becket. He despises me.*
Jess: *He's used to getting his way. Sports players have a God complex apparently. You need to learn to work with each other, this article is important.*

She's right. The article isn't going to write itself and it's important for us both. A chance for us both to put the past behind us and better our careers.

Me: *Leave it with me.*
Jess: *Keep me updated. And Brit … show him who's boss.*

I smile to myself at the last comment then click out of the message thread. I quickly find the number Becket used to get in contact a couple of days ago, then send him a message asking him when we can meet. I don't expect him to reply as quickly as he does and hesitate before opening it.

Instead of a blunt response or onslaught, I get a more amenable Becket, interesting. Perhaps the space we've had over the past couple of days has served a purpose. For the first time since landing in Jacksonville, I feel optimistic that maybe, just maybe, we might be able to move forward, and I can get some research for the article done.

We decide to meet at a coffee shop in a few hours because it's his day off. Discarding my cell at my side on the bed, I settle back into the swing of my Netflix marathon for a little while longer, praying he's willing to behave.

86

***

The coffee shop where we agree to meet is halfway between The Bank and the hotel where I'm staying. Neutral territory. I try to keep my nerves at bay as I push open the door and step inside, wondering what kind of mood Becket will be in. Looking around, I tug at my dress, wishing I'd gone for something longer. I find him sitting in a quiet corner, with his head down, wearing the same cap he had on in the airport, the day we first met. I smile when I notice he hasn't bought a drink for himself yet. Maybe he has manners after all.

He looks up and his eyes settle on me, there's no backing out now. I walk to his table and sit down on the chair opposite, pulling out my notebook and a pen from my bag. He looks at me confused, clearly having forgotten the reason why we're here.

"The article ..." I say with one brow raised, a hint of a smirk on my lips.

"Right," he replies.

My eyes might be deceiving me, but he almost looks sheepish. I look around awkwardly and my eyes focus on where the Baristas are dancing around each other, completing people's orders. "Are we going to get some drinks before we start? I know you're famous, but I think we still have to buy something if we want to sit here."

Ignoring my comment, he pulls out his wallet and stands up. "What do you want?"

"A caramel cream please," I reply, going for the sweetest thing on the menu.

"No coffee?"

I shake my head no. "I need sugar. Coffee makes me act a bit crazy on an empty stomach."

Not missing a beat, he says, "So what's your excuse the rest of the time?"

I narrow my eyes. "I heard that."

"I wasn't trying to hide it." He stalks to the counter to order our drinks and I wonder to myself if he does it so I can't bitch at him again over being courteous. Great start.

A couple of minutes later he returns with my creamy drink and a black coffee for himself. I open my notepad and write down *black coffee.*

He looks confused.

I remind him again, "The article."

"Ok, what have you managed to get so far? Can I see?"

I spin the notepad on the table and the words *black coffee* stare up at him. "That's it?"

"We've seen each other twice ... and both times you've been less than amenable. That's me putting it nicely." I pick up my drink and suck through the straw. When my eyes flick upward, I find Becket staring at me with such intensity I almost gag on my drink. "What?"

"Can you not suck on the straw like that?"

"Excuse me?"

He leans in, so the people sitting at the tables around us are less likely to hear. "You look like you're auditioning for a role in a porno."

My eyes widen in shock. He really is an asshole.

He leans back with that annoying smirk of his and folds his arms across his chest. "Maybe I had the wrong companion in that little movie you made. I think you would have been much better suited for the job."

"You're an asshole!" I snap, louder than intended. Not my finest moment.

He smirks again. "I never said I wasn't."

"Why am I here Becket?" I sigh.

"You know why."

"This article is a ruse. Admit it."

His posture softens ever so slightly. "Actually, it isn't. I have the NFL still on my case after that not-so-little stunt you pulled. Thanks for that by the way."

"How am I supposed to inform the world who *The Real Michael Becket* is, when it's clear you're exactly who they think you are?"

He leans forward and I hold my breath. "The world sees what I want them to. You included. Don't forget that when you throw around your judgmental looks and act like you're better than me." He stands abruptly and walks out of the coffee shop with his head down low. It's a pointless effort if you ask me because he stands about a foot taller than most of the people in the room.

I'm left wondering what the hell just happened when my cell vibrates on the table. I pick it up and open the new message from Becket:

We have a ball to attend tomorrow. Bring your A-game Brit.

***

Me: *I can't go. I have nothing to wear.*
Jess: *It's a job requirement.*
Me: *It's a ball Jess. It wasn't on the agenda when I was packing. I. Have. Nothing. To. Wear.*
Jess: *You didn't go back in time when you flew down there. There are stores you know.*

Unfortunately, she has a point.

Me: *I have no money.*

89

Jess: *There's a little thing called a company credit card. This is classed as business so shop yourself into the ground and charge it to the magazine.*

I roll over on the bed and scream into the pillow. I'm not getting out of this. She has an answer to everything. There's a reason she's my boss—she gets what she wants, and she wants this article.

Me: *Fine. You win.*
Jess: *I always do. By the way, it's a masquerade ball.*

Great. In case Becket wasn't enough of a mystery, now he will be wearing a mask.

***

Standing in front of the hotel mirror, I give myself a once over. Acceptable, I think. I've never been to a ball, let alone a masquerade one, so I don't have a clue. I spent the morning traipsing around store after store, with plenty of video calls to Jess, figuring out what to wear. In the end, we settled on a long, fitted dress, oozing old-school glamour. It's silk with a lace overlay, completely open at the back.

Slipping on my mask, I take one last look in the mirror, applying an extra layer of deep rouge lipstick. It complements the paleness of my skin while matching with the red dress and mask perfectly.

Accepting I can't put off leaving any longer, I make my way down to the hotel lobby, then step outside. I find a sleek, black vehicle with tinted windows waiting, just like Becket's PA said it would be. Sitting in the back, I clasp my hands then unclasp them, trying to focus on keeping my breathing level. It's just a ball—a ball in which I will be surrounded by his friends and teammates who all hate me. Thank God I'll be wearing a mask. The irony isn't wasted on me, that I'm trying to get Becket to remove his, while clutching at my own.

All too quickly, the driver pulls up outside a tall building. I look out the window and watch a couple of players walk inside. Their hulking frames are the only things familiar thanks to their masks. The dates on their arms are the same: unrecognisable. It dawns on me I'm probably one of the few people here without a date and no one to talk to. Great.

"Ma'am," says the driver, breaking me from my thoughts.

"Yes?" I reply.

"Are you ready to go in? If you don't get out soon, you're going to be late," he says kindly.

Why can't *he* be my date? He's the first person since I touched down in Jacksonville who's actually been nice to me. I nod.

He exits the car, walks around to my side and holds open the car door.

I thank him for the ride as I step out onto the sidewalk. I pause before heading inside, readjusting my dress and mask, making sure everything is in place while working up the courage to face whatever awaits me. A throat clears at my side and a chill runs over me, even though the air is warm and humid. I wish I had a jacket.

I turn to face the inevitable. Becket.

I suck in a sharp breath when my eyes land on all six-foot-plus of him in a perfectly tailored tuxe, which shows off every sculpted part of his body. His hair, normally ruffled with sweat after wearing his helmet, is styled neatly. I fight the urge to step in closer and inhale as his cologne hits my nose, overwhelming my senses with the musky scent of lavendar and birch. Get it together, Brit.

"Hi," I say awkwardly, unsure how to act because of the way we left things at the coffee shop yesterday.

His eyes trail down my body, taking in each inch of the fitted red dress. He grimaces.

Not quite the reaction I was going for. "What's wrong?"

"Nothing," he replies, bluntly.

"It's just you loo—"

"Nothing is wrong." He gestures towards the doors of the building, where the ball is being held. "We should go inside, it's going to start soon."

I notice there's one thing missing. "Where's your date?"

"She's running late." He walks off without looking back.

I follow behind, careful not to walk too close. I don't want him thinking I'm following him, like a lost puppy. Inside he makes a detour to a group of players from his team still standing in the foyer. I don't wait for him, he didn't wait for me.

So this is how the other half live, I think as I enter the grand ballroom. I've stepped into a scene from a movie. The only light comes from the hundreds—possibly thousands—of candles strategically placed around the entire room. They're dressed with dark-green, satin table cloths that sweep the polished hardwood beneath. Sparkling silver cutlery, glasswear, and intricately designed porcelain plates have been carefully set in front of every satin-dressed chair. In the middle of each table is a huge glass vase as a centerpiece, filled with gold and black beads, finished with a display of white and gold venetian masks and plume of deep green ostrich feathers at the top. The image it creates is striking. I'm in over my head and try not to look pathetic as I figure out what to do next. A large display in front of all the tables catches my attention.

Thank the Lord there's a seating plan. My luck stops there though. I'm assigned to the same table as Becket and Coach Langford. But where else would I be sitting? This is the reason I'm here.

Throwing my shoulders back and standing as tall as my five-foot-two frame allows, I strut to my assigned table and settle in my seat, offering a small smile to the people already there. The masks make it impossible to recognize anyone, so I focus my attention on the wine. Without a date or a friend to interact with, alcohol is the next best thing. The remaining players and their dates start to make their way in, signalling that it's almost time for the event to begin.

Coach Langford walks across the room with a woman on his arm. Without even trying he commands attention from his players. They nod with respect when he passes by—a dead giveaway that it's him, even with his mask on. Following suit, I nod and smile politely when he sits down across the table from me with who I assume is his wife. Becket walks over and sits at my side. Of course he couldn't choose one of the other empty chairs at the table that are further away. He wouldn't be able to spend the night torturing me when no one is looking if he did.

The main stage at the front of the room lights up and an older man walks on, clearing his throat to silence everyone when he reaches the podium. When he welcomes everyone to the Jacksonville Jaguars annual ball, the room fills with a round of applause. I subtley roll my eyes at how cliché it all is, then zone out for the rest of the speech. The wine at the center of the table becomes the focus of my attention, and I

93

relish the feeling of the crisp, white liquid as it passes down my throat, settling in my stomach and creating a warm buzz. My whole body sags as some of the tension lifts away. Alcohol is definitely the way forward tonight if I'm going to come away in one piece. I catch a female walking hurriedly towards our table out of the corner of my eye. She's petite with long, flowing brown hair and although her face is covered, she seems familiar. She gets closer and I think to myself—Christ, it's Abby West. As far as I'm aware, she's Becket's ex. At least she was the day we met on the plane from New York. She's *why* Becket was on the plane—he was trying to get away from her and everything that reminded him of her. That's why he hates New York so much. At least it's one of the reasons I'm aware of.

There's been nothing in the media since that would suggest things between them have changed, but this Abby West lookalike is heading in our direction. Seeing that my focus is on something other than the man on stage giving the speech, Becket turns to see what I'm looking at and a mischevious smile takes over his face. He stands to greet her, obscuring my view. Pulling out the chair on his other side, she takes her seat, and then he slides it back in gently.

Sitting down in his own, he gestures between the two of us. "Britney, meet my date, Lola Fisher."

Nine

Becket

I can't take my eyes off Britney and I hate myself for it. The moment I bumped into her on the sidewalk and clocked her in that red dress, I was a goner. All I can do is stare when she's looking elsewhere, despite having Lola sitting next to me, who was supposed to be a distraction for my mind among other things.

"What are you playing at?" hisses Lola in my ear.

I barely hear her, mesmerized by the woman on the other side of me, whose beauty is striking in the dim candlelight, even hidden behind her red mask. I grind my teeth back and forth, my nostrils flare, and my eyes skim over her cleavage. Why did I think it was a good idea? Trying to act complacent, I reply, "I don't know what you mean."

"You know exactly what I mean, Michael."

Britney looks at us briefly and her eyes narrow. She's not an idiot, she's going to remember who Lola is. Of course she is, after all, she's the one who made our paths cross. Trying to block out Lola, I focus solely on Britney, my expression blank, watching the cogs turn in her brain as she tries to figure out what's going on.

"Why am I really here?" asks Lola quietly.

"You know why."

"No, I don't. This isn't why I came tonight."

An older man makes his way over to our table with perfect timing, mask firmly in place. It doesn't matter that we can't see his face, we all know who it is, and jump up to our feet when he pulls out his chair to sit down.

He chuckles and shakes his head. "I hope you're not all standing for me."

The whole table laughs lightly, otherwise known as being awkward as fuck. Nobody knows how to act because he's one of the big dogs. We follow and sit when he does, then go quiet. In the background, the speech continues. These things are always painfully drawn out and the rest of the room look bored out of their minds. Thankfully, I've got my own entertainment about to unfold. Lola was the starter, now for the main course.

"Sorry I'm late everyone," says the new masked figure at our table, "I was stuck at The Bank." He looks around, trying to figure out who we all are, the masks make it difficult, but he knows his players. When his eyes find Brad, he gives a nod of recognition. His face lights up like a Christmas tree when they settle on me. Even with our history, I'm still his favorite player. Moving on, his eyes look between Britney and Lola.

It's showtime.

I clear my throat and Britney flinches. It's a small movement, but it's there. After the Lola bombshell, she's on edge.

"Stan, there's someone I'd like you to meet."

The table stills and Stan waits for me to continue. You could cut the tension at the table with a knife. Britney probably feels out of her depth, not knowing what to expect next. I know the feeling well, remember it like it was yesterday, feeling completely out of control after she drugged me. I take a deep breath and gesture towards the stunning blonde at my side, in the red dress. The devil in disguise.

"Britney, this is Stan."

Britney, the acting professional she is, plasters on her most jaw-dropping smile. "Sorry, Stan ... Football isn't my strong point, I'm afraid. I'm not familiar with who you are."

Don't worry Brit, you will be.

"It's nice to meet you, Britney." Stan smiles politely then looks back at me confused.

I beam, turn to Britney and loudly, say, "I've been looking forward to you both meeting. You set me up and filmed me with his daughter."

Of course, the speech stops at that exact moment. I couldn't have got my timing better if I tried. A few people in the room gasp, letting me know *everyone* heard and the whole room is staring at us wide-eyed, like they're watching a live episode of *The Kardashians*.

Brad begins choking awkwardly on his drink. Coach shakes his head in despair, and Lola picks up her glass of wine and takes a large gulp. I focus my attention on Stan, who's looking rather red in the face. I should probably apologize to him later for making him part of my game. Britney looks paler than normal if that's possible and I wait for her to say something, anything. The seconds tick by. It feels like an eternity passes before she looks at me, her eyes glistening with unshed tears. She shakes her head, then without saying another word, stands, picking up her purse in the process. She walks out of the room with her head down. Every set of eyes follow as she leaves and my stomach tugs with guilt. I tell myself to ignore it. This is nothing worse than how she made me feel in front of the world: humiliated.

Stan stands awkwardly and says, "I'm just going to speak with some of the other Board Members." For a big guy, he moves fast as he walks away.

It crosses my mind that this whole charade isn't the best idea, but it's a fleeting thought. There's something about Britney Shaw that brings out the worst in me.

"Becket!" barks Coach. "Terrace, now." He stands with such force his chair falls backwards to the floor. He ignores it and stalks out of the room without looking back to see if I'm following. He knows I will. I have to.

The whole room watches as I stand, shoulders squared back, and then follow Coach's footsteps.

Screw them and screw all this. They have no idea who I am, what I've been through. They smile sweetly, suck up to the MVP, the flavor of the week, but it's all for show. I know how they laughed and gossiped behind my back when everything happened. They showed their true colors, proved every person in here, apart from my teammates, is here for their own gain. It's bullshit. Most of the people in here couldn't have cared less about what the implications were for me. They didn't care whether Britney's actions affected anyone else. But they did. Her actions affected *them*.

When I step out onto the terrace, Coach is standing with his back to me. His shoulders rise and fall dramatically, the way they do when he's about to lose his temper.

"C—coach." Now we're away from beady eyes, my mask can come off.

Coach and Shauna are the only ones who know the real reason I have walls built stronger than Fort

98

Knox, keeping everyone out. When it comes down to the nitty gritty, Coach is the only person who *really* knows me, which is why he didn't lose his shit back there. He knows why I did it, even if he doesn't necessarily agree with my actions. I expect his face to be contorted with anger when he turns around, like it would be with any other player. I wish it was, because instead what I see, I can barely stomach: Pity.

"What are you doing, son?" he asks, his mouth turned downwards.

I look away. It's like I'm eight years old again, being scorned by my mother for drawing all over Josie's bedroom walls when I realized hers was the bigger room. There's a pang in my chest and I rub, trying to soothe the ache. I need to stop thinking about *them*. Holding my chin up high, I reply, "It's nothing she doesn't deserve."

"From what I've seen so far, she's not quite the menace you've made her out to be. Don't get me wrong, I'm not her biggest fan, but could you have gotten it wrong? Maybe there's more to the story."

I can't believe we're having this conversation again. He was the one who helped me find the CCTV footage from that night when I was trying to figure out what really happened. He sat beside me and watched it all. He saw her there. "You saw it!" I say, throwing my hands up in the air.

"I'm not questioning what I saw, but perhaps it didn't all play out how you think."

"It's too late, the damage is already done." I look away and stare at some of the foliage decorating the terrace. "I can't believe you're taking her side."

"Son, I'm not taking anyone's side—this isn't high school—but what happened in there was wrong. This path you're going down, is as bad as what you think she did. Be the bigger person, show her who you

99

really are." He sighs and walks past me in the direction of the ballroom. Before he does, he pauses at the door. "You need to apologize to her before she leaves. For good. While you're at it, prepare to do some sucking up. Stan is also on your list of apologies, unless you want to find yourself out of the NFL."

I wait a while, contemplating Coach's words. What he's saying makes sense. If I keep acting the way I am, she's going to be on a plane to New York before the week is out, and then what will I have achieved? It's time to throw in an unexpected play. There's a reason they say, 'keep your friends close and your enemies closer.' It's time for me and Britney to get so close, she forgets why she's even here.

✳✳✳

Britney

I'm about to click *book*, on a flight back to New York when a knock at the door stops me in my tracks. Coming here was a huge mistake. I knew Becket was an asshole, but what he did at the ball ... I thought there was more to him than this. He's intimidating me into feeling guilty about what I did to him. I should tell him there's no need; I've been plagued with guilt ever since that night. I don't need his help. As far as I'm aware, only two people know where I'm staying: Jess and Coach Langford. I glance at the lilies resting in a glass on my dresser. Wrong. One other person knows.

Becket.

Thankfully, there's a peep hole on the door so I can double check. Even standing on my tiptoes, I only just manage to see through. Small people problems.

When I do manage, I can't take my eyes away. There he is, looking as gorgeous as he did earlier at the ball, only now his top button is open and his bow tie hangs casually around his neck.

"I know you're staring at me. I'd say take a picture, it'll last longer, but yo—" he stops whatever he was about to say, and I watch him rub a hand over his face. "Open the door, Brit."

I take a deep breath before opening it, preparing myself for an onslaught of insults as soon as we're face to face. A part of me wants to run back to New York so I can lick my wounds in peace, but another part refuses to go down without a fight. He doesn't know what really happened, the choices I made. It's that knowledge alone which has me opening the door.

His hair sticks up in all directions, like he's been tugging his hands through it over and over. My eyes drink him in. Why can't my mind and body forget how good it felt being in his arms? It would make him and his actions easier to hate. Emerald-green eyes stare intensely into my icy-blue ones. I don't blink, simply step away from the door, leaving it open as an invitation.

When he doesn't move, I say, "Well, are you going to come in?"

He shrugs with his hands in his pant pockets. "I was waiting for an invite."

"The way you've been going around demanding everything, it comes as a surprise that you're actually asking," I snipe.

He smiles, stepping into the room, then walks around, taking in his surroundings. "You've moved up in the world from the woman I met in economy." He looks over at my dresser and frowns. "Nice flowers."

101

I narrow my eyes. "Rehashing the past is getting kind of boring don't you think?" When he doesn't reply, I ask, "What do you want from me?" I hold my breath, scared of the answer.

"I'm not sure I know myself," he answers honestly.

His comment throws me off. He's at odds with his feelings, something we seem to have in common. It becomes even more apparent when he reaches up and pushes a strand of loose hair away from my face, then rests his hand gently against my cheek. Instinctively, I raise my own to hold him in place, but it's the wrong move as the contact startles him and breaks the moment. He steps back abruptly. Michael is gone, Becket is back. The glimmer of the man I met on the plane, the one who told me his secrets, has disappeared. But what else did I expect?

"I'm sorry." I don't know why I'm apologizing or what I'm apologizing for.

Becket seems to understand the situation better than me, and replies, "You have a lot to be sorry for, Brit. But that was all me."

I look away and focus my attention out the window, on the view of Jacksonville below. The lights from the buildings twinkle in the night, giving the room a magical glow. It's out of place—there is nothing magical about the two of us together.

Clearing his throat awkwardly, Becket breaks the silence that has settled around us. "I should get going. I just came to check on you."

"Check what?" I ask, confused.

"That you were ok, after earlier."

That, I wasn't expecting. For now, this is as close to an apology as I'm going to get. But I'll take it. What else can I do? He's forced us into this ridiculous scenario, and now we need to navigate our way out of it.

I stare him straight in the eyes, speaking firmly when I reply, "I'm not ok. Just so you know. What you did back there was wrong, no matter what the reasoning behind it was. But for the record … I appreciate you coming here to check on me."

"Ok." He shoves his hands back into his pockets. "Where do we go from here?"

It's all I can do to stop my mouth dropping open. The guy who stepped in my hotel room is not the same one from earlier at the ball. I wonder to myself whether he underwent a personality transplant on the journey over. Refusing to miss the opportunity, I say, "Help me with the article. Let me see the real you. I know this"—I wave my hand up and down at him— "isn't it. When we met on that plane ride, there was something else there. I know it wasn't an act."

He shakes his head. "I can't do that, I'm sorry. But I promise to show you what I do day-to-day, and be on my best behavior."

It's not a win, but it will do. For now. "Fine," I reply. "When do we begin?"

Ten

Britney

I pull out my cell and check the address Becket sent me in a message this morning when the cab pulls up slowly, outside an old derelict building. Leaning forward, I show the message to the cab driver. "Are you sure this is the right place?" I ask, as politely as possible.

He huffs while looking at the screen. All I get in return is a "yep", before he holds out his palm and looks at me expectantly, waiting for me to pay for the journey.

"You're sure?" I ask again, peering out the window, unconvinced. I don't have a clue where we are. We've been driving for the better part of an hour. Are we even in Jacksonville anymore? I wouldn't have a clue.

"Unless you're ready to pay double, you need to get out of the cab." His finger hovers over a button, ready to set the tariff counter running again.

"Fine," I snap. "Thank you for the hospitality. FYI if I wind up murdered, it's your ass I'm haunting." I throw my hair over my shoulder and exit the cab as dignified as possible after my little outburst.

The driver hits the gas so hard the tires spin, throwing dust up in my face when he zooms off. When my coughing and spluttering subsides, I look up.

Becket is playing games again.

I'm about to throw in the towel and call another cab, hopefully with a different driver, when a sign above a door at the far end of the building catches my attention. There's no harm in checking it out, I tell myself. *Al's* is all the sign says, giving absolutely nothing away.

Movement in my peripheral vision catches my attention. I turn quickly, and in the distance, my eyes focus on a figure in a black hooded jacket. Goosebumps cover my arms. I want to look away, but I can't. I blink, and just like that, they turn and walk away.

I try to shake it off, telling myself it was nothing. I quickly come to the decision that whatever is inside the building can't be any worse than what is outside. With that in mind, I push open the door, and step inside. The door slams shut behind me and I jump. I jump again when a bang echoes along the empty corridor, then another, and another. Then it stops. I daren't move, so I wait, listening. It's not long until there's another loud bang. This time when it reaches my ears, I recognize it's more like a slam.

Seriously, where has Becket brought me? There's trash scattered all over the corridor which I try to step over as I walk and the smell that reaches my nose is questionable. The door at the end of the small corridor is slightly ajar and I pause before opening it. What I find isn't a room filled with strung out squatters as I expected. It's filled with mats, punching bags, and other equipment. In the middle of it all, sparring, is Becket.

I watch as he moves effortlessly around the mats. I wasn't aware football players could move so lightly on their feet. I always pictured them barging up and down a field with a turd-colored ball, being anything but graceful. How he's moving ... it's beautiful to watch.

His opponent goes to take a swing, and I let out a loud gasp. Wrong move. That's all it takes to draw Becket's attention away from what he's doing. He looks in my direction and in the same moment his opponent's fist collides with his jaw. A loud crack fills the room and Becket stumbles back.

When he regains his balance, he dives straight back in. If he's in pain, he doesn't show it. They continue sparring for a few more minutes and I try not to move, scared of distracting him again and the result being more injuries.

When they stop, I move in closer, focusing on the other guy. Brad. I wonder what the NFL would say if they knew two of their most promising players were sparring outside of training sessions, putting their bodies at risk of injury. I put this little tidbit of information away in a box, just in case it's ever needed.

Becket beams, holding his arms out as if he's about to embrace me. "Here she is, our special guest."

I take a step back, raising an eyebrow.

Brad snorts at my reaction and his shoulders shake with laughter.

"You could have told me where I was coming. I thought the cab driver was kidnapping me and bringing me to a drug den," I snap.

"Don't flatter yourself, Brit, no one would want to kidnap you. And drugs aren't my thing. They're yours, remember?"

Here we go again. Whoever turned up at my room last night, it certainly wasn't Becket, because *this* is Becket in true form. I choose to ignore him. We have work to do. Rummaging through my bag until I find my notebook, I grin to myself when I pull it out, grateful I didn't forget my trusty friend.

Becket looks at me bemused. "What are you doing?"

"Working."

"I can see that, but why do you have a notebook?"

"To make notes … that's why I'm here."

"Aaaand I'm going to leave. See you later, man." Brad fist bumps Becket, nods at me then walks away.

"So …" I say, with my pen hovering over the page of my notebook when Brad has left the room.

"Put down the book, Brit."

"Why?"

"You're not here to make notes. You want to get to know me, then this is how we're going to do it. On my terms." He walks to one side of the room, stopping in front of the exposed brick wall. He begins rustling through a bag. When he walks back to me, he has something in his hands. Whatever it is, he tosses it through the air when he gets closer.

I reach out and catch a pair of wraps. "I'm not fighting you," I say, attempting to pass them back.

"What's wrong? Scared you'll lose?" His eyes sparkle, challenging me.

"You're a giant and I'm … not," I reply sweetly. There's actually a strong chance I'll win, not that I'm going to let him know that. He doesn't need to know I'm a black belt in Krav Maga.

I was thirteen when our neighbor heard Mom's boyfriend screaming and smashing up what little there was in our apartment to destroy. One day shortly after, he knocked on the door and told me to

107

get my shit together, that he owned a gym on the outskirts of town and that he was going to teach me self-defense. I didn't question what he was saying, because the place he was talking about had a rep for being one of the best Martial Arts Academies in the country. I told him I couldn't afford it and all he did was shrug, stating that money wasn't an issue. When I asked why, he looked at me sadly and said he didn't like the idea of me living like I did, defenseless. After my first training session, I never looked back, and Mom's boyfriends never laid a hand on me again.

"Ok, I'll play the game," I say, placing the notebook back in my bag and setting it down beside his. Thankfully, I opted for semi-casual clothing. Not as sporty as the black shorts and fitted grey T-shirt Becket is wearing, but enough that I can move freely on the mats. "How about we up the stakes?"

Becket looks at me intrigued. "Go on ..."

"If you win, you get to gloat and bitch about it however long you please."

He chuckles.

"If I win, I get to ask some questions ... with my notebook."

"Ok I'll take that."

He accepts the offer too easily and I know it's because he genuinely believes he's going to win. I'm not about to clue him in that there's a strong possibility he won't. It's more fun this way.

I start to wrap my hands and Becket steps forwards to help. I shake my head and say, "No need."

He frowns, watching as I wrap each hand carefully.

When I'm done, I walk into the middle of the mats, spin around and place my hands on my hips. "So, are we doing this or what?"

He looks suspicious but says nothing.

We start by warming up and I move around the mats, careful not to give the game away. Every now and again I throw in an innocent, "Like this?" Being the hero he is, Becket dives in to help, exactly like I want him to. When he isn't looking, I smirk to myself. He doesn't know what's about to hit him … literally.

When we're done warming up, he says, "Ok, I think you're good with the basics. Why don't we try for real now?"

"Are you sure I'm ready?" I ask, fluttering my eyelashes.

"I hate to break it to you, Brit, but I don't think you're going to win. I promise to try and go easy on you."

Game on, Becket. Game on.

We bounce our weight from side to side, circling each other. Thanks to the Florida heat I'm already feeling hot and bothered and I pray my body can hold out. I might be out of practice, but I shouldn't worry, it's like riding a bike. The first couple of sparring rounds are easy and I can tell Becket is holding back. He barely comes near me, and the fighter in me begins to get frustrated.

Without meaning to, I say out loud, "Come on, show me what you've got."

He pauses, assessing how to handle the situation. I wink. It's the signal he needs. He darts forward going straight in with an eye strike. Brutal, but not brutal enough. I slam the heel of my palm down on his arm, deflecting his attack. Raising my arm, I go straight in with my own strike to the eye. Becket flinches and my hand stops millimeters from its intended target.

I smile sweetly. "Is that a point to me?"

He stands with his mouth hanging open. "What the fuck, Brit?"

"Come on," I say stepping backwards and wiggling my eyebrows, "or are you scared you won't win?"

He cricks his neck from side to side. Shaking his arms out, he darts forwards. The aim: a full-frontal kick to the stomach. One that would result in me tumbling down to the ground. I have an advantage though. Becket is built like a house. My petite frame works in my favor. I'm able to dart away from him.

He's fast, I'm faster.

He charges in, fists raised. I block his extended arm with my own. I then shift my weight and step to the side. It throws him off guard. I swipe my hand up towards his jaw, careful not to put my full force behind it. I can't risk injuring him. Grabbing his wrist, I drive my knee into his thigh. He buckles. I then slam my arm into the crook of his elbow. It folds like I know it will. I use the opportunity to wrench his shoulder forward and up. Keeping his shoulder and torso pressed to my body, I force him to the ground to my two o'clock. I rest both knees firmly against his back.

Keeping his arm pinned in place, I lean forward and say in his ear, "I win."

Shifting my weight off his back, I kneel beside him, watching him groan into the mats. When he's recovered, he rolls onto his back with his eyes closed and I wait.

One emerald eye flickers open and he smirks. "What the hell was that?"

I shrug and make a show of observing my nails. "Just a little something I picked up."

"*You* are little. *That* was *not* little. I've been doing this for years, and by the looks of it so have you."

"What does it matter if I have?"

"It doesn't. It's just ... interesting. Not many chicks know Krav Maga like that."

110

I narrow my eyes. "I guess I'm not a *chick*."

"Come on, I didn't mean it like that."

A couple of butterflies take flight in my stomach at the way his gaze softens. "While we're at it, stop calling me Brit. Only people who know me call me that."

"I think I know you better than you think."

"You know nothing about me."

My heart, settled from the exertion of our sparring, begins to hammer in my chest as I watch Becket move up onto his knees. He shuffles towards me and when he's close, leans forward, getting into my personal space. My eyes are captivated by his and as hard as I try, I can't look away.

"Do you want to know why I know more?"

Through gritted teeth, I reply, "Enlighten me."

"Only people who have something to be afraid of learn to fight like that. Who are you afraid of?"

Blackness creeps in. He's forcing me to think about things I buried deep a long time ago. But that's the thing about burying secrets, there's always someone waiting to dig them up. I close my eyes and focus on inhaling and exhaling slowly. When I regain control, I open my eyes, only to find myself lost in his, again. I swallow hard before replying, "No one. Especially not you."

His eyes trail down to my lips and for the briefest of moments I think he might kiss me, but that would be crazy, because he has a girlfriend, Lola, and he hates me. Backing away, he shakes his head in frustration and I'm left feeling useless. Whatever control I had, disappeared as soon as we finished sparring.

"I—I won. You owe me some answers." I flinch at how pathetic I sound, even to my own ears.

He grabs his bag from the floor, then turns back laughing. "You already know all my secrets, remember?"

"You promised," I huff.

"Actually, I didn't promise anything. You assumed I would comply."

I clench my fists at my sides and watch as he stalks towards the door, leaving me alone in this virtually derelict place. But then he stops, and I watch his shoulders rise and fall dramatically. I stand up from the mats at the same time he spins around and walks back towards me.

"What now?" I snap, as he gets closer. "Coming in for anoth—"

I'm silenced when he closes the gap between us. His lips come down on mine, hot and urgent. Nothing about Becket is discreet or gentle. He's like a bulldozer, taking down anything in his path. I'm no exception. It's instinct to push him away, ask him what the hell he thinks he's doing. But when my hands reach his chest, ready to push him away, I ball them into fists gripping his shirt. I pull him in closer. He groans and kisses me harder. His hands snake round my waist. His fingertips dig into my flesh with the perfect amount of pressure. A moan of pleasure falls from my lips. When he sweeps his tongue slowly against mine, I'm a goner. My knees almost buckle as I become overloaded with sensation after sensation.

The kiss ends as quickly as it began, and Becket steps back. There's a storm in his eyes. *This*, whatever it is, could never work. Too much has happened.

I watch as he walks away, for good this time, grabbing his bag from the floor where he dropped it, on his way towards the exit. Over his shoulder he says loudly, "I'll make you a deal, Brit. I'll tell you some more of my secrets when you tell me yours."

The door slams and I'm left in the empty room, wondering what just happened.

***

Becket

I never should have listened to Coach. There's a reason I haven't played the nice guy in all of this. Britney has a way of getting under my skin. Up until now I've refused to admit it to myself, let alone anyone else. The night we met, kissed on that plane, sparks fired. Even she can't deny it and if she did, I know the truth. I felt the way goosebumps covered her skin when I touched her, teasing her; the way her nipples pebbled when she pressed up against me.

"Earth to Becket," says Brad, snapping his fingers in front of my eyes.

"What?" I bark, looking up from the ground where I'm sitting taking a much needed water break.

He holds his hands up. "Sheesh, B, will you fuck her already?!"

I clench my jaw and grit out, "Don't talk about her like that." Typical jock. He can be as much of a dick as I can, especially when it comes to respecting people's boundaries, which he isn't doing right now.

He throws his head back and starts laughing. "Priceless. You like her, don't you?"

"You don't know what you're talking about."

He narrows his eyes. "Actually, I do. It comes with being your best friend, and as your best friend I know when you're pussy whipped. You have been since the first time you met her. Admit it."

I clench my fists at my side, my blood boiling. I can't do or say anything, because it's true. I love to hate her and I'm losing control. Bringing her here

113

was wrong, I'm losing sight of what we're doing and that kiss we shared at Al's, made me feel alive, made me feel things I haven't been capable of since the first night we met.

Accepting that I'm not going to give anything away, at least not yet, Brad asks, "What's the next part of the plan then?"

I can't chance another moment with her like we had at Al's. "We go to Miami."

Brad frowns. "Lola will be pissed."

I know he's right, but I don't care. "When is Lola ever not pissed?"

Admitting defeat, Brad says, "Whatever, man." He throws his water bottle down on the ground beside his bag, before sprinting off to complete more drills.

I smirk to myself. Nice Becket is gone. We're back to playing the game my way.

Eleven

Britney

I'm stuck in a moving vehicle with three people who hate my guts. Torture is the word I'd use to describe the hours I've been sitting, as they converse between themselves and ignore me entirely. My only friends have been the drink at my side and the notebook in my lap, which I've been doodling in to pass the time. They're the only things of substance that fill the pages. I've been in Florida for two weeks and my progress on the article is virtually zero. Scrap that. It *is* zero.

The only insight I've gained into Becket so far: *Black Coffee*. I'm screwed.

When I've not been avoiding him, we've spent our time bickering. When we've not been bickering, I've shadowed his every move. What I've learned: he wakes up, eats, plays football, sees his physios, and repeat. Every. Single. Day. The most exciting part about him, I'm beginning to learn, is the lack of filter on his mouth. But the more time I spend with him and his team, the more I learn it's just standard jock talk. He's a bit of a hot head, they all are. If I didn't know any better, I'd agree with what Leigh said the day we were standing in Fiona's office—he's as boring as they come.

But he's not.

I know he's not because the plane ride taught me otherwise. I know there's more to him than the two words *black coffee*, the fight club was a prime example of the fact there's more to Becket than meets the eye. He was in his prime at the masquerade ball, wearing a mask, because he has one in place all the time, shielding himself from the world. I just have to figure out a way to get him to trust me again, to let me in and show me who he really is.

"Where exactly are we going?" I ask.

They completely ignore me. My throat goes dry as I watch Lola drape herself over Becket, peppering him with kisses, giggling in that annoying way girls do sometimes. Someone put a bag over her head already. I'm jealous, there I said it. But what else did I expect? He dropped the bombshell of them being together at the ball and nothing's changed since. Apart from that kiss. The kiss that made my heart pound. The same kiss that's kept me awake each night since, tossing and turning, hot and bothered, trying to ignore the ache between my legs, as I imagine Becket's mouth there, torturing me with his tongue in the best kind of way. I might be a virgin, but I'm no prude. I know what sex is, what it entails, and I know what I want.

Him.

But he's not mine to want, which is made even clearer as I watch Lola suck on his earlobe. Seriously?

I clear my throat and repeat louder, "Where are we going?"

Becket's eyes meet mine briefly. "Miami." He turns his attention back to Brad and Lola.

"Why are we going to Miami?"

116

Brad looks at me and with a shrug, replies, "One of the perks of it being off season. We get to go to the festival."

I look at him, totally confused.

"Oh, come on"—he scoffs—"you have to know about the Miami festival. It's like one of the biggest events of the year. People all over the world come for it."

"Never heard of it," I grumble, and go back to gazing out of the tinted window of the limo. I wouldn't know because I haven't had time to do these kinds of things. The furthest my social life stretches is after-work drinks with Jess. The rest of the time I graft. Graft as hard as I can to try and put my own past behind me. Only when I manage to get rid of the shackles of my mom's debts will I be able to actually start living my own life. For now, I'm chasing one payment after another, always looking over my shoulder in case the people she got tied in with turn up unexpectedly. I can't wait to really feel like I can breathe again without a weight on my chest.

"You'll like it," chips in Becket breaking me from my thoughts. "Lots of costumes, masks, drinking. It's one big party."

I blink and nod, not sure how to reply. I expected some kind of jibe, the sort Becket would make, but there's none. Bored, Lola returns to giggling as Becket whispers something in her ear. That's the extent of our communication during the five-hour journey to Miami from Jacksonville. More than once, I think to myself, who does a trip to Miami then back in a day? I already know the answer. NFL players who can do whatever they want, whenever they want.

I'm the first to jump out when we arrive, excited to stretch my legs. Sitting for five hours solid isn't fun. The midday sun beats down relentlessly, and I already wish I'd thought ahead and brought sunblock or at least worn something that covers my pale skin more than the small red camisole and black shorts I'm wearing. I thought I was being smart and beating the heat. What I won't be beating is sunburn. I'll be lucky if I don't finish the day the same color as my top.

I freeze when Becket throws an arm around my shoulders, tugging me into his side. He leans in and says close to my ear, "Ready to have some fun?"

Our skin contact causes me to shudder and when he pulls away there's that stupid smirk on his face again. I divert my attention to Brad, who's rolling his eyes. Lola looks like she wants to shove me in the limo and send me back to Jacksonville. She wouldn't have to force me, I'd happily go.

"What do we do at this festival then?" I ask.

Becket looks at me, intrigued. "You've really never been to a festival before?"

"Nope." I add an extra pop to the P at the end, hoping he doesn't push the matter further. When he raises an eyebrow questioningly, I sigh and, being careful not to give too much away, expand. "I've never had the time."

He carries on staring, but I look away and hear him let out a huff of air. The atmosphere is so tense you could cut it with a knife.

Brad steps forward and clarifies exactly what the festival entails, "We drink and we party!"

I raise my hands in the air, and hoot, "Whooo party time!"

Not missing the sarcasm in my voice, the group walks off without me and I'm left trailing behind without anyone to talk to. Clearly this day is going to be fun for everyone apart from me.

Rather than diving straight into the festival, carnival, whatever you want to call it, we settle for a small bar to begin. I'm still none the wiser to what we're actually doing here, but on the walk over, decide if I'm here, I may as well try to enjoy myself.

"This place is cool," I say, glancing around at the open-air bar attached to one of the many high-rise hotels that sprawl along the Miami beachfront. Music blares from speakers somewhere. The crowd is young and loud, mostly in bikinis. It oozes cool. "I love being by the beach. You don't get places like this in New York." I cringe at how over-the-top my voice comes out but trying to make an effort with three people who have a serious dislike towards me, is grating on my nerves.

"That's because New York sucks," says Becket, his voice sharp and bitter.

It's been a while since he voiced his irrational hatred of the place. I remember the first night we met on the plane, he couldn't wait to get away, claiming it was down to his breakup with his long-term girlfriend Abby, but it seemed like so much more than that.

Changing the subject, he asks, "Want a drink?"

"Please," I respond politely, determined to be on my best behavior. "A cocktail—a strong one." I catch Lola throwing me a death stare. "Make it two."

"No scotch?"

And we're back to the drink spiking references. It takes everything in me not to roll my eyes and retort with a snappy remark. Sweetly, I reply, "It's not something I drink often."

"Same. Apparently, it makes me do crazy things." He holds my gaze, waiting, but I refuse to start rehashing things in a public place.

Lola intervenes, "Let's go get the drinks together."

I'm almost thankful she's here, until I watch them walk away and she entwines her hand with his tugging him along.

"Well, this is about as fun as I expected," Brad says with a laugh, watching the pair of them disappear to the bar.

"Believe me, I'd rather be anywhere but here," I mutter.

"You could have fooled me." His brown eyes twinkle mischievously.

"What's that supposed to mean?"

"I saw the way you were looking at each other."

"I don't know what you're talking about. He has a girlfriend."

"What? Lola?" He scoffs then throws his head back and laughs so loud people begin staring at us. "Please."

"Am I missing something?"

"Just that she *wishes* she was his girlfriend. Becket hasn't been tied down since Abby."

"Then why were they together at the ball? And why didn't she say otherwise?"

"A certain sex tape springs to mind. They're messing with you, Britney."

Before I get a chance to respond to the bombshell Brad just dropped, the pair return with our drinks on a tray. Becket hands over both of mine and I give him a tight smile, trying to cover up how I'm feeling about the conversation I've just had.

It must be more of a grimace than a smile because he asks, "You good?"

"Fine," I reply, picking up the bright-blue one of my two drinks, downing half of it in one go. I then turn to Lola and say, "I didn't get to properly introduce myself at the ball. I'm Britney."

"I know exactly who you are," she says, her voice so icy it could freeze the drink in my hand.

Becket interrupts what clearly has the potential to turn into a face-off between the two of us, and sternly says, "Lola, not now."

Lola's feisty though and chooses to ignore him, keeping her focus solely on me. "Who do you think you are coming here after what you did? Are you trying to ruin him again?"

"I never intended to do that," I admit and my eyes dart to Becket, who frowns at the tidbit of information I've let slip. "If you have an issue with me being here, I'm not the person you should be taking it up with."

"You never meant to ruin him? Exactly what did you think would happen when you aired a sex tape on prime-time television among the other things you did? Just admit it, you're a deceitful bitch." She snuggles into Becket's side, who looks like he wants to be anywhere but here, and we've only been in Miami an hour. "Sucks to be you though, because it's me who has the guy."

I pick my drink back up from the table, taking another large swig before I say, "Bull."

Her eyes widen and she sits up straight. "What's that supposed to mean?"

"I know you're not together."

Brad begins fake choking on his drink, a signal for me to shut my mouth, but I'll be damned if I'm going to let her walk all over me.

"Y—you don't know what you're talking about."

Wrong Lola, I think to myself. The game is up, we both know it is.

"I thought I could do this, but I can't," she says, "I can't watch you be around her, not after what she did." She stands up, grabbing her bag, ready to leave.

When Becket doesn't move, she places her hands on her hips. "Are you coming?"

His eyes meet mine for a split second and my heart skips a beat. *Pick me.*

He shakes his head at her. "I'm staying. We have the article to work on."

She throws her hands up in the air dramatically and in a much louder tone says, "Unbelievable! Don't forget what she did to us, and don't forget who stood by you through it. Me. I'm out of here." Throwing her brown hair over one shoulder, she stomps away to who knows where.

I don't care.

"I'll go with her and check she's ok ..." says Brad, a little too eagerly. "Message me when it's time to leave."

"Look after her." Becket nods, knowing she's pissed and in need of someone to tame her mood.

And then there were two.

The day has taken a turn for the worse quicker than even I could have predicted. When I look to Becket, he's taking in our surroundings, avoiding eye contact with me as best he can. I look down at the two cocktails I ordered, one of which is already almost gone. With the sour mood I'm in, I should have ordered three.

***

I'm a little unsteady on my feet. Not surprising as I've somehow made my way through four cocktails in a relatively short time. Not the smartest idea, but as the alcohol courses through my veins and the world feels lighter than it has in a long time, I don't care. We're almost at the carnival—festival—whatever it is— when I stumble on a perfectly even piece of sidewalk. Ok, I'm *a lot* unsteady on my feet. Becket places his

122

hands on my shoulders to steady me and I look up into his emerald eyes. His hair looks almost golden as the sun dips in the sky and the orange glow makes the color of his tanned skin seem even deeper.

"You look really pretty today," I say, then slap a hand against my forehead. Cool, Brit. *This* is one of the reasons I rarely drink.

Becket chuckles. "I put in the extra effort just for you."

What the hell? Is he flirting with me?

I don't get a chance to ask because we turn a corner and are hit with noise, color and the smells of all kinds of street food. My mouth drops open, the embarrassing outburst forgotten. Thousands of people dance around in front of us, waving their drinks about like they're having the time of their life. Cigarette smoke fills the warm air, drifting over from a large gang of teenagers not too far away. I've never felt more alive than I do at this moment and my heart races with excitement.

Becket leans in close so I can hear when he says, "It's party time, Brit." He pulls a couple of hip flasks out from the backpack slung over his shoulder and waves them at me playfully.

If I have any more, he'll be carrying me away before we get a chance to experience the festival. So, I politely say no, for now.

We spend the next hour walking around, absorbing the atmosphere, laughing, and joking together. It's all so carefree and being together like this almost feels normal, it almost feels right. I have to tell myself more than once to get my head out of the gutter. The kiss at the fight club is plaguing my mind, making me misinterpret things, making me believe something is happening between us that isn't.

"There's a parade soon," says Becket.

123

"What kind of parade?"

The way his eyes sparkle, tells me he's as excited as I am. "You'll have to wait and see."

He navigates us expertly, making it clear this isn't his first time. My mind drifts off and I wonder how many times he's been here and whether it was with Lola or Abby. A stab of jealousy hits me, as images of them dancing and laughing together like we've been doing, flood my brain. They leave a bitter taste in my mouth, which I try to get rid of by grabbing one of the hip flasks out of his hand and then taking a large drink. I wince as the taste of Scotch fills my mouth and burns my throat on the way down. It had to be Scotch. Now my mind is full of other images I'd rather not be there.

There's a lull in activity and people begin to gather for the parade. The crowd splits down the middle, creating enough space for it to pass through and then we all wait.

Seizing the moment, I say, "You owe me answers still."

"You know the deal, Brit. When you tell me some of your secrets, I'll tell you some of mine. But until then ..." He looks away.

My blood begins to boil. The way he's playing this, I'm never going to have an article and am very much at risk of being fired. For as long as I can remember, I've had a mantra: Don't leave things to chance. Plan every moment, pre-empt every twist, then you can't be screwed over. When life walked all over me, I turned around and walked right back. But then I met *him*. I'm out of my depth. Any control I had is being served to him on a plate. I've lost all sense of why I'm here and what I'm meant to be doing.

Trying not to relinquish what little power I have left, I say, "I feel like we're going backwards. Each time I think I'm beginning to understand a little of who you are, you change. I don't get it."

He looks at me, and an amused expression covers his ridiculously gorgeous face. "You don't know a thing about me, Brit. The games I play aren't just on the field."

I sway on my feet, but it doesn't stop me from staring back, refusing to blink or show any sign of weakness. My gut churns with the anxiety of the unknown. Whatever this game is we're playing, it's clear he's writing the rules. I may have fooled him once, but there's no doubt, he's going to fool me time and time again.

Beginning to lose my temper, I open my mouth ready to snap back, when my words are drowned out by music as the parade begins. *Carnaval de Paris* sounds out and Wasamba Carnival Drummers charge forward, filling the early evening air with a beat that vibrates through the ground and travels through my body. It's so loud I can barely hear myself think. The crowd goes wild as the parade moves steadily through the cramped space. I'm pushed around, back and forth as hot bodies dance and press in all around me, causing me to stagger when the world tilts. My vision distorts and everything becomes double, then hazy, bouncing back and forth between the two. Paint bombs and confetti fire through the air, filling the sky with vibrant blues, pinks and yellows. Brazilian dancers strut past, and the crowds mimic their moves. All while I'm pushed around, mesmerized by the neon feather headdresses and jeweled bikinis glittering in the dimming light.

I'm not sure how much time passes, but when I spin around, trying to find Becket, I can't see him anywhere. Shit. I look around helplessly. Even in my drunken state I know this is bad. I haven't got a clue where we are, and in case this all wasn't trippy enough, the music changes tempo. *Silence* by Delirium reaches my ears. The crowd erupts in cheers and whistles, bouncing around frantically, pushing me forwards towards the huge parade floats passing by.

That's when I see it.

On the other side of the parade, there's a figure in a black, hooded jacket. My blood runs cold. It's a brief moment, so brief I'm not quite sure it happens.

A huge float slowly moves past, obscuring my view, filled with cloaked figures, dancing mythically. Their gowns billow in the breeze and one swoops down towards me ghost-like. Piercing blue eyes find mine behind a white Venetian Volto mask, unblinking. They raise a white-gloved finger to the mask's lips, mimicking *shh*. I stumble back, helplessly, closing my eyes as I fall to the ground, bracing myself for impact, but it never comes.

"Brit, what the hell?" shouts Becket over all the noise, taking my weight with his arms.

I allow him to engulf me, relishing his warmth and comfort for a few seconds, shaking like a leaf while he strokes my hair soothingly and rocks me back and forth.

With his lips buried in the nape of my neck, he murmurs, "It's ok."

When I feel like I've regained control of my breathing, I stand tall and look to where I thought I saw the figure in the black, hooded jacket. There's nothing there. "Can we leave? Please." I try to convey to him with my eyes, how much I don't want to be here.

He nods, wraps an arm around my waist and expertly maneuvers us through the crowds. It takes a good ten minutes to get away from all the noise and bustle, and it's a relief when we turn a corner onto an empty block, not a soul in sight. Unable to hold myself together any longer, I fold in half, resting my arms against my thighs, and gasp for air.

Becket crouches down in front of me, brushes my hair out of my face, then grasps my cheeks with his hands, urging me to look at him. "What happened back there?"

I bite the inside of my cheek, unsure whether I should tell him. I could, but he'd most likely think I'd drunk too much, so I give him a garbled version of the truth, "I thought I saw something, but it was nothing … I guess the masks from the parade freaked me out." I look at him sheepishly.

He chuckles lightly. "Are you sure that's it?"

I nod and when he gives up on retrieving any more information from me, he lets go of my face and stands back up.

He passes over one of the hip flasks from earlier, the one that isn't Scotch. "It might make you feel better."

I smile meekly, taking it from him, embracing the burn of Vodka against my throat, allowing the pain to bring me back to reality.

Becket pulls out his cell, and reels off the address where we are to the limo driver. I hate being a party pooper and putting an end to his celebrations so early, but after what happened, there's no way I can go back to the festival.

A few minutes pass and then the limo pulls up alongside the sidewalk where we're standing. I scramble in with Becket close behind and allow exhaustion to take over, resting my head on his shoulder. Being affectionate with each other isn't how we roll, but for today I don't care, I'll take whatever he gives me, no matter how wrong it is.

The steady sway of the vehicle as it passes through Miami almost lulls me to sleep. Before it does, I tilt my head up and say, "I didn't know you had it in you to be so nice."

Becket looks down at me, his face full of sadness. "Is that what you think, Brit, that I'm not a nice person?"

"You've never given me a reason to think otherwise," I reply, sleepily. My eyes grow heavy, and I succumb to sleep before I get the chance to hear him say, "Fine. You want to see if there's more to me. Just this once, we'll play the game your way."

Twelve

Becket

W here the hell is she?

I'm beginning to sweat, sitting in my living area waiting for Lola to arrive. I'm lucky to have experienced her wrath, multiple times, and my nerves are one hundred percent justified. My favorite time was shortly after the video of the two of us together leaked, and her older brothers turned up on my doorstep ready to jump my ass. Luck was on my side and they had more sense than to assault an NFL player; it was most likely to avoid a multimillion-dollar lawsuit over wanting to hear my side to the story.

I frown when the doorbell rings. Lola usually just lets herself in, which means she knows. She knows the conversation we're about to have isn't going to be enjoyable for either of us. When I open the door, she stalks straight past, head held high, without saying a word.

She's pissed, and rightly so.

I follow her into the kitchen part of my open-plan kitchen/living area. Nothing has changed since the first time she stormed in here ... apart from me. That was the beginning of our journey and unfortunately, this will be the end. I've only ever liked her as a friend, and she wants more. She always has. She cares too much and all I'll ever do is hurt her.

"Water?" I ask, breaking the silence. My eyes take in her usually pristine appearance. Today she's dressed down in loungewear, her hair scraped back, not an ounce of makeup to be seen. She would never let me see her like this. She's given up, predicted our breakup.

We're not even together.

Shaking her head, she folds her arms across her chest. "Can we just get this over and done with?"

I rub a hand on the back of my neck and awkwardly say, "Why does it feel like we're breaking up?"

She shrugs and looks anywhere but directly at me. "I guess in a way we are."

"You know what I'm going to say?"

"I'm not an idiot." Finally, she looks up at me. Her eyes glisten, making me feel like even more of a dick. "Do you know how I feel?"

I nod. She must read something on my face, because hers drops in defeat. She knows I'm not going to change my mind. After our little bedtime buddies stint, we agreed to stay friends and since then I've never led her on, but I should have known better. We should have had a clean break. This is my fault.

"I'm sorry I can't give you more," I say sadly, wishing I could. Lola's a dream and she will make some guy happy one day. There's one guy in particular I know who would be really happy to have her, if only he had the balls to make a move.

"I knew what I was getting into when I said yes to being friends, even though I wanted more. I never thought we'd stay friends for this long," she admits.

"We work well together ..." Christ this really does feel like a breakup. If only Abby had been as heartbroken over parting ways.

"Too well, and for me that's the problem." She takes a deep breath, about to say more, but then stops.

"Were you going to say something?" I ask, trying to catch her eye.

She mutters, "Fuck it," under her breath then almost pleading, says, "Is there no way we could ever give us a try?"

Part of me wants to make her happy and say yes, but it would be for the wrong reasons. In the end, I would wind up breaking her heart. I'm not the asshole everyone thinks I am, and the mask I've been wearing for years has come loose, thanks to the firecracker who's been constantly at my side these past few weeks. "I'm sorry, you're not the one I want." My eyes widen when I realize what I've said.

Any warmth in her expression disappears and her face turns hard. "It's her..."

"That came out wrong," I backtrack, but it's too late. Lola isn't stupid.

"I know exactly who you're talking about."

"Lola, I'm sorry." I take a step towards her, reaching out to grab her hand so I can pull her in for a hug or something that will hopefully pacify her. I'm an idiot. She's feisty as fuck when she wants to be and there's no way, she's going to let this go.

"Sorry for what? Wanting the same woman who set us up? Who filmed us having sex and then aired it on national television? Almost ruined both of our lives?"

I rub a hand along the stubble on my jaw, trying to relieve some of the tension. This couldn't have gone

131

any worse. So much for parting ways on good terms. "I don't know what you want me to say."

"There's nothing to say, Becket. You seem to have a thing for women who aren't all in. Why is that do you think?"

She knows I keep people at a safe distance on purpose. I never allowed her to get close enough to figure out why, but she's always been suspicious. "Leave it, Lola," I say sternly.

She shakes her head. "No. I'm tired of being your lapdog, it's time you heard some hard truths. Britney ... that girl you're pining after—even if you don't realize you are—will screw you over again, whether you want to believe it or not. Just like Abby did. You know, the one you thought was the love of your life. She wasn't by the way. I know you just loved that she didn't pry, but that's because she didn't give a shit. She was already in love with someone else, right?

"You go for women who are unattainable, so you don't have to worry about the future with them; so you don't have to fully commit and let them in. Let *me* in. Let me be that person you tell all your secrets to. *I care*, and I promise I won't go selling your stories to the media, unlike some."

She's unrecognizable to the woman who stormed in here and chewed my ass eighteen months ago. That's why this can never happen. I'm doing this to her. I'm no good for her.

"This is why we can't stay friends, Lola. We're in completely different places and we want different things."

"All I want is you."

I go to pull her in for one last hug goodbye, but she steps away, refusing my gesture. She walks to the front door to let herself out, turning back with one last thing to say, "She's screwed you over before and she will do it again. You can't trust her Michael. If you do ... then you're a fool."

***

Britney

My stomach fills with dread when my phone chimes on the dresser, alerting me to a new message from Jess. I don't want to know what she has to say, so I chose to ignore it.

It chimes again and again.

Resigning myself to the fact I'm not going to be able to avoid her forever, I place my laptop to the side and clamber off the bed. I grab the phone from the dresser, then walk back over to the bed, getting myself settled before opening the message thread, preparing myself for her 'feedback'.

Jess: *What the fuck have you just sent me?*
Jess: *Answer*
Jess: *Me*
Jess: *Brit*

I struggle to swallow. I knew she wouldn't buy into it, I don't even know why I tried. I'm screwed. I quickly begin typing back before she can bombard me with any more messages:

I sent you the article about Becket.

Maybe if I feign ignorance, she might be a little kinder.

Jess: *That wasn't an article. Why would anyone want to read about the fact he drinks black coffee?*

So much for being kind.

Me: *Some people like to read those sorts of things.*
Jess: *The only thing you've done is map out his schedule for all his crazy stalker fans. Unless that's your plan, to lead them to him so they can see him off for you?*
Me: *It wasn't that bad.*
Jess: *No, it wasn't bad, it was shit. If I put that forward, you won't be the only one getting fired. Now, get your ass off that bed before you become permanently engrained in it. Find Becket and find some information worthy of an article!*

A strangled cry fills the room and I drop my phone.

What the hell was that?

My phone chimes and I pick it back up with a shaky hand. My eyes dart around attempting to figure out what it could have been. A minute passes and there's nothing, so I read the message, trying to distract my brain.

Jess: *Why aren't you replying?*

Another strangled cry.

Fuckety fuck fuck fuck! I dart off the bed, looking around frantically. My heart pounds so hard it feels like it's about to burst out of my chest. I walk to the hotel phone on unsteady feet, pick it up and press the button that automatically directs calls to reception.

"You're through to reception, how may I help?" comes a male voice down the line.

"I—I think there's something in my room ..."

The guy on the other end of the line pauses before replying, "Something in your room, ma'am?"

"Yes," I say more assertively this time. "It sounds like someone is being murdered."

"I'll be up right away."

My hand trembles as I place the phone back down on the cradle. Another cry fills the room at the same moment I pick my cellphone up off the bed.

Fuck this.

I run out of my room, not caring that the door locks behind me. It means whatever's inside is locked in, while I'm out. I don't have to wait long before the guy from reception appears. It's all I can do to stop myself from jumping into his arms with relief. He smiles awkwardly at what is no doubt my crazed expression.

I hold my breath when he enters the room, terrified for what he's about to find.

A couple of minutes later he walks back out looking bemused, with a tabby cat purring in his arms. "Is this your cat, ma'am?"

"If it were my cat, do you think I'd have rung reception?" I try to keep the snappiness out of my voice, but I'm not sure what he expected my answer to be. I rang him less than ten minutes ago, clearly fearing for my life, thinking someone was dying.

"Strange. The only time we've ever had a cat in the hotel was when we had mice." He chuckles at the way my eyebrows shoot up. "That was twenty years ago. Don't worry there aren't any mice in your room, I checked. Twice."

I sigh with relief and thank him before he walks off down the corridor, carrying the now purring and content cat with him.

Raising my phone to my ear when it vibrates with an incoming call from Jess, I answer, "Hey ..."

"Why have you stopped replying to me? Someone better be dying."

"I thought someone was," I reply.

"Wait? What?"

"There was a cat in my room, making that God awful noise they do sometimes. I thought someone was being murdered."

"Ew, that means there are mice."

I frown at her comment. "There isn't. Reception checked."

"Weird."

"Very," I agree.

"Back to more important matters. You shouldn't be worrying about a cat in your room, because you shouldn't be in your room. Get your ass out and get following Becket. You're a better writer than this, Brit. Don't make me look like an idiot for putting you on the job."

She's baiting me, I know she is, and it gets the desired response. It gets me back up, lighting a fire inside me, a need to prove to everyone I got this job due to talent, not because of my association with Becket's media scandal.

"I'll have it for you soon," I reply, before hanging up, ready to make plans with the thorn in my side.

***

Being blindfolded was not what I had in mind when Becket and I agreed to meet. He said that it was a secret. He met me outside the hotel, waving a piece of material in my face. I shook my head and told him

136

not a chance in hell, to which he turned around and stalked off towards his car, refusing to take me anywhere unless I followed the rules.

It was then that I realized I had no choice.

"Can we take it off yet?" I ask, the Florida humidity hitting me as I step out of the vehicle.

"No," he replies sternly.

I don't have a clue where he is, but I don't have to wonder for long. He slips his hand around mine and tugs me forwards. My feet follow, stumbling.

"Seriously, I'm going to injure myself if you don't let me take this off," I grumble.

"A couple more minutes. Promise."

I huff and try to focus on carefully placing one foot in front of the other, so as not to risk breaking my neck. Finally, his steps slow, and then he comes to a standstill. The next thing I know, the blindfold is removed from my eyes. I wince at first. Having been in darkness for so long, the light is stark and my eyes struggle to adjust. I look around and find we're in a large, virtually empty room, apart from the mats on the floor and chairs surrounding the perimeter.

"Where are we?"

Becket backs away eyes twinkling. "I'm not allowed to tell you. This was the only way they'd let me bring you in. Just watch and see."

I swallow, nervous, but I shouldn't be. Women of all ages, races, and sizes, begin filing in, smiling warmly in my direction.

"Is this your first time?" asks a woman with tight, red curls and a southern twang.

"Yes," I reply honestly. Just in case I might be mistaken for being here for the same reason she is, I nod at Becket and confirm, "I'm with him."

"Ah," she replies. "Lucky you."

As far as I was aware, the world had Becket slotted in the same asshole category I did. Not here apparently. The room goes silent when he clears his throat and starts to speak. I follow suit as the women gather around closely so they can hear.

"Ladies. Here we are again, you lucky things."

The women hum their approval and I try not to roll my eyes as I watch them visibly swoon.

"You know the drill!" He pulls out his cell and walks to a set of speakers where he syncs them, and electro music fills the room.

The women all pair off and begin sparring against each other. I blink rapidly as I look around. A part of me expects Becket to come over and explain what is going on, but he avoids eye contact and bounces between the partners, correcting their form and showing them different stances. He observes and jumps in when needed, showing them how to make their moves more effective.

He's teaching them self-defense.

I take one of the seats off to the side, not knowing what to do.

The redhead walks over with a friendly smile. "Would you like me to teach you some moves?"

With expert timing, Becket swoops in. "She's the last person who needs help. She's already kicked my ass once and that was enough."

The redhead laughs and returns to her original partner.

I'm about to ask a question, but Becket holds his hand up stopping me in my tracks. "No questions here. Later, I promise. I have work to do."

He walks away and I spend the next hour watching as he interacts with each of the women, making them feel at ease and answering any questions they have. It's like I'm observing a completely different person.

This is the Becket I met on the plane. The one who revealed his secrets and showed vulnerability. Not the dick who turns up nine times out of ten and puts a show on for the world.

I'm confused. He's hiding who he really is, and I want to know why. This is the purpose of the article after all, to find out who he really is. When the room empties at the end of the session, I remain in my seat, waiting for him to come over. Instead, he mills about doing pointless tasks, putting off the inevitable.

When I've had enough, I say, "Becket ..."

He stops what he's doing and turns to look at me, emotions swirling in his eyes. I can't pinpoint what they all are, but my heart aches, wanting to make whatever it is he's feeling, whatever it is he's been through, better.

"They're survivors," he confirms.

I don't need to ask of what. I set my notebook down on the chair next to me, closed. The information he's telling me is for me, only me. "How long have you been doing this?" I ask.

"Years."

"Why?"

"They need help."

"No, not why are you helping them—I get that. What's your reason. There has to be something ..."

He looks away. "I can't tell you that."

"I promise, I won't say a word. You can trust me."

His demeanor shifts and coldly he says, "Like fuck I can."

"Why did you bring me here if you think you can't trust me?"

"To show you I'm not an ass like you think. These women need protection. You can't tell a soul you were here."

"Like there's anything to tell. I don't even know where we are."

"And that's the way it will stay." He steps forward, pulling the piece of material he used to blindfold me earlier out of his pocket.

I frown. "Is that really necessary?"

"You know the deal, Brit. I'll tell you my secrets when you tell me yours. So, what will it be?"

I stare him in the eyes. Images flash through my mind of all the things I've been through, all the things he did. Things I haven't told a soul. "Go ahead and put it on," I sigh, resigned.

Today, no secrets will be revealed, from either of us. I'm not ready and neither is he. The fact we're hesitating, proves how little trust there is. It's not the right time.

When it comes to Becket and me, I wonder if we will ever be able to trust each other.

Thirteen

Britney

T here's a charity game organized for the Jacksonville Jaguars which I'm scheduled to attend. I wouldn't know the difference between a charity one and a normal one, because I've never been to a football game. Rather than fretting over what's to come, I use the morning to catch up on other work projects in my hotel room.

I'm trying to focus when a message flashes on my phone. I don't have to guess who it's from, she has a sixth sense for when I'm procrastinating and when I'm keeping something from her. As I'm doing both, the pull must be strong.

Jess: *The powers that be would like an update on the article's progress.*
Me: *You're using them as an excuse to find out gossip now?*
Jess: *Possibly.*
Me: *You have no shame.*
Jess: *What choice do I have? You keep screening my calls. Now, tell me something about the big blond giant. Besides how he takes his coffee and what his daily schedule is.*

At least she's being playful; it means she's in a better mood than the other day.

Me: *There's nothing to tell.*
Jess: *If there wasn't anything to tell you would answer my calls. It's lucky you're all the way in Florida.*

I roll my eyes, thankful for the distance and that she can't see my reaction.

Jess: *I know you're rolling your eyes.*

Damn it.

Me: *Honestly. Progress is poor.*
Jess: *What do you mean progress is poor? There isn't a never-ending timeline on this. You have to produce an article. Soon. I can't keep putting the deadline off. People want to know when it's going to run.*
Me: *Things are complicated. We've barely spent any time together and the time we have has been a catastrophe. This would have worked a lot better if we'd done the interview over the phone or by email. You know, like we do with most clients.*
Jess: *But Becket isn't a normal client. He set his own terms and he wanted you in Florida. Sorry B. This will be the first big interview he's done in years. It's exclusive and it's huge. It has the potential to be a bestselling issue, so you need to think outside the box.*
Me: *It's an article with a football player how exactly am I supposed to think outside the box?*

Jess: *I don't know but it's your job and what you're getting paid for.*
Jess: *P.S. Is he as sexy in person?*

I pause before replying, wondering whether I should let Jess in on the mixed feelings I'm having. The professional part of me wants to hold back. She's my boss, but she's also my best friend and if I can't speak to her, I have no one.

Me: *He's as sexy.*
Jess: *You'll be dropping your panties in no time. But I didn't say that. As your boss I do not approve. However, as your best friend, I say ride that horse.*
Me: *Slightly inappropriate ...*
Jess: *You gotta lose that V-card someday baby. Might as well set the bar high.*
Me: *I'm ending this conversation now. I have a football game to get ready for.*
Jess: *Wear something skimpy, have fun and don't forget to think outside the box.*

***

There's apparently one perk of doing the article: Free seats. At least it would be a perk if I followed football. I shuffle along my designated row, smiling to myself that I've managed to score another point. Becket wanted me to be in one of the boxes where all the VIPs go. I outright refused, especially after the charade at the masquerade ball. The last thing I wanted was to be around people who were there and witnessed my embarrassment.

Now that I have a great seat, even I can appreciate how great it is, close to the field, where I can see Becket clearly. It might be out of season, but I can feel the fans' excitement in the air. The stadium is buzzing and alive. I'm beginning to understand why he fought so hard for his career. When he walks out onto the field, he has the unwavering support of his fans, but it's not just that. Looking around, taking in the enormity of the stadium, the excitement, the feeling of being a part of something much bigger, I realize he does it for the love of the game. Nothing else could compare.

I feel out of place in my black suit pants and white blouse. I don't know why I opted for my standard New York uniform; it's the first time I've worn it since the day I arrived. Maybe it was to try and keep some distance between our worlds. Something to serve as a reminder of how different we are and why we can't be together.

The crowds start to chant as it gets closer to the start of the game, waiting for each team to run onto the pitch. When the Jaguars appear, the stadium erupts so loudly I think I might have burst an eardrum. My eyes hone in on Becket and become glued to his broad chest and spandex-covered legs, watching as he runs across the field with the crowd screaming their appreciation. He's in his element.

Before running off the field with his teammates at halftime, Becket's eyes scour the crowd until he finds me. He cocks his head to the side as a signal for me to follow. Even behind his helmet I can see the playful glint in his eyes, and my body starts to hum.

I maneuver my way along the row of seats and head inside the stadium, walking the same corridors I did just a few weeks ago when everything felt different between us. The corridor leads to the locker rooms and is clad with giant security guys, making sure no crazy fans get past.

"Ma'am," a particularly burly one says as I approach.

"Britney Shaw," I respond, knowing it's my name he wants.

He looks down the list he has in his hands and when he finds my name, lets me through. It's like wading through treacle the closer I get. I'm almost at the locker room, when a hand reaches out and pulls me along a dark corridor. I go to yelp, but a large hand covers my mouth, silencing me.

"Don't scream, it's just me," whispers Becket.

He spins me around and the first thing I notice is that he's removed his helmet, then my eyes lock on what he has in his hands. "What's that?"

"Hello to you too." He smirks.

I nod at what he's holding, and he takes a step back, holding up a Jaguar's jersey.

I frown. "What's it for?"

His eyes burn each part of my body they pass over. "You're not exactly dressed for the occasion. You look like you're ready for a day at the office."

"It's called being professional." I sniff.

"Consider it a gift." He goes to pass it to me, but I shake my head.

"I'm not wearing it."

He takes a step forward.

I gulp. "What are you doing?"

He doesn't answer, just takes another step closer and then another, until he has me backed up against the wall. I'm not sure if it's with fear or excitement, but my heart races and every part of my body feels jittery. When he grasps the edge of my blouse in his hands, his smirk is back and I look up into his eyes, hoping he will give away the next part of the game. I get nothing, he's a closed book.

Without any warning, he rips my blouse open, and I squeal as the buttons scatter, bouncing when they hit the floor.

"What the hell!" I slap a hand against his chest. It's wasted effort because he's in his football gear, pads and all. He doesn't even flinch.

"Ow," he says, making fun of me. Ignoring my scowl, his eyes travel south, taking in the white, lacy bra I chose to wear under my now ruined blouse.

"That was my favorite shirt."

"It's now my favorite. I like the buttonless look. I was going to make you put my jersey on, but I think I prefer you like this."

Where is this even coming from? Becket couldn't have been more closed off since our kiss back at the fight club. I'm not sure what's happened but it feels like a switch has been flicked and he's done a complete U-turn.

I have no choice but to snatch the jersey out of his hands. Game on, I think to myself, making painfully slow work of stripping away the blouse and covering up.

He lets out a groan when the jersey with his number settles over my frame. "I like seeing you with my number on."

I roll my eyes at the typical jock comment. "How cliché. You need to come up with something more original."

He raises a brow and holds my gaze. "My fame doesn't bother you, does it?"

"Nope. If anything, I prefer you behind closed doors." My eyes widen when I realize what I've said. "I didn't mean it like that."

"Of course, you didn't."

He's being an asshole, but this time I don't hate it, quite the opposite. The ache between my legs is back and I'm dying to feel what it would be like having him rip away my thong in the same way he ripped away my shirt. I want to know what it would feel like having his fingers slip inside me, rubbing at the spot I want only him to touch.

I'd never tell him that though.

Instead, I lift my head defiantly and say, "Confident much?"

"Very much ... Admit it, Brit, you want me as much as you did the night we first met. I know you can't forget about that kiss."

Which one? Each time his lips find mine I feel more alive than I ever have in my life. I've forgotten what life felt like without him in it. A lump forms in my throat as I imagine leaving him behind. I don't want to.

His lips hover, millimeters from mine. I'd only have to lean in a fraction to give in to what we're both feeling. I'm torn between my head and my heart. Temptation proves too much and I'm about to close the gap when there's a noise along the corridor.

We both turn to find Coach Langford standing with his hands placed firmly on his hips.

"Is this a new thing we're doing at halftime, Becket?" he barks. "Last time I checked, we recovered with the team and went through plays, which you don't appear to be doing. Unless Miss Shaw has some insight into your performance that I don't?"

Knowing better than to challenge him, Becket steps back. I shiver when I'm hit with cold air as he walks away, after being surrounded by his body heat.

I hear him mutter, "Sorry, Coach," before he heads back to the locker room.

I don't move and neither does Coach Langford.

His expression is stern, clearly not impressed with the little show we just put on. "I didn't know a sports article required you to get so up close and personal."

"It was a mistake," I say, my voice low.

"It would appear this whole thing could be one big mistake. I asked you to help him, not screw him. Are you purposefully trying to mess up his life ... again?"

I shake my head, I can't believe he's jumping to these sorts of conclusions. I don't know what it will take for people to move past what happened and accept that it's just that, in the past. "No! I swear that wasn't what this was," I exclaim.

"Britney, he's only just got his life back on track after you so kindly messed it up. You have one job. The article. When you're done, move on and let him live his life without his past following him around."

What he's saying stings, but he's right. It's what I need to hear to bring me back down to earth and remember why I'm here. He leaves without saying another word and I walk back to my seat before the second half begins. This time, I pull out my notebook, determined to get some work done. Sitting, I make notes to take my mind off what almost happened between us, again. I need to finish up this article and get back to New York as soon as possible.

The Jaguars return to the field and I watch Becket interact with the other players, beginning to understand what he's about. He's loyal and caring in his own unique way and the team is his family. He will do whatever he can to protect them, even from his own actions. I should stay and watch him play but I suddenly don't want to be here. The game we're playing is confusing and I no longer know which team I'm on. The need to be with him, feel him, get to know every part of him, is getting stronger.

The Jaguars begin running their next play and I decide to go while Becket's distracted and won't notice me leaving. Shuffling along my row again, I apologize as I move past fans, disgruntled I'm disturbing the game. I'm almost at the exit when the noise of the crowd changes, and excitement fills the air. Maybe there's no harm in watching one last play. I should keep walking and leave Becket behind, but I don't want to miss the moment, so I stand and watch as the ball is passed between players. Becket catches it and begins sprinting along the field. The speed he moves at is incredible, and I jump up and down with excitement. At the same time the crowd goes wild and does the same.

That's when a flash of black catches my attention. It's the calm, eerie movement that makes it stand out, where everything else is frantic. Time slows as I swallow, then turn my head, taking in the figure in a black hooded jacket, standing, just a few feet away. I place a hand on the wall beside me, trying to keep myself upright as my legs tremble.

That's when I hear it. Everyone does.

There's no mistaking the almighty crunch that fills the night, and my attention is drawn away from the figure as I quickly look back to the field, praying it's not as bad as the churning in my gut tells me.

I don't know if it's me or the crowd screaming, as my eyes take in Becket, lying on the grass, lifeless.

When I manage to turn back, the figure is gone.

***

Becket

"Sorry Coach," I mutter, as I walk past, leaving him and Britney alone in the corridor.

149

When I get to the locker room, I open my locker and pull out my phone, choosing to ignore the missed calls and messages from Shauna my PR rep. It's been a while since I've done anything in the public eye, and she no doubt wants an update on how the article is going, but I'm not in the mood. Frustrated at Coach for interrupting my moment with Britney, I slam my locker shut and bang my head against it. Dramatic, even for me.

Brad wanders over, not picking up on the vibe that I need a bit of space. "What's up your ass?"

"Langford. He interrupted something with Britney."

"Something," he says, air quoting with his hands.

"Yeah, something."

"Do you think that's a good idea? The two of you," he asks, frowning.

"Why wouldn't it be?"

He looks at me like I've completely lost my mind. "Dude, she outed your secrets and leaked a sex tape which she set up! Are you sure you can trust her?"

I bend over and pick up my helmet. "There's something about her. I felt it back then and I still feel it now. I don't know. Something doesn't add up."

"You think she didn't do it?"

I shrug. "I don't know. It's a conversation we still need to have."

"What? You're actually planning on being mature and having an adult discussion about it?"

I smirk. "Maybe."

Coach Langford steps back into the locker room, the delay of his following doesn't go unnoticed. After a quick pep talk for the second half of the game, he sends us on our way, refusing to give me any kind of eye contact. I'm not the only one who's annoyed.

Stepping out onto the pitch my eyes find Britney in the crowd. I shake my head, trying to get rid of the image of her in that lacy, white bra. It was an asshole move I pulled, but it was worth every bit of her anger. I could spend all day staring at her body if she'd let me.

We're a couple of plays in, when out of the corner of my eye I see her stand to leave. I wonder where she's going but now isn't the time to focus on her. I catch the ball, tuck it under my arm and begin sprinting along the pitch. I can hear the crowd roaring in my ears. I block them out like white noise, staying focused, my eyes on the target. The line at the end of the field. Nothing else matters.

One flicker of my eyes in the wrong direction is all it takes for everything to go wrong.

I turn my head slightly as I run, wondering if I can still see Britney before I make the play. But it's not her I find. It's a figure in a black hooded jacket, one I haven't seen for years. One I thought was in my past. My blood runs cold, my focus on the game gone.

I'm catapulted through the air, then everything goes black.

Fourteen

Becket

*B*eep. *Beep. Beep.*
   I'm about to jump out of bed, get straight in the shower and start the day, but everything feels foggy. That's when the pain kicks in. It begins as a dull ache in my leg, which then starts to throb, before stab after stab hits. I want to rip my leg off. Don't even get me started on my head. I feel like I've been in a wreck. I try to groan but I'm unable to do anything, stuck in a world of blackness. Somewhere in the distance I hear muffled voices, and I put all my effort into listening. There's a male and a female. It sounds like Britney, but the last thing I remember is her leaving the game. Another stab of pain hits and I groan.

   "Did he just groan?" It's definitely Britney's voice.

   "I didn't hear anything." Brad. What the hell are they doing together?

   Another stab of pain. Fuck my life. What is going on? I groan again, this time louder.

   "That was definitely a groan," says Britney.

   "Yeah, I heard it that time," agrees Brad.

   "Do you think he might be waking up?"

A hand rests on my left leg and the searing pain that follows threatens to consume me. I cry out in agony and this time it isn't in my head. The pain brings me from wherever I've been lost, and my eyes fly open. My eyeballs are like sandpaper and I feel like I'm being blinded by light. Jesus. When was the last time I opened my eyes?

"You idiot! That's the injured leg!" Britney shouts at Brad.

"Shit! I'm so sorry man." Brad stands in front of me, holding up his hands, his face distraught.

I lie blinking while my eyes adjust to the light, until I'm able to take in the room. The room I have no recollection of coming to.

My voice comes out hoarse when I ask, "Where am I?"

Britney and Brad look at each other and even in my delirious state I can see the concern written all over their faces.

"Guys seriously, where am I? Why am I in so much pain?"

It's Britney who clears her throat ready to explain, her eyes full of sympathy. "You're in the hospital."

"Why?" I make the error of looking down at my left leg, which is bandaged and elevated on the bed. It looks swollen and I begin to feel nauseous. "What's wrong with my leg?" I'm terrified of the answer. My body is everything to my career. Nothing can be wrong. An injury could ruin my future.

Brad takes his turn to explain, "There was an accident on the field. You were tripped and then taken down by three players at once. You suffered a head injury which is why you're so confused."

"I don't give a fuck about my head," I snap, then repeat, "What's wrong with my leg?"

153

"Your leg's not in a good way. I'm sorry, man." There are tears in his eyes. This is bad, really bad. "You tore part of your quad and the rest of your leg is pretty bashed up."

I struggle to swallow. Britney catches my wince and rushes over with a glass of cold water and a straw. I take my time drinking, avoiding the question I'm too scared to ask.

"What does that mean for football?"

Football players aren't the idiots people think. We know we're not invincible. Our bodies keep us in the job, but they're also put at risk every second we're on the field. One wrong move is all it takes, and it looks like I've made mine. This sort of injury is rare, painful, and the chances of a full recovery are slim. It's the sort of injury every football player fears.

"They said it depends on your recovery, but for now, no football," Britney answers, with a softness in her voice that I despise. I want the feisty, sassy woman I've spent the last few weeks with, not the one trying to protect me because she feels sorry for me.

"N—no football?" I ask, not quite able to believe it. I gave up everything for this. I gave up *them* for my career. All those years wasted … for nothing. For my career to be over when it was only just starting.

Brad looks heartbroken. "I'm so sorry. Is there anything I can do?"

"Get out," I say coldly, my voice so low it's barely audible.

He looks shocked. "Are you being serious?"

"I said … Get. The. Fuck. Out."

Britney shakes her head, but in the little time she's known me, she's learned not to push when I'm not ready. She knows I need this space and grabs Brad by the arm, dragging him out of the room, giving me time to process. But there will never be enough time to process that my football career is quite possibly over.

***

Britney

Jess: *When I said "think outside the box" I didn't mean sideline him.*
Me: *How did you come to the conclusion this was my fault?*
Jess: *Intuition.*
Me: *Well, it wasn't.*

At least I don't think it was. I wouldn't know, I was too busy being scared to death by a figure in black.

Jess: *Looks like you'll be getting your wish after all.*
Me: *What do you mean?*
Jess: *Well, with Becket injured there isn't much point in you being there. What can you shadow … him lying in bed? You might as well book a flight back as soon as you can.*

I pause, thinking hard before typing out my response. Really, there's nothing to think about, it's the right thing to do.

Me: *I want to stay.*
Jess: *Say what now?*
Me: *I'll be staying and finishing the article here. If I can do his article from the office, then I can do my other work from here, like I have been doing. I want to help him.*
Jess: *You're falling for him.*

155

Me: *I can't fall.*
Jess: *And why's that?*
Me: *Because he pulled the rug out from under me a long time ago. I've already hit the ground.*
Jess: *Just remember something …*
Me: *Go on.*
Jess: *People make mistakes, it's a part of life, and some people deserve a second chance, sometimes more. Not everyone is like your mother.*

***

I knock frantically on Becket's front door. I've already tried the doorbell and got no answer. I'm beginning to panic. There's something seriously wrong and I'm about ready to call nine-one-one when my phone vibrates in my bag. I hesitate, trying to decide whether to answer or carry on knocking.

I choose to answer quickly, not even checking the caller ID. "Hello?"

Becket's voice takes me by surprise, "You remember I'm completely immobile right? Doctors' orders."

"What's your point?"

"Well, part of being immobile means I'm unable to answer the door. Could you please stop hammering on it? You're going to put a hole in the damn thing."

At least he's being playful.

He sounds brighter than he did last week at the hospital. That's how long he's been there—a week. Coach Langford and Brad brought him home earlier this morning, agreeing not to tell him my plan. They also promised not to mention I had to foot the bill for the hotel, while I waited for him to be discharged. He doesn't need to know about my financial worries, all that matters is helping him to recover. I owe him this.

156

"How am I supposed to get in?" I ask, glad he can't see me blushing after going hell for leather on the huge chunk of wood.

"I'll give you the code, but you have to promise me one thing."

I frown. "Go on?"

"You'll be nice. I'm not in the mood for this little game of cat and mouse we keep playing."

"I promise, I'll be nice."

Satisfied by my response, he gives me the code, and when I enter it, I hear the lock click. I let myself in, wheeling my suitcase in alongside me, then stand gawping at the entryway. His place is huge, like palatial. At least it is by my standards. Everything is light and airy, the expertly placed rugs and lamps, the perfect mix of browns and bronzes. The shading of the images on the walls matches the colors of the interiors perfectly. It screams *bachelor pad* in the best kind of way. I guess there are worse ways I could spend the coming weeks.

"Becket?" I call out, my voice echoing through the house.

I hear a strained, "Up here," and follow the direction of his voice, my shoes clicking against the marble floors before I reach the stairs and climb to the second floor.

"Hello?" I call out loudly, hoping he will reply again, as I have no idea where I'm going.

"In here," his voice is clearer this time and I walk to the only door that is ajar.

When I push it open, I find him in bed, leg elevated in a cast, a new addition following his surgery at the hospital. I smile at him uncertainly. "Hey."

He looks up and my heart aches. He looks so … broken. It's at that moment that I know I'm doing the

157

right thing, staying and helping him. Even if he's resistant to it, he doesn't have a choice.

"What are you doing here, Brit?" He doesn't look suspicious, or angry. His voice is flat, devoid of all emotion. He's empty. The Becket I know, the thorn in my side, is gone. I pray he isn't so lost I'm unable to get to him and help him find his way back.

"I live here," I reply, tossing my blonde hair over my shoulder, taking in the rest of his room.

"Erm … no, you don't."

"I do now." I smile and flutter my eyelashes in the over-the-top, incredibly fake way I know he hates. I know him and I know he will hate me feeling sorry for him, the best thing we can do is act normal, well, our version of normal.

"What are you talking about?"

"Well …" I walk over to the bed and sit down beside him, being extra careful not to jostle him and cause any pain. "Jess—my best friend who also happens to be my boss—told me I could return to New York."

He looks bemused. "That doesn't explain how you've come to the conclusion that you live with me."

"I couldn't do it. Leave you," I answer, honestly. My eyes fall, settling on his hand. I reach over slowly and cover it with my own. "I'm here to help. Whether you like it or not, I'm not going anywhere."

He doesn't say anything or come back with a snarky remark like I expect him to. When I eventually look up, he's staring at me, his green eyes full of intensity.

"Thank you," he says, so quietly I could almost convince myself I'm hearing things.

As we're being so open and honest, I decide now is the time to put the past behind us. "I'm sorry for what happened back then. How I set you up." I exhale, feeling all the tension leave my body now my apology is out in the open.

"I know."

That wasn't quite the answer I was expecting. I blink. "What do you mean?"

"I've asked myself over and over, how someone could do what you did."

My heart skips a beat.

"I came up with two answers. The first was that you didn't do it, the second was that you had no choice. Both answers mean that whatever did happen wasn't entirely your fault. I'm not saying I forgive you."

My shoulders sag.

"That doesn't mean I can't, at some point, in the future. Whatever this is," he says gesturing between us, "it isn't going away. I might not forgive you yet, but I don't hate you. Not anymore."

"Who knows,"—I chuckle—"maybe one day you can tell me about the assault case."

The warm Becket whose company I was enjoying, quickly slips away. "Some things are secret for a reason."

I sigh, but don't push the matter, keeping my thoughts to myself. For today, this is enough. It might not be the right time, but that doesn't change things. How can we pursue whatever this thing is between us, if we can't tell each other our secrets, the ones nobody knows? For as long as we hold back, we'll always hit a wall, never able to move forward. If Becket wants me, all of me, he has to remove his mask.

***

Becket

I lay awake in bed for hours until I'm certain Britney has gone to sleep. Trying to keep the rest of my body as still as possible and avoid any unnecessary pain in my leg, I reach awkwardly into the top drawer of my nightstand, pulling out an old cell I rarely use. It contains two of the most important numbers in my life. I hit call on one and listen as it rings a couple of times.

"To what do I owe this pleasure?"

I smile to myself. "If I'd known you were going to be so happy to hear from me, I would have called sooner."

"I'm glad you didn't."

"Has there been any movement?" I ask, we don't have time for small talk.

"No. You know I would have been in touch if something had happened."

"Are they safe?"

"I promise. I'm doing what I can to keep an eye on things."

I nod even though he can't see me. "I appreciate it."

"What's going on? You sound shook up."

I take a deep breath then say, "The figure is back."

Silence.

"Are you there?" I ask, bringing my cell away from my ear to check that we haven't been disconnected.

"Impossible. There've been no visitors for years. I check regularly. No one has been in contact who could restart all this again."

I tug a hand through my hair, why is he challenging me on this? "I know what I saw. It was at a fucking game, Evan. Again."

I hear him swallow down the line. He's as thrown by what I'm saying, as I was seeing the figure from my nightmares up in the stands, feet away from Britney. I clench my free fist, digging my nails into my palm, trying to get hold of my anger.

"I'll keep an eye on things and call you if anything changes. Be on guard, don't trust anyone."

The line goes dead seconds before the call can become traceable.

***

A shuffling noise at the end of my bed has me bolting upright.

"Ahhh!" I roar, as pain sears up and down my leg, threatening to consume my whole body.

Britney's head bobs up from the end, her eyes wide with alarm. "What the hell are you doing?"

"Me?" I rub the only part of my leg I can, that isn't covered by the cast. "What are *you* doing?"

She shuffles backwards a bit more and I clock what's in her hands. "Emptying your bedpan."

No. Fucking. Way. I narrow my eyes. "Put the piss pot down, Brit."

She stares back at me defiantly. Like I'd expect anything less.

"Or what? You're going to chase me down? You're bed-bound, remember?"

I'm transfixed by the way her blue eyes look even more piercing when she's angry. I shake my head trying to regather my thoughts. There's no way I'm letting her do this. No. I'd rather crucify my career than have her cleaning up my urine.

"You need help, Becket. What are you going to do for the next few weeks ... months even? Lie in a bed full of *piss*?"

161

I don't even blink at her choice of words as she echoes my own. "Happily. This. Is. Not. Your. Job." I snap, looking away. There's embarrassing and then there's this.

She sighs, finally puts the piss pot back, then stands up and perches on the end of my bed. I grit my teeth and fight back a groan when I see she's wearing loungewear.

"If you're living here," I say, "we're setting some rules. Number one, you don't empty the piss pot. Number two, you don't even come in the room when the shit bowl is out. Number three, no loungewear."

Looking puzzled, she asks, "Why no loungewear?"

"That's what you got from that?"

"Answer my question," she replies.

Damn that mouth. I can't decide if her living here is a good thing or a bad thing. My dick says good, my head says bad. The final verdict ... I'm screwed. Deciding there's no point in beating around the bush—she's already been handling a pot full of my urine—I answer, "It turns me on."

"Why is that a bad thing?" she asks, with a hint of a smile on her lips.

If I wasn't turned on already, the way her eyes skirt down to my crotch, checking to see if I'm telling the truth seals the deal. "Because I can't do a thing about it," I grit out. Carefully leaning over to my nightstand, I grab the business card the hospital gave me when I was discharged and pass it over to her.

"What's this?"

"The number for a nurse. She'll spend the day. Help with things I need like the bathroom, getting clean, making meals, my meds, the works."

"I'll do all those things for you," she replies, her eyes so wide there's a chance I might get lost in them.

"No, you won't."

162

"I'm trying to help you ... I *have* to."

"That's the problem, Brit," I reply, miserably. "You're trying to help because you feel like you have to, not because you want to. I'm not going to let you do this. I'd rather starve and shit the bed."

She stands and narrows her eyes. Sweet Brit is gone, and her defenses are back up. "I think you're being a little dramatic."

I glance at my cast and her eyes follow mine. "*That* is not dramatic, it's real. This isn't a game. We're not playing house here. The kind of things you're wanting to help me with are what marriage consists of. 'In sickness and in health.' You're not tied to me, so I won't let you do this."

"Even injured you're still an asshole," she snaps, then starts to walk out of the room.

"The joke's on you," I shout after her, "I never pretended to be otherwise." My bedroom door slams shut. I hear her shrill voice as she walks down the stairs, organizing things with the nurse like I knew she would, because I asked her to.

Asshole. A word I've heard so many times when people talk about me, I'm starting to believe it's true. I've been at this game so long I'm starting to forget I'm wearing a mask and it's all an act. I'm at risk of forgetting who I really am.

***

Britney

I lie in bed, waiting to hear the same thing I have each night, for the past fourteen nights I've lived with Becket. Always around the same time. I look at the clock, glowing on my nightstand through the darkness, and hold my breath.

Like clockwork he cries out, "No! No! Josie what have you done?"

There was a selection of rooms to pick from. I chose the one closest to him, even though I could have gone for a bigger one with an en-suite. I wanted to be close so I could hear him if he needed me. I never expected *this*.

The first night was the worst because it was unexpected. *Nightmare* is putting it nicely. The vividness, the fear in his voice—they're night terrors. He's reliving something, over and over. Each night I want to go and help make things better, but I don't know if I would make things worse. Stepping into what he's experiencing would be crossing a line in our relationship we wouldn't be able to come back from.

I hear him cry out again. His words are muffled. Maybe it's instinct? He's hiding a piece to the puzzle, the next part of the story. His mind is protecting him from revealing the truth. Fourteen nights I've listened and fourteen times my heart has broken for him, each night a little bit more. Becket revealed a lot of his secrets the day we met on the plane, but I now know, with absolute certainty, he still has one left to tell.

Fifteen

Becket

She's heard, I know she has. You'd have to be deaf not to. Even if I wasn't one hundred percent certain she'd heard me crying out in the night, the way she acts with me in the day—awkward as fuck—is a dead giveaway. I never should have agreed to her staying with me. I knew what the implications were and still I agreed. Basically, I'm a fool.

I'm losing control of the situation. The walls I built are at risk of being brought down by one of the very people they were meant to keep out. A person capable of tearing apart my heart. If I don't do something now, everything is at risk of coming undone.

I have to push her away and I know exactly how.

***

Britney

It's a few weeks after the accident and I'm sitting in the living room on Becket's huge leather couch, the coffee table lined up with movie snacks. During his recovery he's slackened off his training diet, claiming

165

it's the one time he can go AWOL and if his career is going to pot, he's at least going to enjoy the food he's not been able to while being in the NFL.

I'm trying not to feel put out, sitting, waiting for him to return home from his post-surgery appointment, which he attended with Brad and Coach Langford. After everything I've done for him over the past few weeks, he still chose to go with them, not me. He's the same hot-and-cold Becket he's always been. Each day I get up, I never know which one I'm going to be faced with.

When I hear the front door open, I stand, rubbing my palms against my thighs. This appointment was important. It's supposed to inform us how his leg is healing, if there is a chance of a full recovery, and what the odds of him returning to football are.

Brad wheels him in and I clock his solemn expression. My breath catches in my throat, it wasn't good news. I don't know what to do or say. He'd just got his career back on track after my meddling and now ... this.

Hesitantly, I say, "So?"

Becket looks at me, his expression sombre, and I brace myself for the answer I don't want to hear.

"They said they expect me to make a full recovery."

I step forward with tears in my eyes. "I'm so sorry. I wish I could change thi—" It registers what he said. "Wait. What?"

His eyes sparkle, and they seem brighter and greener than ever before.

"You're an idiot," I say, unable to stop myself from laughing.

"Tell me something I don't know." He smirks for the first time in weeks, and I can feel my armor beginning to crack.

166

Brad laughs from behind him. "You make it too easy. Always so serious, Britney."

My cheeks heat up at the way they're both laughing at my expense. "I thought it was bad news," I grumble.

Becket looks to Brad and says, "Thanks for taking me today. I'll see you tomorrow after practice, to go over plays?"

Brad looks at the table where the snacks are lined up, ready for us to have our movie night. "Am I not invited to the party?"

"Not today you're not," replies Becket.

"Come on, bro. It's meant to be. The triple B-team. Let's make it happen."

I don't know much about Brad, but from what I do know, I'm able to conclude that his eagerness to stay has little to do with the company and more to do with the variety of snacks on offer.

"No," replies Becket, firmly.

Brad shakes his head and chuckles, but then his expression changes when he leans down and murmurs to Becket, "Be careful."

He does a crap job at lowering his voice, because I hear him loud and clear, and know what the meaning behind his words is. Unfazed, he looks longingly at the snacks, gives me a reluctant wave, and then leaves, taking the bad vibes with him.

Once we're alone, Becket wheels himself in my direction. "Let's get started. I know we've got snacks but I'm starving. I thought we could order pizza?"

"Sounds good," I reply. "How about you get the television set up and I'll ring in our order. Half and half?"

"Yeah, I'll hav—"

"American hot, no onions, extra jalapeños," I say, repeating the same thing he's had each time we've

167

ordered. It's been a long few weeks and I'm not a good cook. There's been a lot of pizza.

He frowns then clears his throat awkwardly. "Great. I'll pick something to watch."

I walk out of the room, pulling out my phone and hitting call on the delivery number that has now entered my favorites list. When I'm done, I make my way back into the living area to find Becket has maneuvered his wheelchair close to the corner of the couch where I usually sit. I don't say a word, not wanting to give away that I've noticed.

We settle down quietly, watching what's on the screen. Well, Becket watches what's on the screen. I can't focus because I'm hyper aware of his presence. I wish he was closer. Even with the gap between us, I can feel the heat radiating off him. I'm struggling to remember why I can't climb into his lap as I'm overcome with the urge to feel what it would be like to be in his arms again. I don't just want it, I need it. His breathing steadily increases and the way his chest begins rising and falling, gives away that he wants the same thing. I'm about to turn and say as much, but I'm stopped in my tracks when what's on the screen changes.

My mind goes blank when the room is filled with the sounds of panting, groaning and flesh slapping against flesh. I'm about to snap and demand to know what he's playing at, why he's put porn on, when it comes flooding back to me.

The sounds, the outline of the bodies on the screen. They're all too familiar and I feel physically sick as I realize it's *them*. It's the tape I made for the world to see. The torture I'm watching on screen and hating more than anything, I created.

I can't find my voice, which is fine, because Becket leans in so close I could turn and kiss him if I wanted

168

to. I stay still as a statue, afraid of what I might do if I move. My eyes remain transfixed on the screen watching him push in and out of another woman.

I feel his breath, hot on my neck when he leans his head in close to my ear and says, "It could have been you. Now it never will be." He pushes away, ready to leave the room. But he isn't just pushing away from me, he's pushing away from how far I thought we'd come.

Who knows if we'll be able to find our way back?

***

What little progress we made feels like it was a figment of my imagination. In the week that's passed, what little conversation we've had has been awkward, cringeworthy. When we do speak, we're simply going through the motions.

His recovery gets better every day, but he still has to be careful. One wrong move is all it would take for everything to come undone. I'm beginning to question whether it's worth me even being here. He's begun to delegate more and more tasks to the nurse, avoiding me at all costs. Impressive considering he's bed bound and I know exactly where to find him. I could push, but I don't. He just needs space and a little time. But I don't have time. My notepad remains in my bag in my room, unopened since the day I moved in. I'm screening Jess' calls left, right and center. My life is at risk of falling apart, all for a guy who doesn't want anything to do with me.

The day I walked out on my mom, I made a promise to myself I would protect my heart. I locked it and hid away the key, in the hope that one day Prince Charming would ride in and sweep me off my feet. Instead, Michael Becket, the biggest asshole in the NFL, is the one who's taught my heart how to beat again. But he doesn't want it. I need to leave before any more damage can be done. I'm sitting in the living room mindlessly watching some program on the television, when I decide that's what I need to do. I need to tell him this whole thing is pointless and that I need to go back to New York and get on with my life. I give myself a mental pep talk before heading up to his room where he's been resting all afternoon.

Without knocking, I open the door and step inside, expecting to find him spread out on the bed where I left him earlier, but he's not there. I frown. He's not supposed to do any big movements without assistance, not until he's been given the all-clear by the doctor, which I know for a fact he hasn't.

"Hello?" I pause and listen but there's no response. "Becket?"

I hear a whimper at the same time I notice the door to his en-suite is slightly open. Quietly I walk over and hear the whimper again. Looking through the crack, I find him sprawled on the floor and waves of different emotions slam into me all at once. My first instinct is to barge in and demand to know what the hell he was doing, tell him he's an idiot for being so stubborn and risking his recovery, but I don't. Instead, I take a deep breath and give us both a moment. The last thing he needs is me bitching at him, despite how angry and frustrated I am. Right now, he needs a friend and support.

When I'm ready, I push the door open fully and walk over to him. "Are you ok?"

He doesn't look up, just whimpers, hugging the floor. I never knew my heart could break so many times for a person, like it has for Becket, but seeing how alone and defeated he looks, it breaks again. The football God has literally been brought to his knees. He was king of the field and now, he has nothing, no one around him apart from the girl who screwed him over. What a shit reality to have to come to terms with.

The tide is turning, I should walk away and leave him. That's what I'd do if I were smart. He's too stubborn for his own good, brash, shuts the world out for reasons unknown. He's the complete opposite of everything I thought I needed. Standing, I try to understand why, even though I tell them to move, my feet remain firmly in place. And then it hits me. Even though I don't know his past, what fuels his nightmares, I recognize the pain in his eyes, because it's the same pain I see in the mirror when I look at myself. We're two of a kind. I can't walk away and leave him, because if I did, I'd be leaving part of myself behind. My heart, which I thought would never be fixed, is in his hands and he's slowly putting it back together, piece by shattered piece.

I always thought I'd pulled the trump card, having been thrown into one shitty scenario after another. Maybe it was life's way of pushing me onto the right path, to find Becket. Maybe we were meant to tear each other apart. Sometimes you have to break, so that when you put yourself back together, the new version is better, and the flaws, the scars, are what make you unique.

Kneeling next to him on the floor, I'm careful to avoid his injured leg. The cast should have ensured the damage done was minimal, I hope. When I scoot closer, he finally acknowledges my presence, pushing up on his hands, then meekly placing his head in my lap. I don't say a word, just sit, stroking his hair until his body relaxes and his whimpers stop. I don't know how much time passes, but the sun sets, and the room glows, fiery orange, as the remnants of daylight filter in from outside.

I know he's about to speak because his body tenses.

"People think this is living the dream—the big house, fancy cars, money. It's not though, because everything in my life is empty. I don't keep people around, Brit, I drive them away. Without football, I have nothing. I'm alone."

Everything now makes sense. This past week, he's been pushing me away, guarding himself in the same way I have all these years. But he doesn't need to, I'm not the enemy he thinks I am.

"You're wrong," I say quietly. Even though I can't see his face I know his brows are drawn together, in the same way they do each time I challenge him.

"How so?"

I swallow before answering, the truth making my throat feel suddenly dry. "You're not alone because you have me."

To the outside world, the two of us together wouldn't make sense, but I learned a long time ago that the world often works in the opposite way to what you expect. I should know, all I ever found was pain where I should have found love and comfort.

As the room goes dark, I remain sitting with his head in my lap, watching as his breathing settles and he falls asleep, wishing we could stay in this bubble where we don't hate each other for longer than time will allow.

***

Becket

My neck's stiffer than a plank of wood. I groan as I try to move it, the pain radiating up and down. The moon shining through the window provides a dim light for me to take in my surroundings and I realize that it's not my bedroom window the light is coming through, it's the window in my en-suite. Everything comes flooding back.

Stupidly, I tried to prove to myself I still had some independence and didn't need her. I tried to walk the distance from my bed to the toilet on my own, and not so surprisingly my leg gave way. I'm an idiot. I collapsed onto the same leg I'm meant to be allowing to heal and the searing pain has my eyes watering. I've potentially whittled away what little hope there was of me making a full recovery, and for what? My pride. Now I'll be left with nothing.

"You're not alone because you have me." Those were the words she whispered to me, the words that made my heart pound in ways it shouldn't. I shouldn't be feeling all these things for her because I can't let her in. I can't show her who I really am. It's not safe for her and it's not safe for *them*.

Shifting my head slightly, I feel the damp patch beneath my cheek on her jeans. Not my finest moment. She's settled with her head tilted to the side, back resting against the bathtub, eyes closed. She hasn't witnessed me blushing like a schoolgirl, thank God. I try to lift myself up with my arms but being stuck in the same position for so long has made one of them numb and I slip back down into her lap with a thud. "Damn it!" I hiss.

The movement makes her stir and her eyes flutter open, staring into mine. Her blue eyes glow in the moonlight and her white-blonde hair looks like a halo. Like a halo? What the fuck? I'm officially a goner.

"How do you feel?" she asks.

"Like crap," I answer honestly.

"I bet." She smiles and I feel less like an idiot, until her eyes trail to my leg and she frowns.

I follow her gaze and when I see what it is she's looking at, I curse under my breath. I thought things couldn't get any worse. I was wrong. In case her seeing me a mess on the bathroom floor wasn't bad enough, I've pissed myself. It's official, I've hit rock-bottom.

"Please, don't be embarrassed," she says gently. I know she's being sincere, but it doesn't change anything.

"Easy to say when you're not the one covered in your own urine," I grumble.

She shakes her head and looks away. There's nothing she can do or say to make this better. I watch her throat bob as she swallows and then says so quietly, I can barely hear it, "Would you like me to help you clean up?"

I want to say no, but I don't have a choice. There's no way I can get up and get clean on my own. My attempt to prove I can be independent has made me the complete opposite. Sheepishly, I nod. "Please."

She leans away from the tub and winces in pain. "Are you ok?" I ask.

"I'm fine," she replies, brushing me off. "Let's get you clean."

I manage to shift my weight off her and she stands, quickly wheeling over the shower chair the nurse uses to help me wash, before helping me to get to my feet. It's a struggle, but we manage it without causing me any more injuries. When I'm sitting comfortably, she doesn't hesitate as she begins to help me strip down. I try not to think about how wrong this all is, that she should be stripping me down for other reasons—not to clean me up.

She helps remove my boxers, diverting her gaze and allowing me my modesty, then carefully wraps my casted leg in plastic wrap so it doesn't get wet. When she wheels me into the shower, she turns the chair so the water hits my back, and my leg remains as dry as possible, then grabs the shower gel and a sponge. I quickly wash my front, then pass them to her and she cleans my back. Her hands on my body feel amazing and I spend the whole time she's cleaning me trying not to let my mind wander.

When I'm finished, she steps away and passes over a towel. I do what I can to get myself dry, then place it over my lap. Only when I'm covered and with my modesty intact does she look me in the eyes. Hers are hard, giving nothing away about how she feels. Mine are full of respect.

She bustles away and returns with my wheelchair. I wrap an arm around her shoulders, and she helps to transfer me over, then wheels me back into my room. We go through the same motions, transferring me onto the bed. Getting my boxers on proves just as difficult, and she helps me to maneuver them on, being careful not to jostle my bad leg. She waits for me to get comfortable, then sources the leftover supply of painkillers the doctor prescribed. I've not needed them for a while, but after tonight, I might be due a top-up. I swallow them down, then settle as she tucks me in.

At no point have we spoken. She never asks what I need, she's one step ahead each time. I'm in safe hands. She's about to leave, when I place a hand over hers, pinning it to the bed.

Looking up, I say, "Stay, please."

She looks at me, surprised. "Why?"

"Because I want you to." It's a simple answer, but we both know we're overcoming a huge hurdle.

175

"But you said the other night ..."

"I freaked out," I reply honestly. "I didn't mean what I said. I've tried to stop whatever this is, Brit, but I don't know if I can keep doing it. I don't know if I want to."

***

Britney

Becket passed out after his little confession. Lying next to him and hearing him breathe so peacefully almost lulls me to sleep, but my clothes are damp and uncomfortable after helping him shower. I carefully lift his arm that is draped over me, trying not to disturb him, as I get up from the bed and go in search of clean, dry, clothes.

When I find some, I change and quickly go back to his room, determined not to break the promise I made—that I wouldn't leave. When I walk back in, I sigh. His room's a mess, not that it's his fault. I mill around, picking up discarded clothing from the floor, placing it in the wash basket. I'm bent over, tidying up a pile of books that have been knocked over when I hear a loud crash.

I freeze, book in hand.

I look over my shoulder at Becket. The drugs have done the job they're supposed to and he's still out cold. I wish he wasn't, especially after hearing that mysterious crash. I'm on edge, which is why I don't miss the shuffling sound that comes from outside.

I crawl carefully along the bedroom floor to the window, then crouch on my knees out of sight. Taking a deep breath, I slowly lift a hand, parting two of the slats and peer through. I don't see anything and look away. Watching horror movies on Netflix has to

176

stop. Just to be certain, I look again. As my eyes adjust to the darkness, they find a vehicle in the distance, out past Becket's high-tech security gates, on the road that is almost always empty. Goosebumps cover my skin.

"Come back to bed," grumbles Becket, drawing my attention away from the window. He lifts himself up, resting his weight on his elbows, his face full of sleep. "What are you doing over there?"

"I thought I heard something. It was nothing," I lie.

He flops back down onto the bed and begins snoring. Before I climb in next to him, I turn back and peer out the window one last time.

The car door opens and shuts without a sound. The gentle rumble of the engine reaches my ears, before the vehicle pulls away. As it does, the streetlight it passes under illuminates the driver's side for a millisecond, highlighting a figure in a black, hooded jacket, and then the car disappears into the night.

Sixteen

Britney

I t took me hours to get to sleep, even with Becket by my side. I should tell him what's been going on, but I'd sound like a lunatic, rambling on about a figure in a black jacket, that one minute is there, the next minute isn't. It's my mind playing tricks, remembering how things used to be before I had enough money to start paying Mom's debts. The scare tactic they used worked too well, now I'm seeing them everywhere. It's my guilty conscience—I've missed one of the few payments I have left.

I should never miss a payment.

"Brit ..." A large pair of hands shake me gently and I groan. I must only have been out for a couple of hours if that. "Brit," hisses Becket, closer to my ear. Why isn't he getting the idea that I'm not ready to get up? "Brit, it's one in the afternoon, you have to wake up."

Ok, maybe I was out longer than I thought.

My eyes feel like sandpaper and I struggle to open them. My mouth tastes as good as they feel. Holding a hand up over my mouth, I look up into Becket's gorgeous, ruffled face. He looks even better when he's just woken up, better than he does in his football uniform, which I didn't think was possible. I could get used to waking up to this, I think, then scold myself for getting carried away. With Becket's record, we're most likely back to hating each other today. Yesterday's truce was probably a fluke.

"Why are you holding your hand over your mouth?" he asks, his mouth tugs at one side as he tries to fight a smile.

"Morning breath. Be right back." I dart out of bed, heading straight for his door, but pause when I get there and spin back around. "Do you have CCTV?"

He frowns. "Erm, yeah ... Why?"

"I thought I heard something last night," I answer, trying to keep my voice as blasé as possible. "It was probably just a cat, but I thought I'd check it out."

"Check away, but I have a security team. You're safe, Brit. Nothing's going to happen to you when you're with me."

"I know, but please, let me check it out?"

He nods. "The screen is set up in my office downstairs. First door on the right, past the stairs."

"Be right back." I grin, praying my face looks more relaxed than I feel.

Hurrying down the stairs, I quickly find his office and slip through the door. I'm on edge, not sure what I'm going to find when I look back over the footage from last night. The screen is full of little squares with different angles of the house, just like Becket said it would be. It takes me a couple of minutes to navigate the software, but once I get the hang of it, I rewind the video to around midnight, then set it to play.

I see myself walking along the hallway and back into Becket's room. I begin to pay extra careful attention, my eyes moving from one grid to the next, looking for anything. There's nothing.

179

I let out a breath I didn't realize I was holding, relieved that my past hasn't found me in Jacksonville. Yesterday was a long day and tiredness can make the mind do funny things. Before I push away from Becket's desk, my eyes trail slowly around his office, taking everything in.

Like the rest of the house, it's been expertly decorated and flows perfectly with the other rooms, but among all the perfectly placed décor there's something amiss. He has no past, no pictures. No family. There's nothing in the whole house. Everything is perfect, too perfect.

The only thing I managed to find that seemed slightly out of place was a spare phone in his nightstand which I've never seen him use. I found it when I was searching for his pain meds one day when the nurse was late and he was sitting in the living area. I've not been prying, just searching so I can understand him better. But there's nothing to be found. Anything that could give insight into who Becket is, is gone.

Remembering what I initially left Becket's room to do, I shoot back upstairs, feeling a little lighter knowing there's nothing to be worried about. There's a niggle, but I stamp it down. I walk back into his room a couple of minutes later and wave my toothbrush and toothpaste in the air.

"Did you find anything?" he asks.

"Nothing. Like I said, must have been a cat."

When I walk into his en-suite, he shouts after me, "That's it, you just sort yourself out."

I roll my eyes as I start to brush. When I'm done, I walk over to him with an empty cup and his toothbrush.

Keeping hold of the cup, I nod at it, and say, "You can spit in here."

He stares at me blankly, then when he can't keep a straight face any longer, throws his head back laughing. "Anyone listening would think we were up to something kinky," he winks.

"Well, both of us know there's not."

"I'm not spitting in a cup, Brit."

"I know, I was kidding." Sort of. Not that I'm about to admit my error, forgetting that he still needs help to go about his morning routine.

When he's finished in the bathroom and I've helped him get settled back on the bed, he grabs my hand before I can leave. "Why are you still a virgin, Brit? There's nothing wrong with it, but it is a bit ... odd."

I wasn't expecting to have this conversation with him so soon, if ever. Awkwardly, I look away towards the window, but then images of the figure from last night flood my mind and I wind up looking back at him. There's no avoiding this. "You're not the only one with secrets," I reply, cryptically, hoping he will give up.

He doesn't. He's as persistent as Jess when she knows there's something, I'm not telling her. "You can trust me." He gives me a look that has my resolve crumbling.

I'm about to tell him that no, I can't, not after everything he's put me through while I've been here, when I remember Jess' email:

Some people deserve a second chance, sometimes more. Not everyone is like your mother.

I take a deep breath, hoping Becket is prepared for what he's letting himself into, because this box we're about to open belongs to Pandora, and what's kept inside, I can't deal with alone. "Scoot over a little," I say.

"That serious, huh?" he replies, shuffling carefully sideways, giving me room to climb on the bed.

I don't say anything as I sit and stretch my legs out, then scoot myself in as close to him as I can. He wraps an arm around my shoulder, tucking me into his side and I inhale his comforting scent. Lavender and birch, the two things I'll now always associate with him.

I hear him swallow. He's as nervous about this as I am. "What is it, Brit?"

I close my eyes, it's time to open the box.

My body jumps in terror as the bedroom door flies open, slamming against the wall. Light floods in and I wince, shuffling down under the covers, trying to keep them wrapped tightly around me. Not again, please, not again.

Mom, where are you? Why aren't you here? I hold my breath, trying to stay as still as I can. Maybe if he thinks I'm asleep he'll leave?

Of course not, he's the devil. Like something so simple would deter him.

His footsteps get closer. I hear the click of the metal as he unfastens his belt, a swoosh as the leather passes through each loop on his pants and the clunk as it hits the bare wood floor.

Cold air hits me when the cover is ripped off. He looms over me, a black silhouette against the stark light from the hallway. He crouches down, his face almost touching mine, the smell of Scotch hits me.

"Why were you hiding pretty girl? I'm here to look after you."

Becket's hand grasps my chin, bringing me out of the darkness. "Brit, where did you go?"

The softness in his voice is all it takes. I shake as sobs wrack my body and we sit for minutes, maybe hours, entwined, letting years of pent-up grief take over me.

When I feel like I can't cry anymore, I look up at Becket through bleary eyes, finding his face full of pain. "My mom was a drug addict."

His throat bobs and his eyes harden as he waits for me to continue.

"Things were never easy. I didn't have a happy childhood. I never knew my dad. He and my mom were as bad as each other, and he died of an overdose not long after I was born. My mom gave up drugs long enough to have a healthy pregnancy with me, but when he passed away, she slowly started to slip back into old habits. I may as well have raised myself.

"She'd drag me between rentals, all over town. We'd live in one place just long enough, then leave before we were served an eviction notice. The early years were bearable. It's when I got older things started to change. There was only so long before the boyfriends she had coming through the door, would no longer turn a blind eye to me ..."

Becket tenses and I pause. It's too much; no one wants to hear my sob story, not even him. I expect him to say as much, but instead he begins stroking my hair soothingly, in the same way I did to him on the bathroom floor.

"Don't stop." That's all he says, so I don't.

"She'd disappear for days on end. There was one boyfriend who was worse than the rest. He'd get angry, turn up when he knew she wasn't around, letting himself in the apartment because of course she gave him a key. He always came at night when it

183

was dark. The first time was the worst. I woke up, terrified, not knowing what was going on.

"I was numb to everything after that. There was nothing I could do. What chance does a thirteen-year-old girl stand against a fully grown, intoxicated man? That's what my neighbor said to me when he took me to his gym and began training me in Krav Maga. It was after one particularly bad night when Mom's boyfriend beat the shit out of her, and he heard it all from his apartment."

"Brit ..."

"Want to know the worst part?" I ask bitterly.

He nods.

"Whenever he'd beat her, I felt thankful. Thankful that it wasn't me he was putting his hands on for once. Does that make me a bad person?" I hold my breath as I wait for him to answer, expecting the worst, expecting him to say yes and be repulsed by me.

He stares back at me, his face is full of understanding. "No," he replies. "It makes you human."

***

Becket

It's not often I'm lost for words, but right now, I don't know what to do or say. I knew there was more to Britney's story the day she showed up at the club and literally floored me, but I never expected this. It's taking everything inside me to keep control of my anger. Each time she tells another part of her story, reveals more of the pain she's experienced, I bite down on my cheek, so hard I can taste blood.

The bastard. I want to find who did this to her and put him through the same pain she's been carrying around all these years. I ache for her in ways she'll never understand, because she can never know the truth. Like her parents, we're two of a kind, but not because of addiction or poor life choices. Because the people who have been thrown in our way, knocking us off the path we were meant to follow, have caused us unbearable pain, and we have witnessed things, carried burdens that no child should ever have in their arms.

It takes me a while to work up the courage to ask the question I've been dreading. "Did he ..."

She looks up, utterly broken and shakes her head. "No. It never got that far. The things he did to me were bad enough, but I suppose the only saving grace was that he never got as far as he intended."

I exhale and some of the tension leaves my body. Small mercies and all that. It doesn't change what he did though. Bile rises in my throat when it hits me how similar our realities are. I want to tell her that on some level I get it, what she's been through, more than most, but doing so would give the game away.

I can't.

She's told me her deepest, darkest secrets. I can never tell her mine. If I did, it wouldn't just put *them* at risk, it would put her at risk too.

"What happened to your mom?" I ask.

She looks down and sniffs. "I left my gym gear at home one day and was already in trouble at school, so I went back to get it. When I got there, I found her strung out screwing my boyfriend. That's when I left. I accepted that however hard life was, it couldn't get much worse. At least without her there dragging me down, whatever bad happened to me, it was because of my actions not hers."

"It sounds to me like you did the right thing."

She smiles. "Maybe I did. But I still made my mistakes; I am her daughter after all."

"People make mistakes, Brit."

"My biggest one was you."

I blink, not quite understanding what she means.

She lets out a small laugh. "Sorry. I should have said, my biggest one was what I *did* to you. I know I said I was sorry, but I want to say it again. I really am sorry, Becket, I never meant to hurt you and there's something mo—"

I hold a finger up to her lips, stopping her in her tracks. For now, enough secrets have been revealed, we both need time to process what's been said.

I'm tired of fighting whatever this is between us. In a world where I had no one, I've found myself with Britney goddamn Shaw. No matter what the circumstances for why we're here together, all that matters is that we are.

Staring deep into her eyes, my pulse starts to race. "Can I kiss you?"

She smirks. "It's not like you to ask."

There she is. Even after what she's revealed, she's still my little firecracker and I don't doubt for a second, that it would take a lot to put out that spark. Leaning in slowly, I press a featherlight kiss against her lips, testing the waters, checking she's not all talk. When she presses back firmly with her own, without any hesitation, I know there's nothing to worry about. Her lips part, waiting for me to take her, and that's exactly what I do.

I sweep my tongue over hers, teasing until she's begging for more. My hands find the curve of her waist and she climbs onto my lap. Straddling me, she cages me in with her thighs. Our new position sparks something in her. Her movements become more hurried as she takes control. Her tongue moves faster. She presses harder against my lips. She grinds down onto my dick. I'm rock hard and dying to feel how wet she is for me. I want to taste how crazy I make her. But I can't rush this with her. Trying to relieve some of the tension, I trail my hands down to her ass and squeeze it firmly. The same ass that's been taunting me since she put on her little show at our first training session.

I groan in frustration. "I can't wait for you to find out what you've been missing out on."

She stills and for a second, I think I've said the wrong thing.

"Show me," she says breathlessly, grinding down against me. She licks her lips and gazes at me hungrily, through hooded eyes.

It takes everything in me to say, "No."

She sits up straight, lifting her hips off mine, and my dick instantly mourns the loss of her against it.

Before she gets a chance to say anything, I continue, "As much as I want to, I want your first time to be memorable." I gesture down at my leg, the logistical nightmare she seems to have forgotten. "I never run a play unless I can give it my all."

She throws her head back and laughs. It makes the whole room light up and I can't help grinning back.

"You're such an ass," she says.

"Never pretended to be otherwise, Brit." I'd be an ass to her all day long if it made her laugh like that again, anything to take away the pain from her eyes. "How about I promise that when we do the deed, it will be worth the wait."

"You actually just said 'do the deed', didn't you?" She snorts.

187

"It sounded better in my head," I admit, my cheeks feeling warm. I'm about to have my man card revoked.

Before she can laugh again, I stop her with a searing kiss. She moans and bites down on my bottom lip. This woman is trying to kill me. My body hums, craving every part of her, it's been a long time since I've wanted someone as much as I want Britney Shaw. The kiss grows deeper, and my hands move up and down her body, then begin toying with the waistband of her pajama pants, forgetting why we can't take things further. My fingertips skim lightly under her top, over the soft skin of her back and she shivers. It's a small movement but it brings me back to reality.

I pull away and press my forehead to hers, panting. "Brit, trust me, I really don't want to, but we have to stop."

"Ok," she says reluctantly, pulling away.

I watch, confused as she moves off the bed and walks towards the bedroom door.

"Where are you going?"

"I'm leaving, because if I don't, I'll keep wanting more." Looking back over her shoulder, she winks. "Make sure you rest that leg, no more silly stunts. I know what I want; don't make me wait."

Seventeen

Becket

L aying back on the bed, I let out a groan of satisfaction. "Damn that feels good."

"I thought we discussed this before. You can't speak to the physios like that," Brad scolds.

"This isn't a physio though. And he doesn't mind, do you, Doc?"

I wiggle my eyebrows at Doctor Greenman and he laughs in return. He's been the Jaguars' team doctor for years and loves to think he's a part of the gang and in on the jokes.

He smiles and says, "I'd be saying the same thing if I got a cast off after six weeks."

"Six. Weeks." I let out another groan.

"You're a lucky man," says Brad. "These injuries normally take months to recover from. Does Britney have magical powers or something?"

"I hope you're going to be more careful in the future," says Greenman, sternly. "You might not be so lucky next time, and this is nothing short of a sporting miracle. Please remember before you go trying to skip out of here that you're not out of the woods yet."

"Yeah, no getting distracted ..." Brad rolls his eyes, he thinks it happened because of Brit.

Nobody knows the real reason for the accident.

Ignoring Brad's underhand comment, I look at Greenman and ask, "When do you think I will be able to play again?"

"It will be months yet. You're going to have to build your strength back up and make sure the muscle repairs fully so there isn't the risk of another tear." When I frown he adds, "You should be thankful I'm not saying years."

Trying not to show the disappointment I'm feeling, I nod. "I am."

He gathers his notes and forms together and looks between the two of us. Before leaving the room, he says, "I have some paperwork to fill out, but I will see you in a week to check on how you're doing."

Brad looks at me hopefully when he's gone. "Celebration time?"

"You read my mind."

***

I look out the window of the cab skeptically at the bar only a few people know the significance of. It's the same bar Britney and I went to after our flight from New York, where the last thing I remember is kissing her in the restrooms before blacking out.

"Why are we here?" I ask, as Brad wheels me through the doors.

Any possibility of an answer flies out the window, when my eyes land on the tables filled with my teammates.

"Becket! Becket! Becket!" They all begin chanting, slamming their hands and drinks on the tables.

"Surprise!" says Brad. "They demanded to come when I told them what we were up to."

"I said why are *we* here, not *they*."

He shrugs. "I heard it was a good place to drink that's all."

I don't get a chance to push it further. He wheels me to one of the tables, quickly putting an end to the conversation. One of the guys takes a drink order and I watch as he walks to the bar. Everything looks and feels the same. The dark oak of the bar. The neon signs flashing on the walls. The smell of beer and liquor. Even the music sounds familiar. It brings all the memories of that night to the forefront of my mind.

This is why he brought me.

"It hasn't changed," I say.

"I'm surprised you remember ... being drugged and all."

The drinks arrive and it's clear the guys are taking advantage of the opportunity to celebrate, with the quantity set down on the table. We each hold up a shot of Tequila and toast to my recovery. I wince at the burn, chasing it down with a drag on my beer.

When the team settles and the attention is no longer on me, I ask Brad again, "Why here?"

"Can't we just come somewhere for a drink?" He's being a prick on purpose.

"No, because this isn't just *somewhere*. You know where we are."

With a sigh he gives me the answer I already know, "I wanted you to remember that night—what she did to you."

"This is pointless. I've already forgiven her."

Brad groans and rubs a hand over his face. "So what? You screw her and all is forgiven?"

"We haven't slept together. I thought you liked her. You've been the one telling me to hear her out."

191

He picks up his beer and takes a long drink. "I did, until she messed with your career. Again. She's the reason you're in this mess."

"I've already told you. The accident wasn't her fault. I was distracted."

He looks confused. "By what?"

"I thought I saw someone from my past."

The snippet of information is enough to make him settle and the scowl on his face disappears.

"For the record, I haven't slept with her."

He blinks. "Serious?"

"Serious."

"Why not?"

"On my best behavior, remember?" I say, gesturing at my leg.

He narrows his eyes, wanting to pry some more.

I level him with a stare and ask, "What's got up your ass anyway? Did Lola turn you down or something?" His face turns sour again, and I know I've hit the nail on the head. "Sorry, man."

He looks down into his drink. "She's hung up on someone else." We both know who that someone is, but neither of us say it out loud. "I know I said to give her a chance, but I don't get it. Why Britney?"

"What do you mean?"

"Even if she had her reasons, she still screwed you over. Do you really want to be with her? I've got your back, whoever you chose, I just think you could go for someone who doesn't have as much drama following them around."

"She's sorry and that's all that matters."

"Whatever you say. Just remember, the past will always be there, lingering between you. You might be able to forgive, but it's hard to forget."

***

I blame the shots of Tequila for what I do when I return home.

Britney welcomed me at the door and with Brad's help they managed to get me up to my room in one piece. I wait until I know Britney is asleep before I reach into my nightstand drawer and pull out the same phone I used to call Evan a few weeks ago. This time it isn't him I need to speak to.

"Hey, baby."

God, it's good to hear her voice. "Hey, Mom," I reply wearily, unable to hide the tiredness in my voice.

"How's the leg holding up?"

Of course she knows about it. Just because we can't speak, doesn't mean she can't keep tabs on my career. The same career we all made sacrifices for. "It hurts like hell, but I got my cast off today. Doctor Greenman thinks I'll make a full recovery." Even saying it out loud it doesn't feel true. I'm a lucky son of a bitch.

"And football?"

"It could be a few months, but hopefully I'll be back on the field in time for next season."

"That's great. I'm happy for you," She couldn't sound less happy if she tried.

"You'll never win an Oscar for that one, Mom. What's wrong?"

I hear her sigh. "Oh, I don't know. Maybe I'm being silly, but would it be such a bad thing if you couldn't go back to football? Think of all the new things you could do with your life ..."

"I don't want to do anything else, Mom."

"Football has a shelf life, and so does starting a family. It's the most important thing you could want."

"Football?"

"A family," she says, her voice stern.

"Forgive me for not thinking it's the be all and end all," I grumble back.

"Don't," she scolds.

I picture the stern expression on her face, the way her eyes crinkle when she's angry, that's if she still looks the same. It's been years since I last saw her and a lot's changed, including me. "What did you expect me to say?"

"Exactly that, but don't let the past taint your views or change your expectations. Don't let it hold you back from being with someone you love and starting a life with them. You could have your happily ever after."

"Whatever."

"Don't dismiss me. I'm still your mother. Now what's the real reason you've called?"

"I've met someone ..."

"I knew it." I can tell she's beaming, by the way her voice lightens. It comes out like a song.

"Are you keeping tabs on me?"

"Let's just call it a mother's intuition. Now, tell me about her." I hear a ruffle as she settles down to get comfy. She's in this for the long haul.

"It's complicated," I huff.

"Love always is. Tell me more."

"I never mentioned the word love."

"If you're mentioning her, she must be important. It's an easy conclusion to come to. The fact you reacted so quickly tells me what I need to know."

"Remember that media scandal a while back?"

"Yes ..." she replies, hesitantly.

"She was the one responsible."

I frown thinking back on my night with Brad, then all the things Britney told me. I'm at odds with myself. My head is telling me to be cautious but the

194

beating organ in my chest, the one that runs the show, has other ideas.

A few seconds pass before she replies, "We don't always get to choose who we fall in love with. Love—when it's real—is all consuming. It's messy and sometimes it hurts. And that's the point. Nothing worth fighting for ever comes easy, and the most beautiful things can be found in the most unexpected places."

I'm about to speak when I hear her snuffle. Damn it she's crying. "Mom?"

"Don't let my mistakes ruin you. Don't let them hold you back and stop you from letting someone in. I am not the example you should be following, and I could never forgive myself if I thought for a second that I was the reason you were holding back."

"It wasn't your fault, Mom. You didn't know."

"Yes, and I've come to terms with it. I hope the same can be said for you. Give yourself a chance to love and feel how good it feels to be loved back. *Really* loved. Not like Abby."

I chuckle. "You just had to drop that one in there didn't you?"

"She was never the one for you. I could always tell by your voice when you spoke about her. You deserve to be happy. Just remember, there will come a day when you won't be able to find it running around a field with a ball."

"Thanks, Mom."

"No, thank you."

"For what?"

"For never holding it against me that I brought that monster into our lives."

We hang up shortly after that. It's late and we're both tired. I don't know when I'll get to speak to her again, but I know her words will stay with me for a long time. She knows me better than I know myself, even despite the time and distance between us.

It's time to start taking down those walls I built to keep everything and everyone out. They've done a good job, too good of a job. I meant it when I told Britney on the bathroom floor that without football I have nothing. But now I do. I have her.

Eighteen

Britney

I never thought I could feel for someone the way I feel about Becket. He's one of those people who fly under the radar, then suddenly there they are, entwined in every part of you in such a way that you forget how to live without them. I always thought he would be hard to love, but I was wrong. He's impossible to hate.

Jess has well and truly embraced the art of me working remotely. She's using it as an opportunity to send all the crap jobs my way, knowing there isn't a thing I can do about it. Not if I want to stay here with Becket.

Sometime soon I need to leave. Then what?

A message flashes up on my phone and I open it before she can bombard me with any more.

Jess: *I'm all for seeing how this love story is going to pan out, but at some point, you need to return to New York. People are asking questions and I can't put it off any longer. This is your boss speaking now, not your best friend.*

I sigh, thinking about how to reply.

Me: *I know.*

Jess: *That's it? That's all you're going to say?*

Me: *There's nothing else to say. I know I need to come back.*

Jess: *You could at least pretend to be excited about it.*

Me: *We kissed … again.*

Jess: *Forgive me for not being surprised. Without even meeting the guy I can tell the two of you have chemistry.*

Me: *How? I've barely mentioned him.*

Jess: *The fact that you mentioned him at all was enough, B. You never talk about guys, like ever.*

Me: *I'm working with him of course I'm going to mention him.*

Jess: *You're also working with Six Seconds to Barcelona, one of the biggest rock bands in the world, but you don't name-drop them as much as you name-drop Becket.*

Me: *Hmm.*

Jess: *So, here's the big question: How hard are you falling?*

Me: *I'm at risk of breaking every bone in my body.*

Jess: *Basically, you're screwed.*

Me: *Well and truly.*

Jess: *I hate to break it to you, but we need you back by the end of next week at the latest. There's a big awards ceremony we need you to attend, so I'm officially putting an end to this little hiatus you've been on.*

Me: *Great. What do I do about Becket?*

Jess: *Christ, B. We're not in the dark ages. We have these little objects called cell phones that people use to stay in touch. You've found it easy* *enough being away from me for two months and we all know even if Becket takes your V-card, I will always be your number one love.*

Me: *Hoes over bro's.*

Jess: *Amen. Why don't you invite him to New York? With his injury, it's not like he has anything better to do.*

Me: *Easier said than done.*

Jess: *Why?*

Me: *He hates the place. Like literally despises it. I'll be lucky if I can get him on a plane, let alone to New York—not a chance.*

Jess: *What could he possibly hate about New York?*

Me: *I don't know. When we first met, I thought it was simply because he'd broken up with his girlfriend there. But now I think there's more to it.*

Jess: *Well, there is a certain article you're meant to be writing, and might I add, have yet to send me a draft of—it's the perfect excuse to do a bit of digging.*

Me: *Leave it with me.*

Jess: *I will. But one thing I'm not leaving with you: booking your flight. Sorry, B. Times up. It's time to come home.*

I stare at the screen, eyes glazed, digesting what Jess has just said. It's time to go back. When I first arrived in Jacksonville, I would have happily turned straight back around and hopped on a plane back to New York. Now ... I can't think of anything worse. The hardest part isn't that I have to go back, it's that I have to provide Becket with a choice. Am I worth following, despite whatever issues he has with the place? The strong possibility of him giving me an outright 'no' is why we haven't broached the subject yet. It's the big fat elephant in the room. We both know it's there. We're just choosing to ignore it.

I shut my laptop down, predicting not much work will be done after *the* conversation. I don't have any other choice than to bite the bullet and get it over and done with. There's no point in putting off the inevitable.

At first there's no answer when I knock on his bedroom door. For the love of God, I hope he hasn't tried to attempt the bathroom on his own again. I knock loudly and lean in closer so I can hear better.

His gruff voice filters through the door, "Come in."

He's pulling his headphones out when I walk in, which explains the delayed response.

"We need to talk."

"I gathered," he replies.

My eyes trail to his chest, he doesn't have a shirt on. The reason I'm in here, making life difficult for myself, becomes unclear. All I want to do is climb on the bed with him and forget about everything, forget about New York.

"I have to go back ..."

"Ok?"

My stomach drops. That's it? After the other night, and the things I shared with him that I've never shared with anyone apart from Jess, all he can say is *okay*? Maybe I've misinterpreted this situation, made him out in my head to be something he's not. The Becket I'm staring at right now is not the same Becket I revealed my darkest secrets to. He's not the same guy who held me and made me feel like I could move on from the past and be a better, stronger person. The way he's looking at me right now—it's like he couldn't give a crap.

"Is that all you're going to say?" I ask, completely stumped.

"I don't know what you want me to say ..."

"Why are you shutting me out? What's in New York that's so bad?"

He frowns and looks down.

Please, give me anything. Something more than this.

When he looks up, his eyes are cold. "I don't know what you want from me, Brit."

"What the hell?" my voice gets louder with each word I speak. I'm so pissed with him right now. "After the other night, that's all you can say? You practically dragged my past out of me, and now, all I want is a few days in New York with you, and you're pushing me away?"

"I can't go back to New York. I won't."

He's unbelievable. I've been here for months and what do I have to show for it? Absolutely nothing. The words *black coffee* on my notepad and a pathetic attempt at a first draft. This was his plan all along—that's what I want to believe, but I don't. I know him and I know us. The other night was as real as it gets. Everything I felt, he felt too, I know it. I can't give up, not yet. "I'm leaving, Becket. I know there's something more to this whole New York story than what you're telling me. Jess is booking the flights. Please, come with me?"

"I can't go to New York, Brit. Please don't push this." He looks back up at me and, in his eyes, there is nothing.

We're right back to where we started.

***

Becket

Last night was a disaster of epic proportions. I couldn't have handled the situation worse if I'd tried. And now, Britney hates me. There's a strong possibility she won't write the article. I've messed up, big time.

I'm sitting in my wheelchair in Coach Langford's office, waiting for him to arrive. He called earlier, demanding I drag my sorry ass in. When I tried to put up a fight, claiming I wasn't up to it, he wouldn't hear of it, texting:

A lovers' tiff with the blonde residing in your home is not a valid excuse to not come to this meeting, Becket. Three PM. Do not be late.

Nothing gets past him.

So here I am.

A bleep comes from the door. A sign that the security code has been entered into the keypad. The door opens and in walks Coach Langford.

His eyes roam over my face and bluntly, he says, "What bit you in the ass?"

"Britney."

His eyebrows raise.

I rectify my mistake. "Not literally."

"Hmm."

He sees her as a distraction. He's not wrong, he never is. She's all I can think about. Years I've spent dwelling over my past. Now my mind has been taken over by her. I'm not sure which is worse. Both serve as a reminder of things I can never have.

He walks behind his desk, pulls out his chair and takes his sweet time getting settled. He's doing it on purpose, and I huff impatiently.

"Why am I here, Coach?"

He grunts. "You did it, son."

"Did what?"

"Please don't tell me you've forgotten."

I wrack my brain but come up trumps. "Not a clue what you're talking about, Coach."

"Damn players. You're aging me beyond my years. The award, Becket."

I stare at him vacantly.

"I guess I'm going to have to spell it out for you. You won the award with Sports Elite, the biggest sports magazine in the country."

I blink, still none the wiser. "What award?"

"Damn it, Becket. Maybe we should put you up for idiot of the year?"

"Bit harsh, Coach."

"You won Sports Personality of the year!" he explains, exasperated. "Although I'm beginning to wonder if they got you mixed up with someone else."

I vaguely recall him mentioning my name being submitted for it. It was meant to be a chance to get back in the NFL's good books, but I never thought I'd win. Especially not in the personality category, everyone knows it's not my strong suit.

I sit wide-eyed, digesting what he's just told me. "Wow."

"Is that all you've got to say?"

"I think I'm in shock. This is good right?"

His face softens and he smiles. "This is the break we've been waiting for. The NFL might finally stop following your every move and looking for a reason to push you out. Along with the article Britney's writing, it's a done deal, you're finally out of the woods."

Damn it. Here we go. His good mood is about to turn sour. "About the article ..."

He rolls his eyes. "What did you do?"

"We may have hit a roadblock."

"Well back up and drive in another direction. We've spent months trying to put that night to bed and I'm not about to let our hard work come undone because you can't keep your dick in your pants."

"I haven't slept with her," I reply through clenched teeth. I don't add how much I wish I could change that fact. Somehow, I don't think he'd be pleased if he knew how my head is well and truly in the gutter when it comes to Britney Shaw.

He gives me a look that says he doesn't believe a word coming out of my mouth. "Right."

"I swear. We may not see eye to eye on a few things that's all."

"That's because you're as agreeable as my mother-in-law."

This conversation isn't going great, and now he's likening me to his mother-in-law? No way. I met her once, never again. "Can we get back to the awards?" I say trying to change the subject.

He narrows his eyes. He's not done berating me about the article, but he knows better than to get me fired up. "Fine. But you need to clear up the Britney situation ASAP. I'll be checking up on it. Anyway, the awards are next week, so start getting your speech ready."

"So soon? I'm assuming they're in Florida?"

He's lost complete interest in the conversation, his attention focused on some paperwork on his desk. He doesn't even look up when he replies, "Nope. New York."

"No chance."

That grabs his attention. "Excuse me?"

I shake my head defiantly. "I'm not going."

He of all people should know that this was always going to be a no. He knows why—he's one of two people who know the truth about my past. Bad shit happens when I'm in New York. I can't go back there.

He leans back in his chair and sighs, clasping his hands together. "You don't have a choice, son."

"I do and my choice is no."

Looking to the ceiling, he mutters under his breath, "Lord help me. These players are going to be the end of me."

"You're being a bit dramatic."

"Which part is dramatic, Becket? The part where I watched a video of you motorboating the NFL commissioner's daughter or how about when I watched you being carted off the field, virtually in a coma, with possibly one of the worst sporting injuries you could have obtained. Oh no, wait, the porn video aired to everyone including the President of the United frickin' States. That was a really good one. So, tell me again I'm being dramatic and this isn't a really big deal."

"I messed up," I reply quietly.

"Messed up would be burning toast or forgetting your gear for practice. This ... was colossal. Do you know what it took for me and Shauna to sweep this under the rug?"

I look away, focusing on the awards and trophies presented proudly on his wall. I should have known he was going to pull the guilt card.

"Don't look away, you know I'm right. I've worked with you for years, watched you grow, and the worst thing I've ever witnessed was the way you almost threw your career away ... because of a girl. No, actually, there was something worse—when I found out about your past and how you put *them* at risk, all because of a blonde. If you don't do this and detract

205

the attention away from that scandal, people will come searching Becket, mark my words. Secrets don't stay buried for long. You know that better than anyone."

"It was out of my control ..."

"That might be so, but you know what *is* in your control? What you do next. If you care about your career and you care about *them*, then you will get your ass on a plane to New York."

He doesn't need to dismiss me. I know the conversation is over.

Before I go to leave, he says, "And if you know what's good for you, you'll take Britney Shaw with you, and don't bring her back!"

***

It's been three days since Britney's spoken to me. Pretty impressive considering we technically live together. Even when she's around, helping, she doesn't say a word. She's proving to be as stubborn as I am, and that's saying something.

"Michael Becket?" calls out a voice, from the side of the waiting room.

I look up, beaming, ready for what I hope is about to come next. I know what I need to do to win Britney over. But first I have something more important to deal with.

Nineteen

Britney

He leans in, licking his lips hesitantly. Do it, I think to myself, please just do it.

His eyes flick down, and I know this is the moment I've been waiting for. Right when he's about to close the gap, the screen freezes.

"What the—" I mutter to myself, my hand full of popcorn frozen midway to my mouth.

The screen unfreezes and I sigh in relief. I'm one hundred percent emotionally invested in this movie and these characters. I'll be pissed if anything stands in my way of watching the angsty sex scene—the point of the whole movie. It's taken over an hour of my life to get to this point.

Right when their lips are about to meet, the screen freezes again. Unlike the last time, it remains that way. Netflix and I are about to have a serious falling out. "Gaaaah!" I'm being over the top, but the past few days of animosity between me and Becket has me wound up. If I can't get my happy ending, I need to watch these characters get theirs.

I stand and stray pieces of popcorn fall from my loungewear onto the floor. The words *hot mess* spring to mind. I stalk over to the one-hundred-and-twenty-inch flat-screen TV and stare at it coldly, hoping that scolding it with my eyes might spark it back to life. Nope. There they are, larger than life, Britt Robertson, and Dylan O'Brien, ready to make sweet love, and what do I get? Nothing.

Leaning forward, I tap my knuckles against it, then tap it again. "Piece of shit," I mutter to myself.

I mean who needs a TV this big? The people on the screen are literally bigger than me. I'm ready for rapping my knuckles against Dylan's perfect brow once more, when a pair of hands swoop in front of my face, and everything goes black.

Instantly, the figure in the black jacket flashes through my mind and my heart stops.

I'm about to fight back, when Becket's scent invades my senses. Lavender and birch. A deep throaty chuckle follows that sends a reaction straight down to my lady parts. If I weren't so on edge and sexually frustrated, I might have been able to see the funny side to all this, but hell hath no fury like an orgasm-deprived woman. If that's the case, Becket's screwed, because this has been building for years and I'm ready to combust.

"Get off me," I grunt.

He removes his hands and I'm staring at Dylan.

I should turn around and face him, but I can't. The past few days have been awful. All I've wanted to do is apologize for pushing the New York thing too much. I knew what it meant to him and I should have backed down. Unfortunately, Becket and I are equally stubborn, so instead of settling things like grown adults, there's been an increasingly awkward silence building.

Accepting I can't avoid him forever, I spin around, ready to unleash my wrath. "Are you trying to send me to an early grave? Who sneaks up on someone like that?"

Gone is tortured Becket and back is the smirk. I'm not sure which is worse. Tortured Becket has me weeping inside and out, wanting to take on whatever demons he's fighting. Smirking Becket has me wanting to slap it straight off his face, then tear his clothes off. I've never met someone who could draw such polar opposite reactions from me. He's infuriating.

What's more infuriating? The way he towers over me, and says, "It's my house, Brit. I was hardly sneaking around."

He has a point.

"Your fancy TV is broken."

He smirks again. "Alexa ... Play TV." Dylan leans in and devours Britt Robertson's mouth, sexy soundtrack, and all. "What's wrong, Brit? Don't you want to finish watching the movie?" He takes a step closer, getting so close our toes are touching.

I have to lean my head back in the same way I did, that first day in the gym, only this time I know he doesn't hate me. Quite the opposite. And I'm one hundred percent certain he's going to kiss me.

Then it hits me: he's standing.

"What are you doing? Where's your chair!" I shriek, looking around frantically.

He holds his arms out wide and says, "Surprise."

"Alexa ..." I say, "Pause TV." There's no way I'm missing watching my fellow Britt lose her V-card, but for now, she'll have to wait.

I reach up with my arms, wrapping them around Becket's neck before slamming my lips against his. He groans when I part his mouth with my tongue, deepening the kiss and pressing my body into his.

From what I can feel, this game we've been playing has been as frustrating for him as it has for me.

I'm done playing by the rules, I've waited long enough.

My hands begin roaming, finding his belt and attempting to unfasten it. I don't get far when Becket's hands cover mine, stopping me from completing the task at hand. I try to bat him away and begin fighting with the surprisingly challenging metal object. Our lips never break contact until Becket's hands firmly pull mine away from his belt, and pin them to my sides.

I narrow my eyes. "What are you doing? Why are you making me stop?"

He looks almost sheepish when he replies, "I thought we could have a date?"

"What ... like right this second?"

Letting go of my hands, he takes a step back and runs a hand through his hair. "Yeah." He looks at the screen, raising an eyebrow. "Unless you're busy?"

Oh, Britt you're just like me. You're never going to seal the deal. "What did you have in mind?" I ask, trying not to think too much about the fact I couldn't be dressed any less appropriately for a date if I tried.

He shrugs. "I thought we could order in. Maybe a bit of Netflix and chill."

My eyes widen. "'Netflix and chill?' Are we talking literally or metaphorically?"

"I'd like to say I don't put out on the first date, but it's been so long I can't remember if I do or don't. How about we wait and see?" He winks.

I roll my eyes playfully. After the animosity of the past few days, it feels good to be back to the normal Britney and Becket. The B Team in full force. Oh my God. I just did that thing social media couples do where they no longer refer to themselves as separate beings, instead becoming one and give themselves a single name. I'm in deep. Deeper than the Titanic.

"Why are you doing this?" I ask, backtracking, trying to regain control of the situation. The last time we attempted anything like this, he had me sit and watch him screw another woman.

The smug expression on his face disappears and he answers, "I fucked up, Brit. Last time we tried this ... I shouldn't have done what I did. Can we have a do-over?"

Damn it. I can't not forgive him, especially when he looks at me with puppy dog eyes. "Fine." I sniff. "But we're ordering pizza because I'm starving. And I get to pick the movie."

"What did you have in mind?"

"Well, as you spoiled Britt and Dylan, we're starting again."

He looks at the TV screen skeptically. "Ok, what's the movie called?"

"*The First Time*."

"Seriously?" he groans.

"The most serious I've ever been in my life. I was just getting to the good bit and you ruined the momentum, so now we have to start again."

He leans in and places a sweet kiss on my lips.

"What was that for?"

He shrugs. "Just because I can, and it feels right. I like this."

"What?"

"Us. Being normal, rather than fighting or trying to take on the world. It feels like we're a normal couple."

"Throwing the couple card around already? Careful, Becket, your teammates won't think you're cool if they find out what a softy you really are."

This time when he leans in and kisses me, he pours every emotion he's feeling into it. I know because I'm feeling it too. We're teetering on the edge, ready to fall. I just hope that when we do, it's together.

"I don't care what they think. I don't care what anyone thinks. Apart from you."

Every part of me swoons, and I scold myself. After all, this could just be another one of his games.

***

Two supersize pizzas and a whole lot of candy later, we're back to the pivotal point of the movie.

My mouth drops open. "Please tell me it's not *that* bad."

The whole point of the movie is the build-up to their first time, and then it turns out to be crap? Is that what I have to *not* look forward to? I swallow nervously and look at Becket out of the corner of my eye. His broad shoulders shake as he laughs silently. "Why are you laughing at me?" I huff.

"You look like someone just told you Santa isn't real. It's a movie, Brit. Of course, it's not like that."

"I don't have a clue what to expect," I admit. "In my head I've built it up to be this huge thing, and what if it's not? What if I'm disappointed?" Ok, so that was anything but cool. Spewing the inner working of my mind to Becket is probably not the best way to handle this.

He grabs the remote control off the coffee table and presses pause, then turns his whole body to face me and stares me directly in the eyes. "Do you want the truth?"

Breathlessly, I say, "Always."

He takes me by surprise when he shuffles in closer and starts kissing me. He doesn't break for air, and within minutes, I'm riled up, the conversation and any worries, forgotten.

I moan when his lips leave mine, but I'm not disappointed for long as he begins placing small kisses along my neck. He varies the pressure between nipping and sucking gently, and warmth spreads throughout my whole body.

Hovering close to my ear, he says in a hushed voice which has me trembling and that I hear in every part of my body, "The first time might hurt. But you'll forget when you're begging me for more." He pulls away with a serious expression on his face. "I won't ever make you do anything you don't want to. All you have to do is tell me to stop."

I nod, letting him know I get it.

He stands and offers his hand out to me.

"Where are we going?"

"Your first time isn't going to be a quick fumble on the couch."

Alrighty then. We're really doing this. I totally swooned over Dylan, but he's got nothing on Becket. Who knew the brute without a filter could be so ... sweet? With the expectations of what's to come, it all feels very heavy and becomes a little too much. Panicking, I have no control over what comes out of my mouth, a bit like someone else I know. "I totally dig you right now," I blurt out, trailing behind him on the stairs.

A rumble of laughter fills the house, but it doesn't stop him. He says over his shoulder, "You did not just quote the movie?"

"It felt fitting," I squeak.

The door to his bedroom opens. This is really it. Britney The Virgin will be a virgin no more. They say your first time is a big deal. When you get to where I am in life, it isn't just a big deal, it's a *huge* deal. I trust Becket with this more than I've ever trusted anyone, but my stomach is still in knots. I'm only human after all.

Following him inside, I try to swallow but my mouth is drier than the desert. When he switches the lamp on his nightstand on, I pause, staring at it.

"Brit?"

"I don't have a clue what I'm doing."

Tugging me towards him, he wraps his arms around my waist and trails his fingers back and forth along my lower back. It's soothing and calms my nerves.

"Stop overthinking it," he whispers.

Easier said than done when you're in the arms of one of the hottest NFL players in the country. I don't get a chance to overthink it, because Becket does everything he can to make sure my mind is shut off. His mouth devours mine and I'm incapable of doing anything but respond to his kisses.

He pulls back, and in a way that is only fitting to me and him, he quotes the movie and the words of Dylan O'Brien right back to me, "I totally dig you too." Before taking things any further, he asks, "Are you sure this is what you want?"

It's the first time someone has asked. That's when I realize I'm starting to fall for him, the moment he respects me and my body and all the emotions that come with my past.

I nod and he peels away my clothing, one piece at a time, then backs me up to the bed. Falling back, I relax into the sheets, watching as he strips down to just his boxers, and as he does, every hard trained muscle flexes.

He's about to climb over me, when I clear my throat and boldly say, "Take them off."

All I get is a smirk before he pulls his boxers down, then stands up tall. My eyes zero in on his huge erection and of course, my mouth takes over, not in a good way. "It won't fit."

Becket freezes. I've completely fucked up getting fucked. Mortified, I'm ready to scurry off the bed and leave Jacksonville, naked. Getting clothed would take too much time, I need to get away from this situation as quick as humanely possible.

The worst possible thing happens next. Becket begins to laugh. I cover my face with my hands.

"Seriously, Brit, what now?" he wheezes out.

"Your cock—it's waving at me ... you have to stop laughing." I watch as he begins to stroke himself up and down slowly. "What are you doing?"

He stops laughing and his expression turns serious. "Showing you what I want you to do with your mouth." My mouth forms an O. "Brit, you're a natural."

Suddenly I don't want to run away from Jacksonville, the only place I want to be is right here. Shuffling towards him on the bed, I lift my hand up and replace his, stroking back and forth in the way he showed me. When I move forward, licking my lips, ready to take him in my mouth, he shakes his head.

Gently, he pushes me back onto the bed, covering my body with his, as he whispers into my ear, "We'll save that lesson for later. Tonight, is all about you."

That's the moment I'm ruined for all other men. I might not be experienced, but I know finding a man who's happy to put my pleasure above his own is a rare find.

I arch my back as Becket reaches around and unclasps my bra, tossing it to the ground. He trails kisses from my collarbone down to my nipple, sucking and teasing with his tongue. At the same

215

time, his hand wanders, circling my stomach, waiting, gauging my reaction. I buck my hips upwards, rubbing myself against his cock, trying to find some relief as the ache between my legs builds.

It's the signal he needs that I'm all in. I want more.

When his hand skims under the lace of my thong and his fingers slide inside me, stars fill my vision. All the time his movements are slow, teasing, he's giving me time to accept that what he's doing is ok. The way he's touching me is because I want it, and my eyes are being reopened to how things always should have been. Two fingers move in and out, while one circles my clit in a way that almost drives me over the edge. When a shudder starts to take over my body, he stops.

I lift my head and stare at him with daggers. What the fuck does he think he's playing at?

"I want the first time you come to be around my dick."

I'm about to filter my response, but I stop myself. Polite isn't us. "I can't come on your dick if it's not inside me ..." I don't know what to do when Becket's face starts to turn purple. "What's happening right now?"

"I'm trying not to laugh," he says breathlessly, "because if I do, I'm literally going to tickle you with my dick."

I cringe. The moment is slipping away. "This isn't working, I'm broken."

He stops laughing and his face turns serious. "You're not broken, you're just overthinking it."

"I've been waiting a long time for thi—"

I'm silenced as Becket's mouth devours mine, and everything I was fretting about, suddenly seems trivial. Seconds—that's all it takes for me to forget what I was worrying about.

216

"Fuck me," I moan. There's no uncertainty. I've never wanted anything as much as I want him right now.

He slides his dick inside me slowly, a little at a time, giving my body time to adjust around his size. "Ready?"

Yes. No. Never. Always. All the thoughts that flood through my mind. What it comes down to—this moment will never fit a fairytale, we're both too flawed for that.

I don't answer with my voice. Instead, I grab his hips, forcing him in deeper. I can't hide the wince or the hiss of breath that escapes my mouth, when he finally pushes through that barrier, taking away my virginity. But I don't want to. The moment is raw. Real. Perfectly imperfect. When the pain begins to subside, I wrap my legs around his waist, wanting more. I want to be closer to him, but he's holding back, and I know why.

I hold a finger up to his lips, stopping his kisses and say, "Don't hold back."

"I'm scared of hurting you," he replies.

We both know he doesn't just mean physically.

"You can't break me. I was already broken. This here, what's happening, is you putting me back together again."

"Brit ..."

"I'll say it one last time. Fuck me. Now."

He must see something in my eyes because that's exactly what he does. He thrusts his cock in and out of me at a relentless pace, hitting just the right spot. When I'm at the edge, ready to tumble into bliss, he slows down, teasing. When it becomes too much for us both, he doesn't ease back. His fingers circle my clit at the same time he drives inside me, tipping me over the edge. Electricity courses through my body in waves, a pleasure that feels like it might never end but stops too soon.

Becket slides out of me, spent, and rolls onto his back, his chest heaving as he closes his eyes.

"I hope you don't think you're going to sleep," I say, and he smirks in the way he does that drives me mad. One eye opens and meets mine. "I'm not finished with you yet."

***

"Favorite color?"

My pen hovers over the page of my notepad, waiting for his answer. Kneeling beside him, my eyes linger on his exposed chest, then find their way to where the bed sheet settles across his waist.

"Blue, like your eyes."

I jab him in the ribs with my pen, hard. "Now give me the real answer."

He chuckles. "Ok. Red. My favorite color is red."

I tug his oversized shirt down, over my legs, awkwardly. "Weird."

"How is that weird?"

I shrug. "I dunno. I always associate red with bad things. Blood. The devil. Hate."

"Maybe you're wrong," his tone is a little defensive and I'm determined not to ruin the night for the sake of one silly question.

"What's the one thing you've always wanted?" I ask, choosing to ignore the change in his mood.

"You."

"I'm being serious! I have to get some answers for this article, or I'll be fired."

"You won't be."

"Excuse me? What's that supposed to mean?"

He rolls his eyes. "The article is about me. I can pull a few strings, especially if the reason you can't do it is because I'm not being compliant."

He has a point, but it still doesn't feel right. "I can look after myself."

He pecks me on the lips. "I don't doubt that for a second. But I'm not about to let you get in shit for something that is my fault."

"How about you answer my questions, and we don't even let it get to that stage?"

"Brit ..." he warns.

I'm pushing us over that fine line. The one where he closes off and leaves me questioning what I really know about him.

"Come to New York with me," he says out of nowhere, stretching his arms up above his head like he's asked for something simple like a glass of water. Not like he just dropped a major bombshell.

"You're going to New York? I thought you hated it?"

His tone is flat when he replies, "I do."

"I'm completely lost."

His face changes and he's wearing the same cocky expression he does for the rest of the world. "You're looking at Sports Elite's very own Sports Personality of The Year."

"Sports Elite? Like the biggest magazine in the country?"

"The one and only," his voice gives away his excitement.

"That's huge! I'm so proud of you!" I toss my notepad to the floor and throw myself at him. Without realizing I've wound up straddling his lap in nothing but his shirt. Pulling away, I stammer, "Sorry I—"

"I want you to come with me."

His comment catches me off guard. "Why?"

"You know why."

Do I though? One minute he hates me, the next he doesn't. One minute he's refusing to go to New York, the next he's asking me to go with him. I can't keep up.

But if we're going to move forward, we need to learn to trust each other. "Ok."

"Really? That's it?" he asks, surprised.

Looking down at my notepad on the floor, I sigh. I'm as close to getting the article written as I was when I first touched down in Jacksonville. How can I tell the world who the real Michael Becket is, when one moment, I feel like I know everything about him, then the next I feel like I know nothing at all?

The moment is gone though, I can see it in his eyes, he's back to being a closed book. Admitting defeat, I begin planting kisses on his bare chest, teasing him when I slide my tongue just beneath the waistband of his boxers. I pull them down, slowing my kisses, prolonging the inevitable. He sucks in a sharp breath of air when I grasp his cock in my hand, and his eyes widen when my mouth hovers right where he wants it.

I wet my lips and say, "I was going back to New York anyway."

***

Becket's in the shower when I go about my new morning routine. I don't want him to know how anxious I feel. My past is humiliating enough without him having to worry about my mom's 'friends' turning up for money when we least expect it. I'm supposed to be helping him, not burdening him.

Checking the CCTV each morning helps to put my mind at ease. Like every other morning, I slip into his office when he's distracted and begin playing the footage back from the night before. I speed it up and my focus jumps between looking out of the window and the screen. There's never anything to see anyway.

Until there is.

It's a small movement on one of the grids. With the footage sped up it's one of those blink-and-you-miss-it kind of moments. But I don't blink. I see them. A pair of feet right at the edge of the grid. Almost out of sight, but not quite.

Frowning, I look at the time of the footage. One AM. Becket and I were still up. We were up most of the night. Stopping the footage from playing, I rewind it back to the point where the feet appear. Eleven PM—when Becket's security team swap shifts. I frown and fast forward to the point where the feet disappear. Two thirty-six AM.

The rose bush to the side catches my attention next. What are they looking at?

Setting the CCTV back to real time, I quickly leave Becket's office and run upstairs, shouting through to him in the bathroom that I'm heading outside to get some air. Once outside, I begin scouring the grounds, looking for anything that seems strange or out of place. Everything is fine. You're acting crazy, I tell myself. But I saw them, I know I did.

It takes me ten minutes of walking around to find the single rose bush. There are no others. Positioning myself in the same place I saw the feet peeking out on the grid, I look up to the house. To Becket's window, where the curtains are parted a little, like they were all night. My blood runs cold.

'I like to look at the moon, it calms me,' I had told Becket.

But for two hundred and sixteen minutes, there was someone in the shadows who liked to watch us more.

My past has found me.

Twenty

Becket

B ritney's mouth drops open as she looks out of the tinted window of the limo, and her eyes settle on the private jet, waiting to take us to New York.

"What's that for?" she asks, frowning.

"I'm not doing a standard flight," I answer, "not after last time."

She looks confused. "Last time? As in the first time we met ..."

"Yep."

"You haven't been on a flight since? How? What about all the away games you have?"

"Forward planning and one of those large objects that move on wheels."

She looks at me like she's having some kind of epiphany. "Wow. The Great Michael Becket has an Achilles Heel after all."

"More than one," I mutter under my breath. I've added a certain blonde to my list.

She turns her attention back to the plane and says, "It's huge. Like a flying house."

"Courtesy of the NFL," I shrug.

The novelty of these things wore off a long time ago. Nothing matters apart from the game, the feeling of the ball in your hands, the euphoria of crossing the line and hearing the stadium erupt around you. Everything else is just stuff. Things that aren't needed, replaceable.

"This is great, but you know you're not God, right? You can't control the weather."

My pulse elevates. I'm freaking out inside, but I plaster on a smile. Stop being a pussy, it's a plane. People fly all over the world in them each day and what we witnessed was a rare occurrence. I hate how weak my voice sounds, when I say, "At least if we're going to die, it will be in luxury." There's no point in putting off the inevitable. I nod in the direction of the plane. "After you, my lady." My eyes settle on her perfectly shaped ass as she steps outside of the vehicle and I struggle to fight back a groan.

Bending over, she looks back into the limo, her white-blonde hair falling over her shoulders. "Are you just going to sit there all day? Come on."

I shuffle out, awkwardly with my leg and we make our way onto the plane together.

Britney's mouth drops open again when we step inside. "Seriously? This is unreal!"

"It's impressive isn't it?" I reply.

My eyes follow hers. The spotlights reflect off the perfectly polished, rich, wooden tables, a stark contrast to the white leather of the wrap around coach, filled with perfectly plumped up cushions. There's even a goddamn chessboard. Britney's right, it's not a plane, it's a flying house. It's too pristine for my liking and couldn't be further from where I started out, but her mood and seeing the way her eyes light up as she looks around, drinking everything in, is infectious.

"Would you like the tour?" I ask.

"You've got to be kidding? It's so big it needs a tour!" she squeals, which tips me over the edge.

I throw my head back laughing. "Come on."

She doesn't respond, just stands, looking around hopelessly.

Grabbing her hand, I pull her behind me. "We haven't got long until take off, so I'll just show you the bar."

"It has its own bar?" She scoffs.

"No. I just thought I'd say it for the hell of it." Looking back over my shoulder, I find her scowling at me. When I wink, she shakes her head, trying to fight a smile.

We walk through a door at the back of the main seating area and step into a smaller room. The blinds are down and the black glossy bar, gleams under the dim lighting. Walking over to it, I pull out a bottle of Scotch.

"For old times' sake?" I ask, waving it in the air playfully.

Britney's expression darkens. "No thank you."

"Am I missing something?"

"I don't like it." She sniffs, looking away.

"You did when we first met. If I remember rightly, you were knocking back shots for fun."

"I had to. You know that night was an act ... right?" She looks down to her feet and mumbles, "Well, some things were an act."

Placing the bottle down on the bar, I walk over to her and grasp her chin, lifting it gently so she's looking straight at me and can't hide.

"What aren't you telling me?"

"The smell ... it reminds me of *him*. It was always on his breath."

I grit my teeth. It's a trigger. I see it in her eyes, read it all over her body. They say it takes one to know one. Right now, truer words have never been spoken. Loosening my grip on her chin, I skim my fingertips along her jaw and watch as her whole body begins to relax. I place a quick kiss on her lips, before walking back to the bar where I unscrew the lid off the bottle of Scotch and pour it down the sink. When the bottle is empty, I pop the lids off two bottles and say to a bemused-looking Britney, "Beer?" She doesn't answer, so I walk back over carrying the beers in one hand and grab hers with my other. "We better get to our seats."

"Are you allowed to just take them like that?" She glances over her shoulder as if she expects the flight attendants to jump out and tell us off.

"This is my world, Brit. Anything goes. Come on, before we actually get in trouble."

We head back to the seating area and once we're settled, I grab my beer and down it in one.

"Is everything ok?" Britney asks, concerned.

"I'm nervous," I admit.

"Don't be," her voice is soothing as she tries to calm me down. She draws the complete opposite reaction from me, when she begins rubbing my thigh. Each time her hand moves upwards it gets closer to my dick, which is very much aware of what she's doing.

"Brit." My warning doesn't stop her.

She keeps moving her hand higher until the Captain walks in to introduce himself, and she snaps her hand away like she's been caught stealing from the cookie jar.

I don't listen to anything, completely oblivious to the flight attendants talking us through the emergency procedures as the plane slowly sways along the runway, ready to take off. All I can concentrate on is the spicy perfume that reaches my nose each time Britney moves. The same one she wore the first time we met.

Distractions aren't enough though. When the plane runs over a slight bump, my back goes ramrod straight and I choke on my own breath as my eyes dart around, looking for an escape. "I can't do this."

Britney grabs my hand and squeezes it. With her help, I focus on keeping my breathing steady as the plane takes off.

"Would you like anything, sir?" asks one of the flight attendants when we're moving smoothly through the air.

My eyes trail to Britney staring dreamily out of the window. "If you could leave us alone for the rest of the flight that would be great."

Eyes caked with black mascara blink back at me. "For the whole flight?"

I nod and lower my voice, so there's no room for discussion, "The whole flight."

"Was that really necessary?" asks Britney, watching the flight attendants both leave the main seating area.

"Yes, it was."

She huffs and picks up her beer, then swipes away a drip on the rim with her tongue.

My dick twitches in my pants. "Stop it."

"What?" she asks, fluttering her eyelashes.

"I know what you're doing. Stop it."

"Or what?"

"Be careful, Brit, you're poking the bear with a stick."

"I don't have the stick, you do."

"You just referred to my dick as a stick?" I growl, then move my lips close to her ear and whisper, "If

227

you'd like to join the Mile High Club, please, carry on."

She undoes her seatbelt, straddles my lap, and not so innocently says, "Yes, please."

I'm struggling to keep up. She's acting as crazy as the first time we met. This time, I love it even more. "Fuck it," I grumble, lifting her away.

Once standing, I pull her behind me, into the bar, and walk to the back of the small room where there are two closed doors.

"Where are we going?" she asks, trying to slow me down.

Ignoring her, I carry on walking. I open the door to the small bedroom. Her throat bobs when her eyes find the bed. She steps inside without missing a beat. The door clicks shut. I move towards her, grasping the hem of my shirt and pulling it over my head as I do. I hear her breath hitch over the hum of the engine. Her eyes move hungrily over each part of my body. When I finally close the gap between us, I place a finger on her bottom lip. I push down gently. She follows my lead, taking it in her mouth and sucks. She sweeps her tongue over it like she did the rim of the bottle. Like she did with my dick this morning. I can see how turned on she is through the thin material of her top. A groan rumbles through my chest.

She's still new to this and I don't want to push her too far too quick, so I ask, "Can I?"

She nods and I pull the top over her head. She gives me the invitation I need when she unclasps her bra and lets it drop to the floor, then does the same with her denim pants.

"Fuck," I rasp out.

When she sits down on the bed, I step forwards but move my injured leg into an awkward angle. Pain shoots through it and I grimace. Excellent timing.

228

"What's wrong?" asks Britney, panicked.

"Nothing," I grunt, trying to sound better than I feel. Nothing's interrupting this for me, not even my leg. "You might have to take the lead ..."

"Wha—"

She doesn't have a chance to finish her question because I tug her into my arms and flip us on the bed so she's straddling me as I lay on my back. Eagerly I grab the grey, lace thong she's wearing and try to tug it down. It rips, coming away in my hands. Crap.

"What the hell?!" she exclaims. "What am I going to put back on?"

"That's what's on your mind right now?" I smirk.

"No bu—" I thrust my hips up and she stops, letting out a moan.

I'm about to tell her to take off my pants when, reading my mind, she expertly whips my pants and boxers off at the same time. I stare at her open-mouthed when she lowers herself down onto my dick and I feel exactly how wet she is for me.

"What do you think porn is for?" she giggles, replying to the question I never actually asked.

My hate of flying disappears. My fear of the past is being replaced with new memories, watching as Britney rides me straight to her orgasm, thirty-five thousand feet in the sky.

Twenty-One

Britney

A gentle tapping on the exposed skin of my back stirs me awake. At first, I'm confused about where I am. It all comes flooding back when my eyes flit around the room, taking in my surroundings. I'm tucked under Becket's arm, using his bare chest as a pillow. "Hi," I say, sleepily, when I find him gazing down at me.

"Hey," he says back, his voice, too, thick with sleep.

I can hear the steady thrum of his heart beating in his chest as I make a pattern with my fingertips over his skin.

"Sorry I had to wake you, but it will be time to land soon."

I can't hide my disappointment. I want to stay in this bubble forever, away from real life. "How long was I out?" I ask.

"Maybe half an hour?"

"That's it? I'm so tired."

"Sex does that to you," he smiles.

He begins drawing patterns on my back and my skin tingles, goosebumps raise. I want him again.

His chest vibrates when he chuckles. "Unfortunately, we don't have time for round two."

I let out a frustrated groan, then remember a not so minor detail. "You ruined my underwear."

"Now we can share a secret." He places a gentle kiss on my lips, sits up slowly and climbs out of bed. I watch, mouth open, as he gathers up our clothing from the floor, muscles flexing each time he bends. He looks around and catches me ogling him.

Throwing my clothing at me, he says, "Head out of the gutter, Brit."

The clothes hit me in the face. "Ass."

"What? You love my ass?"

I roll my eyes at his comment.

He sighs. "We really need to get moving."

With excellent timing, one of the flight attendants calls out from the other side of the door, "Mr. Becket."

"Damn," I grumble, climbing from the bed and throwing on my clothes haphazardly.

"Don't worry, we'll have all the time in the world when we get to the hotel."

"Hotel?" It never even occurred to me that he might have somewhere else to stay.

"Yeah, the NFL booked me a hotel."

"You could always stay at my place ..."

His eyes light up. "Done. I hate hotels. Ready?"

I walk to a small mirror on the wall and take in my appearance. My hair is a mess, and my clothes are crumpled. At least my skin is glowing. Accepting there is nothing I can do, I smile and say, "I'm ready."

***

When Becket enters my apartment, he walks around, observing. Not that there's much to observe. His bedroom has the same size floor plan as my entire living space. The joys of living in New York.

My eyes settle on the console table at the side of the living room, and I walk over before he can get there, placing the picture of me and my mom together face down. It's one of the only happy days I can remember us having, shortly after one of her stints in rehab. When she came out, she promised me the world. The image was taken in one of the local diners, and the waitress who took it captured us both grinning. My cheeks ached for hours afterwards. We had the biggest cheeseburgers and strawberry milkshakes I had ever seen, thanks to the extra money we had from Mom not sinking it into her supply. Three days later, she had a relapse and left me without a dime, and no food in the cupboards for two days. She sent her boyfriend to look after me, the one who only appeared at night. I keep the photo as a reminder to keep my guard up. People can't be trusted, not even my mother.

"So, this is your place," says Becket. He spins around, frowning when he sees I've changed position.

I shift my weight to hide the photo and smile at him sweetly. "This is it."

He circles the room, observing the odd trinkets I've collected over the years. Besides a bit of décor, there's nothing much of significance, no overly personal touches, just like his home.

"Do you mind if I make an observation?" he asks.

"Hit me with it."

"This place ... it's not very *you*."

I blink. "What do you mean it's not very me?"

He shrugs. "It's empty, lifeless, and Brit, you're anything but. It doesn't fit you."

"I suppose not."

He takes a couple of steps towards me, his eyes never leaving my face. "Care to share why?"

"After what happened with my mom, I never knew if I'd be able to settle anywhere permanently. I made a promise to myself that I wouldn't get attached to places, things or people. I didn't expect to stay in New York for as long as I have."

His eyes bore into mine, full of understanding. But how could The Great Michael Becket, surrounded by his team and friends, understand what I've been through?

"It sounds like a pretty lonely way to live."

"It is," I admit. "But I've gotten used to it."

He nods. "I get it."

"Do you really though? Have you ever lost someone close? Been let down by someone you thought you could trust? And I'm not just talking about Abby."

"Yes, and yes," he answers cryptically.

"That's it. You're not going to expand?"

He sighs and his face looks pained. I know he wants to tell me more, but he won't. "I can't. Don't push this. You know how it ends."

Ignoring him, I ask, "Why do you hate New York so much?"

"Stop asking questions you know I can't give you the answers to."

Standing tall, I cross my arms over my chest and through gritted teeth say, "So, it's ok for me to tell you everything. It's ok for me to let you in, put my heart on the line, but you won't do the same?"

He groans, rubbing a hand over his face. "That wasn't the point of this conversation."

"But this is where it's ended up. When are you going to trust me?"

"I do. But this—what you're asking—I can never tell anyone."

"Fucking wonderful," I snipe. It's only been a few hours since we set foot off the plane and already our bubble has popped.

"Yes, you are," he says playfully, walking closer to me.

I know what he's doing. He's trying to make me forget the almost fight we were just having. It pisses me off even more when he leans down and places a kiss on my lips that makes my resolve start to crumble. I try to hold it together, to stand my ground, but when I look up into his green eyes, I forget what we were talking about.

"I could do with some food," I say. The conversation isn't finished, we're simply pressing pause, for now. "There's nothing in the fridge so we will have to go somewhere."

"Great, I'm starving. Mind if I freshen up before we head out? I smell like sex."

I try to ignore the mischievous glint in his eyes because I'm still pissed with him. Pointing to a door on the other side of the room, I say, "Bathroom's over there."

He picks up his bag and heads to the bathroom, closing the door behind him. I'm left, consumed by my thoughts, wondering what this all means for us. Reality is beginning to set in, and the honeymoon phase is quickly coming to an end.

I frown when the door reopens and Becket walks back out, shirtless with his pants unbuttoned. He stalks towards me with purpose, picks me up, and walks back to the bathroom, where he's left the shower running and steam billows out into my chilly apartment.

"Your leg!" I gasp when my mouth manages to catch up with my brain.

Ignoring my protests, he steps into the shower—me still fully clothed, him semi-clothed. I'm silenced when he kisses my neck then sucks on my earlobe. Giving in, I allow my head to roll back in pleasure.

"I don't give a fuck about my leg," he grunts, then places a searing kiss on my lips.

My legs wobble when he places me down, but I don't fall, because he anchors me against the wall with his hips. He raises my top over my head and makes quick work of my bra, discarding them out of the shower, onto the bathroom floor. When he undoes my jeans and pulls them down my legs, there's nothing left for him to do—my thong was left destroyed on the plane. I look down through hooded eyes and watch as he kisses along the inside of my thighs. When he looks up at me, water droplets stick to his eyelashes, framing his eyes and making them even more mesmerizing.

"The only thing I give a fuck about is you."

His kisses move higher. I throw my head back, letting out a moan that fills the whole apartment when his tongue circles my clit. I can barely catch my breath when he slides two fingers inside me. He draws them out, continuing the motion at a relentless pace that has me coming apart on his mouth.

Only when my breathing settles and I come back down to Earth, do I acknowledge that what we're doing is avoiding the inevitable. If we want to be together and really make this work, he needs to let me in. If he can't, whatever this is we're doing, will end as quickly as it started.

***

A couple of hours later we finally leave my apartment for food. We end up at a hidden gem away from the usual tourist traps. It's my favorite.

235

"That's disgusting," I comment, as Becket all but licks his fourth plate clean.

He leans back rubbing his stomach and belches loudly. "You don't get a body like this by not eating."

"You're gross, and not very modest," I reply, throwing a straw at him.

He holds up his hands and laughs. "I never said I was a gentleman."

My phone flashes on the table with a message from Jess. I open it and mutter to myself. She wants me to swing by the office for some important work stuff apparently.

"What's the problem?" asks Becket, midway through shoveling another forkful of food in his mouth.

"I need to go to the magazine. Do you mind?"

"Not at all. Can I tag along? It would be good to see part of your life, after you've lived in mine for so long." He grins and any lingering animosity from our conversation earlier blows away.

We finish up and make our way to the office. It's getting late and I know I'm not alone in wishing we could go straight back to my apartment and get comfy in bed. When we step inside, Becket looks around, taking everything in, just like he did at my apartment. For someone who apparently hates New York, he seems almost at home being here.

"Bitch, get over here!" comes an ear-splitting shriek. Ever the professional, Jess bounds out of her office and covers the distance between us at an Olympic pace.

Becket watches, amused, as Jess jumps at me and engulfs me in her arms.

"Can't breathe," I say, struggling for air.

She doesn't hear me, so I give her a firm whack on the back, and she pulls away.

"That hurt!" she exclaims.

"I couldn't breathe."

"All you had to do was say so," she huffs.

"I tried!"

She loses interest in what I have to say and focuses her attention on Becket. I watch like a hawk, knowing exactly what she's thinking.

"Are you going to introduce me?" she preens.

I roll my eyes. "Jess, this is Michael Becket." I then turn to him and gesture back at Jess. "This is my boss and slightly crazy best friend, Jess."

"It's great to finally meet you," she says, holding her hand out for him to take. "I've heard a lot about you."

"Oh, really?" He smirks and I jab Jess with my elbow.

Realizing her mistake, she tries to backtrack, "For the article I mean."

Becket's expression makes it obvious he's having none of what she's saying.

"Sorry," she mutters.

Looking to Becket I say, "You're not the only person in my life who lacks a filter."

They both look at me like they don't have a clue what I'm talking about.

Becket laughs and says, "I'll step out and let you two catch up." I'm about to say that it's fine and he can stay, but he holds up a hand, stopping me in my tracks. "You've not seen each other for weeks, it's fine. I've been here before. I can find my way around and could do with some air."

"But your leg ... You shouldn't be using it too much."

He leans in and whispers into my ear, "You weren't saying that earlier. I'm a big boy. My leg is fine, Brit." He walks away.

237

I turn to Jess. "Looks like it's just me and you."

She doesn't waste a second and drags me into her office, then walks to a small fridge where I know she keeps her emergency stash. Pulling out a bottle of wine, she holds it up in the air and with a little shake, says, "Celebratory drink?"

"What are we celebrating?"

"Losing your virginity, of course."

"Wha—"

"Oh please," she tuts. "I'm not stupid. That nice glow you have reeks post-sex. I'm jealous."

Awkwardly, I run a hand over my hair and my cheeks burn, making it painstakingly obvious she's hit the nail on the head.

"Don't worry. I don't think it's quite as obvious to everyone else, if that's what you're worried about ..."

I take the glass of wine she's holding out to me across her desk and gulp it down.

"He's so hot!" she squeals. "And the way he looks at you ..." She begins fanning herself. "Tell me, is the sex good? Is it everything you thought it would be?"

"Slow down!" I giggle.

"No way. You've left me here, on my own, with these bores, for almost two months. You owe me this. I want details, B."

"There's nothing to tell," I lie.

"What a load of crap. You just gave a guy your virginity after holding on to it forever. You can't tell me that doesn't mean something."

"I like him."

Her shoulders shake with laughter. "Of course, you like him. I'd be concerned if you didn't."

Admitting defeat, I hold up my glass for a toast. "To the loss of my virginity—it went with a *pop*." I place emphasis on the word *pop*, but rather than joining in like I expect her to, Jess pales and remains

238

quiet. I close my eyes and take a deep breath. "He's behind me isn't he?"

She nods and mouths *sorry*.

Looking back over my shoulder, as expected, Becket is standing in the doorway with his arms folded and a stupid grin on his face. "You might have lost your virginity, but there's one thing about you that hasn't changed."

"What's that?" I ask.

"You're still crap at keeping secrets."

Twenty-Two

Becket

I'm struggling to form a coherent sentence. Scrap that I'm struggling to form a coherent thought.

"You don't like it, do you?" asks Britney.

I shake my head. "You're right. I don't like it."

Her face falls, distraught.

"I love it."

The dress in question is low cut, but tasteful, and the champagne-colored silk complements her fair skin. It's outstanding. I can't stop staring.

She shifts nervously under my gaze.

"Don't worry. You've broken the unbreakable. My dick needs a break." Her mouth forms the perfect O and I peck her nose. There are a lot of ways I could describe her right now, but the simplest—no frills— seems the most fitting. "You look beautiful."

Her cheeks turn a shade of pink, visible even under the makeup I watched her apply not so long ago. I curse to myself that we have to leave the comfort of her small apartment and delve into the shit show that is New York City. I hate it here. It doesn't matter how much time has passed, my feelings for it remain the same.

"We should get going or we're going to be late." She walks away and grabs her bag from her room. When she returns with it in her hands, she asks, "Have you planned a speech?"

I tap at my temple. "It's all up here."

"That doesn't fill me with confidence."

I actually don't have a clue what I'm going to say. I hate giving speeches, but I'm not about to tell Brit that.

My phone lights up with a message informing me our driver for the night is outside. "We need to go," I say reluctantly.

"I wish we didn't have to." Her eyes tell me she feels the same as I do.

I kiss her and her lips help to calm me, when inside a storm is brewing. I slip my tongue into her mouth, deepening the kiss and my hands trail over the silk of her dress. Losing what little control I had, I back her across the room.

"Becket ..." she moans when I suck down on her neck and begin a path of kisses to her breasts.

We're brought back to reality when my cell rings loudly. "Damn it." I step away from Britney and answer. "We'll be there in a second," I say to the driver and hang up. Our time is running out, I can feel it. Something is about to be thrown in our path, making sure that no matter what we do, or how we feel, we have no chance of survival.

***

I try and fail to shake off my feelings of unease when the limo pulls up outside the venue for the awards. My skin is crawling. I know that New York is going to screw me over somehow ... again.

Britney leans across my lap and looks outside, taking in the frenzy of the paparazzi. "Let's get this over and done with," she says, sounding as resigned as I feel.

At some point on our journey, the clear blue sky was replaced with stormy greys, and rain bounces off the sidewalk. An assistant runs over holding an umbrella over our heads as we climb out of the limo. Cameras flash all around as we walk towards the red carpet. Britney stops dead in her tracks and I almost slam into the back of her and take us both to the ground.

"Can we just go back to my apartment?" she asks.

I shake my head. "Coach will kill me. The NFL are looking for any excuse to boot me out. I have to do this."

"I have a bad feeling ..." she sighs, flinching as the flashes become relentless and the noise unbearable.

Through gritted teeth, going against everything I'm feeling, I say, "We *have* to go in."

We look ridiculous when I plant my hands on her shoulders and march her to the red carpet. That's where the shit show begins. The paparazzi go wild. I've flown under the radar since the media scandal, and this is the first big event I've done. Everyone wants a piece of Becket.

"Becket, give us a smile."

"Becket! Long time no see, smile for the camera."

"Becket, baby, where've you been all my life."

"B, is this the broad from the sex tape? Baby, give us a moan."

It's the last prick that has he me stepping forwards with my fists clenched. Britney grabs my arm before I have a chance to follow through and drags me off the red carpet and into the building. The doors shut and the noise stops, I feel like I can breathe again.

242

When I face her, she's plastered on the biggest smile possible, hiding what I know. That she feels the same as I do. Destroyed by the media.

"Well, that was interesting," she says.

"Tell it as it really is ..."

"It was bad."

Rubbing a hand over my jaw, I try to relieve some of the tension before I look back through the floor to ceiling windows, where I find some of the paparazzi have breached security, and have their cameras pressed up against the glass.

I shake my head and grumble, "Why do you think I've always hidden away."

"I just thought you were boring," she replies, a hint of a smile on her lips.

Even feeling the way, I do, the sparkle in her eyes calms me. "You know better than anyone, that's not the case."

When I wink, all I get in return is, "Asshole."

"You love it."

"What I'd love more is a visit to the restroom. Do you mind?"

Placing a swift kiss into her hair, I murmur, "Not at all."

She moves through the crowd, turning back when she's almost out of sight, smiling at me like I'm the only person in the room. I wish I could capture the moment in my mind and save it, because at the same time Britney turns her back to me and carries on walking through the crowd, a head full of fiery red hair blocks my view. That's when everything starts to go wrong.

"Who'd have thought the nation's favorite porn star could flip it around and become the Sports Personality of the Year?"

"I'm sorry do I know you?"

The redhead steps forwards, offering her hand out for me to shake. I quickly grab two glasses of champagne from the tray of a waiter passing by.

If she's put out, she doesn't let it show on her face. "Of course, you know me, silly. I met you with Britney, in Jacksonville. I'm Leigh."

I don't know what to do or say, I'm still none the wiser to who she is, so I opt for taking a drink of my champagne at the same time an older woman, with curls tighter than a poodle, wanders over to us.

The bitch I now know as Leigh, turns to the older woman and says with a shrill voice, "Fi, I was just catching up with our favorite football player."

Fi flashes her perfectly straight, whiter than white teeth at me.

"It's a pleasure." I bite back the response that no, it's really not.

Fi's face literally doesn't move. She clearly ploughs as much money into Botox as she does getting her hair curled. Someone needs to tell her that her money would be better spent on other things.

The two of them together make my heckles rise. "What do you want?"

Leigh and Fi, the rhyming duo, don't even bat an eyelid, the latter most likely because it's physically impossible for her to do so.

Leigh says, "We saw you were with Britney ..."

"And?"

She turns to Fi and they share a knowing look. "We were concerned."

"Why?" I scowl.

"Because she set you up, silly." Leigh giggles.

They're not telling me anything I don't already know. Brit and I have already been through all of this, but there's something on red's face that tells me there's more to what she's saying. Who do I trust?

There's only one way to find out. I have to play their game.

"You would know that how?" I say. She smirks. I know she thinks she's got one up on me. I'll let her believe it for now.

"Because I was her boss," jumps in Fi. "Although I never expected her to take it quite as far as she did."

The second part catches my attention. What they're saying doesn't make sense. It doesn't fit with Brit's side of the story.

"The assault case was the most interesting. I didn't think she had it in her to go behind everyone's back."

My stomach turns, this doesn't feel like a game anymore. "What do you mean?"

"*That* leak wasn't to do with us. We don't cover cases relating to minors, they cause a lot of legal problems. Britney was one of the only people who knew. She jumped ship not too long after, got herself a better job at Allure. I wonder how little Miss Shaw managed to catch the attention of such a prestigious lifestyle magazine? Just something to think about. You make a gorgeous couple by the way."

Damn it. I don't know what the hell to think or say. My mind keeps jumping from one scenario to the next, but there's still a lot Brit and I haven't talked about. There's still so much she hasn't told me: how she ended up at Allure, what it took to get there. How much do I really know about her because she knows nothing about me? I feel sick. I don't know who to trust anymore. I can't even trust myself.

I watch as Leigh tosses her hair over her shoulder and starts to follow her boss into the crowd. Before they get too far away, she spins on her heel and says for everyone to hear, "You can't trust her, you know that, right?"

"It's none of your business," I snap, my breath coming out in short spurts, as for the first time in a long while, I begin to lose control of my temper. I lose it because a part of me knows there's truth in what she's saying, I know better than anyone how easy it is to wear a mask to deceive everyone around you.

The room begins to bustle as people make their way into the banquet hall for the awards ceremony. I need to find Brit. I don't even acknowledge Leigh as I start to walk in the direction of the restrooms.

She shouts after me, "You're a fool if you go back after what she did. It was all her idea. Everything. She's the one who concocted the whole plan."

I pause but don't turn around.

"It's one thing outing your secrets but the assault case, knowing what it would bring up, knowing how many people's lives she would put at risk—I'd say that's unforgiveable."

I'm left standing in the crowd, questioning why I ever thought I could let my walls down. I've spent years keeping people out, and now, I've learned the hard way, that I never should have let anyone in.

***

Britney

Placing my hands on the washbasin, I lean forward and stare myself straight in the eye. Get it together, Brit. He's beginning to trust you. Show him it wasn't a waste of time. Outside on the red carpet was a circus, and it almost broke the both of us. But tonight means too much to Becket, we can't let the paparazzi get the better of us. When I'm done with my little pep talk to myself, I throw my shoulders back and stand tall. It's game time.

Pushing through the door to the restroom, I smack straight into Becket. He places his hands firmly on my shoulders, steadying me.

"We should get seated," he says. His voice is flat, off, something has changed.

Following closely behind, I wonder what could possibly have happened in the few minutes I've been gone. We enter the banquet room, full of the rich and famous, all dressed in beautiful gowns and perfectly tailored tuxes. I'm feeling totally out of my depth. Becket does a quick check of the seating plan then walks away, leaving me behind.

We settle in our seats, just as the lights dim and the room grows quiet. I glance at him out of the corner of my eye, but all he does is scowl as he stares straight ahead. Every part of him is rigid, apart from his chest which rises and falls dramatically. He's pissed.

"What's wrong?" I whisper.

I get nothing. He ignores me and listens to the speaker on stage who is welcoming everyone to the ceremony. They finish and there's a round of applause. Before the evening gets into full swing, servers make their way around the room with glasses of champagne.

I take a glass and knock it back in one. Becket doesn't comment. He still won't even look at me. I have the urge to bolt. Everything feels wrong, and the guy sitting next to me who was beginning to feel like everything has suddenly become a cold and distant stranger. The whole night passes in the same way, with him ignoring me.

Then, it's time for Becket's award.

Despite whatever is going on with him, my heart swells with pride when his name is called out. He stills when the room erupts, applauding The Sports

Personality of The Year. The clapping continues but he doesn't move. For a second, I think to myself he isn't going to do it, he isn't going to go up onto the stage. Inside I'm screaming for him to move, he's worked too hard to throw this all away.

I sigh with relief when he takes a deep breath and stands up. Like he has done all night, he doesn't even acknowledge my existence. Unlike the rest of the winners who all shook hands with the people around them or leant down and kissed their dates, Becket ignores everyone. His eyes are devoid of any emotion, lifeless. He walks up onto the stage and takes the award from the presenter's hand with a tight smile.

He clears his throat, and the sound is picked up by the mic, the room goes quiet. My stomach churns. He had nothing planned for his speech and he's not known for being the greatest public speaker.

"Firstly, thank you to everyone who nominated me for this award. It means a lot. More than you'll ever know."

My shoulders sag in relief. He's taken the safe route.

He continues, "A while back ... things weren't going great, but if I'm not on the field, when do I ever have a fine moment?"

The room fills with polite laughter. My pulse starts to race, and I rub my palms against my dress, not caring whether I leave smears of sweat on the silk.

"I owe a big thank you to the NFL for not giving up on me. I wouldn't be standing here accepting this award otherwise. Next, I'd like to thank all the fans who have supported me over the years and inspired me to keep going.

"Coach Langford. Thank you for the lessons you've taught me, the way you took me under your wing and pushed me forward. Because of you, I learned that sometimes it's necessary to fall, because when we do, we rise up stronger.

"In football, we prove our worth when we get back up and carry on playing. So, thank you to those who tried to take me down. If you didn't try, I wouldn't have fought back. I'm standing here because of you. You tried to break me, but you failed."

The crowd titters between themselves and I think I'm going to be sick.

The presenter all but shoves Becket away from the microphone before he can say anything else.

It's wasted effort on their part, the damage has already been done. They might not know it yet, but Becket has announced to the world that everything that happened was entirely my fault.

***

Standing in the afterparty, I search for Becket, but he's nowhere to be seen.

When the crowd parts slightly, my eyes finally settle on him. He looks back, eyes cold. I barely recognize him. Jerking my head towards the door, I signal for us to leave. I don't wait for him to respond. If he doesn't follow, then I have the answer I need: He was never worth my time.

Walking out into the night, I swallow over the lump in my throat. My heels click against the sidewalk and rain splashes up against my dress as I power away, needing space to collect my thoughts. I'm almost at the end of the block when I hear footsteps from behind. I stand on guard. Just in case. Always in case.

"Brit!" Even the sound of his voice makes my skin crawl.

I don't look back. He doesn't deserve it. "Follow me," I snap with venom.

249

I keep walking until we reach an alleyway which I turn down. We need to be out of sight, away from the eyes of the public. He draws attention wherever he goes, but the conversation we're about to have needs to be in private.

When I've walked far enough into the darkness that it hides us from prying eyes, I stop and gaze straight ahead. I don't want to look at him, I don't know if I'll be able to hide how angry I am, how hurt. I can't let him see the fault in my wall, if I do, he'll know exactly where to hit to bring it crashing down. I'm beginning to wonder if this was his plan all along.

"I'm surprised you even came," I say, so low it's barely audible.

"I had to leave out the back to avoid the Paps ..."

Silence. Neither of us know what to say.

When I eventually spin to face him, he looks almost as broken as I feel. There's a ringing in my ears. He's the one that broke us, he did this.

"What the hell was that?" I spit. "I thought we were past all of this?"

"So did I. I met some people you used to work with while you were in the restroom ..."

I roll my eyes. I don't need to ask who he's talking about. I now know the flicker of red hair I thought I saw in the foyer wasn't my imagination. Leigh. And where there's a Leigh there's usually a Fiona. "Let me guess? They told you a great story."

"They told me what you did," his voice is as dark as they alley where we're standing, and chills run over my skin.

"You knew I was there that night!" I exclaim, throwing my hands up in the air. It's all I can do to stop myself slamming them against his chest, trying to knock some sense into him. How can he believe two strangers over me? I thought I meant more to him, clearly, I was wrong.

He cocks his head to the side, almost looking amused. "You missed out a few details. How you came up with the whole plan. How you were the one that leaked the assault case."

The only way to make him feel a fool, for believing people he barely knows over me, is to tell him the truth. "What she told you wasn't what happened that night."

He narrows his eyes and sneers. "Please, enlighten me."

"I had a notepad with me. When you passed out and we were in the car on the way to Georgia, I made notes on everything. It went missing. There was only one person in that car besides you ..."

"Leigh," he says quietly, putting the pieces together. "It doesn't change the fact you planned the whole thing."

I look up at the night sky, exasperated. "You actually believe that? After I just told you that she stole from me." I step in closer and our chests almost touch. When I raise my chin, the rain hits my skin, getting heavier with each second that passes. "You know me. I've told you everything. You know I wouldn't do the things she said. I might have been there that night, but I had nothing to do with fallout."

"Why should I believe you?"

"Because I'm still paying for the past. My mom had a ton of debts with the wrong people. Do you know what happens when you piss the wrong people off?"

He looks down, guiltily.

"Exactly what you're thinking. *They* are the reason I accepted the job because I was running out of time

251

and kept missing payments. I needed the pay raise Fiona promised to get rid of them for good."

He frowns, a signal that he understands what I'm telling him. "I was scared, Becket. I had no choice. So yeah, I might have helped to set you up, but when it came down to it, even with the risks involved, I couldn't do it. I walked away. It wasn't me who spread everything, it was Leigh and Fiona, and after everything we've been through and how far I thought we'd come, you believed two strangers over me."

"Why didn't you just tell me?" he asks softly.

"For the same reasons you won't tell me why you hate New York, why you have nightmares every single night, what the assault case was really to do with."

He groans and rubs a hand over his face.

"You know *everything* about me. I hate you right now for what you did back there, but it doesn't change the fact I'm falling. Please, tell me the truth. Fall with me."

He grimaces. "Don't try and make me do this, Brit."

I take a step back and laugh, but nothing about this is funny. "You're joking right? You just humiliated me in front of hundreds of people, yet I'm still here putting my heart on the line, and that's all you can say?"

"I can't tell you. It's not just about me," he answers, his eyes full of pain.

But his pain isn't enough to make me back down. For us to work as a couple, we need to share our burdens, carry each other through the bad times. If he can't trust me with his darkest secrets, with his heart, then why should I trust him with mine?

I shake my head and through gritted teeth say, "Then I can't do this. I won't do this. I deserve more."

I step around him and begin walking back to the bustle of New York. I need to get away from him.

"Where are you going?" he shouts after me.

"Home. You can stay at your fancy hotel tonight."

"What about my things?"

My anger flares. This is what he's worried about? A bag of clothing. "You're the hot shot NFL player. Buy some!" I shout back, over my shoulder. Turning onto the block, I use the crowds as a shield, allowing them to engulf me as I finally succumb to my emotions and allow my heart to break.

***

The storm set in as I trailed the streets. I was looking for clarity on what just happened with Becket. All I found was rain.

I wring out my hair as I step inside the apartment. Lightning flashes through the windows. I sigh, then turn on the lights. I walk through to the living area, headed straight in the direction of my bedroom. Three things consume my mind: Becket, getting out of my soaking wet dress, my bed. The need for sleep has never been stronger. I go to set my keys in the little dish on the console table. Suddenly I'm plunged into darkness. The sky flashes white outside. I hate New York storms. I stumble my way to the fuse box located near the kitchen.

My breath catches in my throat. All the switches are up.

I slide my hand shakily along the wall. Finding the light switch next to the kitchen I turn the lights back on. Stop being an idiot, Brit. On shaky legs, I walk back towards my room. Apart from the odd rumble of thunder, the silence is deafening. I drop my keys in the dish. They clink when they hit the porcelain. I'm plunged into darkness again.

Lightning flickers. My eyes slowly move to the side. My pulse races. Mom's eyes stare up at me. The same picture I placed face down when Becket and I first arrived at my apartment. In front of it, there's a single white lily. I swallow. A huge rumble of thunder echoes through the night. A lightening strobe fills the sky. The whole room illuminates, highlighting a figure in a black hooded jacket standing in front of my window, stock still.

I open my mouth to scream. Nothing comes out.

Another flash startles me. I clench my fists, ready to fight back. I knew they'd come to find me. All my training was to prepare myself for something like this.

There's a sharp prick to my neck. No training could ever prepare me or make me strong enough to withstand it. My fist flies clumsily out to the side colliding with the picture. The sound of glass shattering fills the room. Consciousness slips out of my reach, and I slump down to the floor.

Twenty-Three

Becket

To say the night didn't go as planned would be the understatement of the century. I deserve every bit of Britney's anger. I shouldn't have done what I did, I humiliated her. That was Becket lashing out, not me, and now I know the truth. I've been punishing the wrong person.

Pacing the hotel floor, only the dim light of a single lamp illuminates the room. The storm that began earlier has picked up and lightning strobes across the sky. The lights flicker and my instant thought is whether Britney is ok.

I shouldn't be here. She shouldn't be alone when there's a storm like this. I'm ready to march over to her apartment when I remember that this is what she wanted. I need to respect that. The least I can do is check on her and see if she's ok. Pulling my phone out from the inside pocket of my tux jacket, I tap the screen, expecting it to come to life. Instead, I get nothing, it's completely dead. *Damn it.* I smack my hand against my head in frustration. This is the worst possible time this could happen. I want to know she's ok, but I can't because all my things are at her place, including my phone charger. In a last ditched attempt, I shake the useless object in my hand as if that will somehow bring it back to life. It does nothing.

My eyes settle on the clock on the nightstand next to my bed. One AM. I could ring the concierge service, have them find out the number for her apartment, but she's probably tucked up in bed fast asleep. All I'd be doing is waking her up and pissing her off even more than I already have tonight. I shake my head, trying to fight the urge to call and hear her voice. Don't be an ass, Becket. Give her the time and space she needs. Maybe tomorrow when the dust has settled, she might see things from my perspective. She might understand that some secrets should never be told, like she never told anyone about her mom's boyfriends. Until she told me.

My gut tugs and I struggle to swallow over the bitter taste in my mouth. I'm climbing into bed when the hotel phone on the other side of the room rings. So much for sleep.

I walk over and pick it up. Hesitantly I say, "Hello?"

"Good evening, sir. It's reception. We seem to be having an influx of calls for you. They're demanding we put their calls through to your room."

"Did they leave a name?" I ask. Stupid question. It doesn't take much to figure out who's trying to urgently get in touch with me at this time.

"Coach Langford of the Jacksonville Jaguars."

He's the last person I want to talk to right now. Having my ass chewed over my little performance on stage, is not on the top of my list of things to do. "Don't put him through," I respond bluntly, "and please don't call again."

"I'm sorry, sir, it's policy. I have to at least attempt to get in touch if they say it's an emergency."

"Attempt?" I say, picking up on their careful choice of words.

"Yes, sir."

"Attempt all you like. I'll be going to sleep now. Thanks for letting me know."

I place the phone down to end the call, then pick it back up and leave it hanging off the receiver. I'll deal with this crap in the morning. The dial tone fills the room, so I place a pillow over it to muffle the noise. Then another. When the room is silent, I grumble while climbing back into bed, then settle between the sheets. I toss and turn, trying to get comfy, but I can't without a certain blonde tucked into my side, like she has been each night this week. I miss Britney more than anything and we've only been apart a few hours.

This wasn't meant to happen. She's gotten under my skin. Somehow, she's become everything and instead of having her with me, my bed is empty, the way it's always been and might always be.

***

Britney

Coming to, I feel like I've been part of a train wreck. Everything hurts. My head is the worst. It pounds so hard that I can barely hear myself think.

Open your eyes, Brit. Blackness.

I close, then open them again. All I see is black.

My breaths come out ragged as I struggle to breathe, the weight of the situation pressing in, as everything comes flooding back. Where am I? I try to move, but I can't. Starting to panic, I attempt to cry out for help. But like I can't open my eyes, I can't open my mouth. There's something there, stopping me from doing so. My whole body aches. My muscles

257

burn, screaming for me to move them. But I can't. I can't do anything.

Muffled voices reach my ears and I hold my breath, wishing my heart would stop pounding, so it doesn't give away that I'm awake. The voices get closer.

"She's coming round. What do you want me to do?"

"It's not time."

"What do you mean it's not time? What exactly do you want me to do with her?"

"Give her more."

"You're sure?"

"Yes. The longer she's here, the more chance there is of him coming."

Becket. They're talking about Becket. I might be in trouble, but the sinister tone of their voices tells me if he comes, it will be so much worse. Don't follow me. I'm not worth it.

Silence.

There's a shuffle of footsteps close by, then a hand pats my head and starts to stroke my hair.

"I can see why he likes you. You're a beauty."

I whimper, it's all I can do.

"Don't worry. I'm not going to hurt you. Not yet."

My pulse starts to race when hot breath tickles my ear.

"It's time to play a game ..."

Footsteps. A prick in my neck.

The voices disappear.

***

Becket

Sunlight beats against my skin—it's like I'm in a sauna. Rubbing away the sleep from my eyes, I sit up and look out of the hotel windows overlooking New York. The view is amazing. Shame. The NFL shouldn't have wasted their money. My eyes stray to the other side of the bed, looking for Britney. I curse when I find she's not there. She's not there because right now she despises me. I need to find her and make things right.

Picking up my phone, I check to see if she's gotten in touch, but nothing happens. Then I remember ... my battery was dead when I arrived at the hotel. I have no charger, no clothes, nothing. I could ring the concierge service, but I'd just be wasting time. I don't care about all of those things. I just need to see Brit. Everything and everyone else can wait.

Jumping out of bed, I quickly use the bathroom then put my tux back on. It's a crumpled mess after being thrown on the floor in a heap and the material sticks to my skin uncomfortably because it's still damp from the storm.

It doesn't matter, none of it does. I could be walking out of here naked for all I care. I just need to see her.

When I get to the lobby, my sights are set on the exit, when the receptionist tries to catch my attention. They most likely want to relay the hundreds of messages Coach Langford and Shauna have left me. They can wait. Ignoring the receptionist, I walk through the revolving doors, out into the stark daylight. A cab screeches to a halt immediately when I raise my hand. Damn it. I pat my trouser pockets searching for my wallet, the same wallet I put in Britney's purse last night. Sliding into the back seat, I say a small prayer to God, hoping that the driver likes football. I don't usually play the fame game, so I'm due a few favors. Straight away my eyes zone in on the football memorabilia hanging from the rearview mirror. Today, the big man in the sky is on my side.

The driver turns around to ask where I'm going to and his eyes widen in shock when he sees my face. "Holy shit. You're Michael Becket!"

Plaster on my best panty-dropping smile, I nod, "The one and only."

"Where can I take you?"

I rattle off Britney's address, and the cab screeches away into the mid-morning traffic.

Before we get too far into the journey, I say sheepishly, "I actually left my wallet with my friend and have no money to pay. I can run straight inside and get some when we arrive?"

The drivers' eyes watch me through the mirror. "How about you sign something, and we call it even?"

I beam back at him, this time it's genuine. "Deal."

"Actually, can we get a picture together too? My friends won't believe me when I tell them you've been in my cab."

I shrug. "No problem." I never do shit like this, but the guy is doing me a massive favor and I'm feeling in a generous mood.

Ten minutes, one signature and a photo later, I'm stepping onto the sidewalk outside Britney's apartment block. Looking up in the direction of her apartment window, I take a deep breath. Here we go. I hope she's in a good mood, but it's not likely after how we left things. When I reach her door, I raise my hand and rap my knuckles against it lightly. No response. I knock again a little louder and listen for movement inside. Silence.

Maybe she's in her bedroom or the bathroom? I bang harder so she can hear me if that's the case. The door rattles from the force. There's no way she can't hear me even if she's all the way in her room. "Brit!" I shout through the thick wood. "It's me, open up."

Nothing.

I frown. Where the hell is she? I briefly remember her mentioning that she might have to go into the magazine today because she had a lot of catching up to do. I was irked at the thought of having to spend a few hours without her. It all feels trivial now. Accepting she's not inside, I make my way back outside. When I get there, the cab driver is gone and I'm in the same position as earlier.

I don't want to push my luck. If Brit's in the mood I think she's going to be, I'll be needing it if I stand a chance at winning her over. Estimating it's going to take at least forty-five minutes to walk to her office, I let out a huff of air and start walking.

***

Britney's boss and best friend, Jess, looks up in surprise when I knock on the door to her office. "Becket. Hi?"

The receptionist almost passed out when she saw me standing in front of her desk. It didn't take much effort on my part for her to let me in.

"Is Britney around?" I ask, shoving my hands into the pockets of my pants awkwardly.

Jess' eyes trail over my crumpled tux. "No ... she's supposed to be with you?"

I frown. "She mentioned yesterday that she was going to come in and get some work done? Hasn't she turned up yet?"

She avoids my question by asking another. "Did you guys have a fight or something?"

"Something like that." I shrug and look out of the window. She must have one of the best views in the city.

She narrows her eyes. She's guarding her friend and I don't blame her. I respect her for it and it makes me happy knowing Britney has such a loyal friend, but right now it isn't helping. I need to know where she is.

"How about I give her a call on her cell and see if she's on her way?"

"That would be great. My phone is dead, and all my things are at hers."

"Must have been some fight ..." she says, her face full of concern.

"I spent the night at my hotel. Don't worry."

"Ok." She taps the screen of her cell then raises it to her ear, all the time keeping an eye on what I'm up to. Seconds pass by and she frowns, bringing the cell away from her ear. She taps the screen again, then raises it back up to her ear, holding a finger up as a gesture for me to wait.

"Is everything ok?" I ask when she lowers her phone, muttering to herself.

"I don't know. Her cell is going to voicemail. It never goes to voicemail. She always has it charged in case of emergencies. She's good like that. Overcautious. Safe."

"Maybe she's on the subway?" I suggest.

She frowns again, this time her brows draw closer together. "Yeah ... maybe."

I try not to let my mind run away and begin imagining all kinds of scenarios. Doing so isn't going to help find Britney.

"Why don't we go to her apartment together?" Jess suggests, pulling a key out of her bag and waving it in the air. "I have a spare."

262

Standing up from her desk, she plasters a reassuring smile on her face, but I see it falter when she thinks I'm not looking. My stomach flips. Brit, where are you?

When we get outside, I look at Jess guiltily and rub the back of my neck. "I'm really sorry, but I don't have any money."

She raises an eyebrow, then refusing to pass any comment, raises her arm in the air to hail a cab. It doesn't take long for one to pull up and soon we're on our way. When we get to the apartment, Jess politely knocks on the door and waits for Britney to answer. I shift my weight from side to side impatiently, trying not to get too annoyed that she's wasting so much time. I want to get in and check that everything's ok. When there's no answer, Jess presses her ear to the door for a minute. She sighs and pulls the spare key back out of her bag, slips it into the lock, turns it and opens the door.

She steps in first and I look over her shoulder, expecting to find the worst. There's nothing. Everything is exactly how it was when we left for the awards. I don't know what would be more unsettling, finding something wrong, or finding nothing wrong that could explain Britney's whereabouts.

"Brit!" Jess calls out.

There's no answer.

I step around her and stride through the apartment looking for any sign as to where she would be but find nothing. I'm walking towards the living room window, when I step on something and stop. Looking down I find a photo frame face down with glass shattered around it. I pick it up and frown. I've looked at everything in her apartment while I've been here. This, I haven't seen. In the picture is Brit, but a much younger version.

263

Jess walks over and says, "Her mom."

"Right ..." Something doesn't feel right. "I'm going to put my phone on charge," I say. It's the only thing we haven't tried and I'm praying Britney's tried to get in touch and there's a simple explanation for all of this. Walking into the bedroom, I find my bag and retrieve my charger. After a few minutes, my phone lights up and the loading sign remains on the screen.

"Come on, you piece of shit," I mutter to myself. Sitting on the bed, I stare at it, waiting. The loading screen disappears, replaced by my home screen and a few seconds pass before it begins bleeping incessantly.

"What's that noise?" asks Jess, walking into the bedroom and looking at me bewildered.

"That's the sound of the big fucking mistake I made."

"The awards ..."

"You watched them?"

She nods. Of course, she did. Half the country did.

"You have that many messages?" she asks, peering at my screen as the alerts continue sounding out into the silent room.

"And missed calls," I reply.

"Who are they all from?"

"People I don't want to hear from." And that's the truth. There's too many to even process. Most with No Caller ID, probably the media. But there's nothing from Brit, nothing at all.

While we're both still looking at it, a No Caller ID starts ringing through again. Usually I'd ignore it, but I can't because it could be Britney.

"Hello?" I answer hesitantly.

"Thank fuck! Where have you been? Why aren't you answering your other phone?"

"Evan? How'd you get this number?"

264

"Do you really need to ask that question?"

He's right, he could get in contact no matter where I was.

"Why are you calling?" My voice falters even though I try to keep my tone even. He never gets in touch with me, it's always the other way around.

"I've been trying to call you all night," he sounds as stressed as I feel.

"My phone died," I explain, "and I couldn't get to my charger."

"Great fucking timing," he grits out, then the line goes quiet.

"Are you there?"

"He got out ..." he says quietly.

Nausea hits me, full force. I know the answer but still, I ask, "Who got out?"

"Don't play dumb."

I start pacing the floor, frantically. This can't be happening. "They can't have let him out, he's in for life ..."

"Listen to what I'm saying. He *got* out. Broke out. Nobody knows how."

"How? How is that possible? He was under maximum security?"

"In the same way he managed to fly under the radar all those years. When he has something in his sight, no one can stop him."

"And who does he want?"

"You. Where are you right now?"

I swallow. "I'm in New York."

"You've got to be kidding me?" he bellows down the line.

I run a hand over my face and groan. "I shouldn't have come back."

"No, you fucking shouldn't." When I don't reply he says, "He would have found you wherever you were.

Be on alert. I'm coming to New York. You can't be on your own right now."

Britney. The broken glass. Please. God. No.

"Are you there?"

"I was with someone last night … We had an argument and I left her alone. I haven't heard from her since and now I can't find her."

"Damn it," he hisses down the line.

"Why would he take her?" I ask, even though deep down I know the answer.

"To try and get to you."

***

Britney

Stop, I tell my heart. It hammers in my chest. Whatever was covering my eyes has been removed. I can just make out my surroundings as I stare straight ahead. I want to look around. Figure out where I am. But I'm terrified someone will hear or see me moving. Eventually I work up the courage to move my eyes. I dart them from side to side. The piercing beam of light through the cracks of a boarded-up window is the only thing that illuminates the room. Sweat trickles down my spine. My eyes burn with tears.

Footsteps sound. My blood runs cold. The figure in the black, hooded jacket steps through the door. Their movement is slow, but all to soon they're uncomfortably close. I scream into the gag that fills my mouth. I writhe against the ties that secure me to the chair. It's wasted effort. The only thing it achieves are burns on my skin from the friction.

"Quiet."

I scream again.

266

The figure raises its fist in the air. It swoops down. A resounding crack fills the room as it connects with my jaw. I'm stunned into silence. The only saving grace ... the throbbing in my face detracts from the unbearable pain the rest of my body is feeling. My gaze settles on my lap. I stare at the now filthy, once-champagne-colored fabric of my silk dress. There's a slight tear at the knee. It's the small details that are helping to keep me grounded.

"It's time to play our game. Answer quickly and this will all be over soon. I promise." The sinister tone fills me with terror. "Where is she?"

I shake my head. I'd never give him up, even if I knew where Becket was, I'd never tell.

Crack.

My face swings to the side and stars skew my vision. The throbbing is replaced by a stabbing pain.

Drip. Drip. Drip. The only noise that fills the room as blood trickles from my nose, over my top lip, onto the fabric of my dress.

"I'll ask again." The figure crouches down and the hood of the jacket casts a shadow over their face, as they clasp filthy, leather skinned hands in front of me. "Where is she?"

They're not talking about Becket.

I whimper and shake my head again. My eyes remain focused on the tear in my dress. I don't have a clue who they're talking about. The only answer I can give isn't the answer they want to hear, which means only one thing for me: nothing good.

The figure stands tall. "It's time to play another game."

One thing they don't teach you in school: not all games are fun.

The figure skulks behind the seat I'm strapped to, then slowly unties the material covering my mouth. I gasp for air when it comes away. It's thick and musty, but it's air none the less.

Seizing the opportunity, I scream at the top of my lungs, "Help!" Over and over, I scream, thrashing from side to side. The restraints chafe at my skin even more and eventually my voice grows hoarse.

A cold laugh fills the room. Every hair on my body stands on end in warning. It's too late for warnings.

"No one can hear you. Tell me where she is."

"I don't know who you're talking about!" I choke out through a sob.

"You're lying." The figure walks to a black bag on the floor, bends over and first, retrieves a knife. It glints as it passes through the beam of light before it's placed on a small table. The way it sparkles and shines is almost poetic, that something used for such evil could, in this moment, look so beautiful. The figure reaches back in the bag and pulls out a handgun, then stands and walks with long, purposeful strides towards me. Without any hesitation, the gun is forced under my jaw, so hard it almost breaks the skin. "There's a theory that in moments of sheer terror our memory can be clearest. I think we should test that theory."

I close my eyes, waiting, as tears pour over my cheeks. Without the material gagging me, they cascade onto my dress, soaking my lap. The click of the safety mechanism being released echoes around the room.

"Let's see what it takes to make you remember where she is."

Twenty-Four

Becket

B eside myself, I pace the floor of Britney's living room, running my hands through my hair, pulling at the ends in frustration. It's been hours. Evan said he would get back to me as quickly as he could, but it's been too long. Each time I call it goes straight to voicemail.

"What's going on?" asks Jess, looking pale.

"My past has found me," I answer.

"Does this have something to do with the assault case?"

I spin around, finding her staring at me with narrowed eyes. "What do you know about the case?"

She shrugs. "Britney didn't tell me much, just that it was one of the things you told her when you met."

I'm about to snap—it's none of her business—but my phone bleeps on the coffee table, with an alert for a new message.

Evan: *Was waiting for WiFi. On a flight to New York. Don't do anything without me.*

My fingers tap the screen frantically and I send a message back:

269

What do you know?

Evan: *CCTV footage a few blocks away from Britney's apartment showed a figure in a black, hooded jacket getting out of a car. We think it's him.*

Black spots creep into my vision. There's no *think* about it. He has Britney.

Evan: *We can't be certain. For their sake don't do anything stupid.*

I stare at the object in my hand, clenching it so hard I'm surprised it doesn't shatter to pieces. This can't be happening. "Useless piece of shit!" I roar, launching it at the wall, watching as it falls apart.

Jess lets out a shriek and demands, "What the hell is going on?"

I ignore her and carry on pacing back and forth. Why would he take Britney? It doesn't make sense. Surely if he wanted revenge, he would come straight for me.

I freeze.

The white lilies in Britney's hotel room ... He's made her part of his game. He's gone back to where it all started.

*** *

Becket 11 years old

Mom seemed different. Happier than she'd been in a long time, especially when she got flowers, big white ones. She'd walk around smiling, singing to herself.

270

Then something changed.

I was sitting in my room doing my homework when she knocked on my door asking if we could talk. She said that one day soon, a friend might come to visit, and when they did, Josie and I were to stay in our rooms and keep the lights off. It was weird. Whenever I had friends over, it was always something to be excited about. But Mom, talking about her friend, looked scared.

It was late, I shouldn't have still been up. I jumped when Mom barged into my room. I went to say sorry for staying up past my bedtime, but she grabbed me, threw back the covers and shoved me onto the bed.

She placed a quick kiss on my head and gave me a sad smile. "My friend is here. No matter what you hear, don't come out. And remember, leave the lights off." She pulled the cover over my head and patted me. Her hand lingered before she walked out of the room and closed the door behind her.

Something didn't feel right.

The door was open slightly, it had never been fixed. It was one of the jobs Dad was meant to do and never got round to. Light spilled in through the crack. Slowly, I crept out of bed, tiptoed over to it, remaining out of sight. I didn't want to get in trouble with Mom and her friend. I listened carefully, hearing as she opened the door to our apartment.

Her voice faltered when she asked, "What are you doing here?"

"It's time to play a game."

There was shuffling, then clattering, as objects hit the floor. I didn't know what game it was they were playing, but it didn't sound right. Then the shrieking started and I didn't know what to do.

Someone had to come and help us, I thought to myself, but I knew that they wouldn't. That was the problem with living where we did in New York. People kept themselves to themselves. The noises my mom was making were often white noise when I was trying to get to sleep at night.

It was when the shrieking stopped that you knew something was wrong.

Suddenly there was no noise.

I knew I wasn't supposed to leave my room. I knew I'd get in trouble, but I had to know if she was ok. I opened my door, being careful not to make a noise. When I stepped out into the hallway, my eyes landed on Josie, who was standing, staring into the living area. "No!" I hissed when she charged forward.

I raced after her, but it was too late. I watched in horror when she collided into the back of the figure knelt over Mom. Their hands were wrapped tightly around her neck. The impact Josie made with the figure made them fall forward. I winced at the cracking noise when their head collided with the coffee table and they collapsed over Mom. Neither moved.

"Josie! No! What have you done!" I cried out.

I raced over, shoved her out of the way, and she backed up against the wall, shaking. It took me a minute of hard tugging to get the figure in the black, hooded jacket off Mom. They rolled onto their back beside her.

It was a man and there was a huge lump on his head. I didn't know if he was still breathing.

My eyes focused back on my mom. Her neck was red where his hands had been. I crawled over her, brought my face close and her own started to glisten from my tears. I let out a sigh of relief when the faint feeling of her breath tickled my skin. She was still with me. She didn't lose the game.

I looked over my shoulder at Josie, little Josie. Before Dad left, he told me it was my turn to be the man of the house, that I had to keep them safe. I couldn't let her get in trouble for what happened, I knew what I had to do.

"What are you doing?" she asked.

"Shh. I'll be right back," I said and then darted towards my room.

She started to cry when I came back with Dad's baseball bat in my hand. She cried even harder when I lifted it in the air and brought it down on the figure's head, covering up the evidence of what she did.

I walked over to her and pulled her into my arms while she sobbed. "No matter what anyone asks," I said, "this was my fault. I did this."

She nodded and wiped her nose against the sleeve of her pajama top.

I walked to the phone. Panic started to set in when I pressed the numbers and lifted the phone to my ear.

"Nine-one-one, what's your emergency?"

"I think I killed a man."

***

Josie was on the swings, singing happily, in her own little world, floating backwards and forwards through the air. Mom was in a corner of the playground with some of the new friends she'd made. I was the only one who was unhappy.

I hated that we were the Beckets. We were the new family in town.

Mom said it had to be that way to make sure we were safe. We packed our bags in the middle of the night and left our old lives behind. I wasn't even allowed to bring my football awards. "*In case anyone finds them,*" Mom had said. "*It has to be this way,*

I'm sorry." No goodbyes. Nothing. It was like we never existed.

I watched Mom throw her head back and laugh. How could she be happy again after what happened? She and Josie had settled into our new life like New York never happened. But I couldn't forget, ever. When I closed my eyes it was all I would see. I couldn't tell anyone. I was already the outsider, the new kid halfway through the school year. I needed to fit in. I couldn't be different.

I looked up to the sky and the rain started. I enjoyed how it felt on my skin in the Florida heat, but it was time to go back to the new house. I couldn't call it home. When the rain started to get heavier, I let out a huff of air, then stood up from the grass and walked over to Mom to get my jacket.

"Ready to go?" she asked, with a reassuring smile.

I nodded. That's when I heard it. Shouting.

Mom looked up in the direction of the swing set and shrieked, "Freya! No!"

The world slowed. Everything became hazy. I turned and there he was. The figure in the black, hooded jacket. Crouched down over Josie who was flat on her back below the swings.

Not again I thought to myself. No. I had to stop him.

Before anyone could stop me, I started to run. I had one focus and one focus only: get him off Josie. I almost lost Mom to him. I couldn't lose her. I charged in his direction. All I could see was red. I put every ounce of energy I had into each stride. I drove my shoulder into the figure side-on.

We both went flying through the air. We landed on the ground with a thud. I heard an *ooof*. The figure was winded from the impact. I couldn't risk them getting back up, or I'd have been their next target. I jumped to my feet then kicked and punched. Over and over with every ounce of strength I had. They couldn't get back up. I wouldn't let them.

My ears rang. I couldn't hear or see anything apart from the black, hooded jacket. I only stopped when a pair of arms surrounded me. They pinned my arms to my side before dragging me backwards.

When the arms around me loosened, I collapsed to the ground, crying at how unfair it all was. Even though we moved state and changed our names, the figure still found us.

I knew he would always find us because he never got to finish his game.

***

I stormed through the front door, slamming it behind me. I was so angry I didn't know what to do.

The door opened again, and Mom walked in slowly. She took a deep breath then said, "A bad thing has happened to us, Ben, but that doesn't give you a free pass to act this way. Let me help you."

I clenched my hands at my sides, then dug my nails into my palms. I scraped them back so hard, I could feel the sting when the skin started to break. All I felt was relief when the physical pain took over. It made me forget. Stopped me from remembering the figure in the black, hooded jacket. For a second, it would get rid of the fear of losing Mom, or Josie.

"Why did you take me there?!" I shouted.

"Because I have to. Let them help you."

"There's nothing wrong with me."

Walking over, Mom crouched down in front of me and tears fell from her cheeks. She grasped my hands, forced her own into mine, stopping me from punishing myself, in the same way I had each day since I saw her on the floor in our old apartment. When I almost lost her.

She opened my hands, looked down, then almost in a whisper said, "Baby, it's getting worse. You have to stop doing this to yourself."

"I don't want to go, Mom."

"I know you don't, but you don't have a choice."

"Why are they making me do this? I don't understand."

"Ben. You attacked someone who was trying to help Josie when she fell off a swing. You thought it was him. People can't know the real us, they can't know our story. That person pressed charges and this is the only way we can help stop you from going to a very bad place. You're lucky the judge understood. This is the third time and at some point, people will stop giving you chances."

I shook my head. I couldn't do it. I didn't want to do it. I didn't want to be Michael, I just wanted to be Ben, my real name, and I didn't want Josie to be Freya either. I tugged my hands away and stormed off in the direction of my room. "I hate this house! I hate this place! And I hate you!" Slamming the bedroom door behind me, I collapsed on the bed, pounded my fists into the mattress, and bit down on my cover to muffle my screams. I wasn't sure if I was screaming because I was angry or screaming because I was afraid.

The only thing I knew was that if friends did what they did to Mom, I didn't want any. I didn't need any. The only person I needed was me.

***

Becket 17 years old

Staring at the end zone, I told myself to just run. My heart was about to burst out of my chest from the expectations of the game. This was it. I could do it. The play was already in motion, all I needed to do was follow it through.

The crowd roared. Everything came down to that moment.

There were five seconds left on the play clock. Players darted by and flashes of color filled my vision, then I saw it. The tan, brown object, spinning through the air. I picked up speed ready to intercept it at the twenty-yard line. I tried to keep the ball in my sight but suddenly the pressure of everything became too much and my eyes flitted to the sidelines. It was the wrong move. What I found in those few milliseconds was what I least expected. The figure in the black, hooded jacket. I blinked and it was gone. But that moment was all it took to make me fumble the ball.

Quickly regaining focus, I charged forward with the ball cradled under my arm. The crowd went wild, not noticing my blunder. But they weren't the ones who mattered. The three people on the sidelines, clip boards in hands, were the ones who did.

I screwed up but there was still time to win it back. Darting left and right, I spun out of reach of the other players. Then, I strode out. It was the biggest, most important stride of my life. Tumbling forwards from the momentum, I eventually stopped. I threw down the ball and drove a fist up into the air. I'd done it.

Coach Martin came racing over to me, grabbed each side of my helmet and stared me straight in the eye. "That was magic, Becket."

The whole team surrounded me, cheering. We'd won the season. Everyone's spirits were high and I wanted to feel the euphoria they did. But then the figure in the black, hooded jacket flashed through my mind. The one that had stood on the sidelines when I fumbled the ball. The same one that was meant to be locked away in solitary confinement in a maximum-security prison. Shaking my head, I tried to get rid of the image.

Eventually the team pressed pause on their celebrations and made their way to the locker room. Rather than following them, I walked to the sideline to meet with the scout from Jacksonville University and Coach Langford. My pulse had begun to settle after the physical exertion of the game, but when I got closer to them it picked back up.

The scout held out his hand and I shook it, waiting. Coach Langford hovered in the background.

"That was some performance you put on out there." His expression was blank.

There was a ringing in my ears as I waited for his decision.

When his face cracked into a smile, he said, "Big things are waiting for you. Congratulations. I'll be in touch."

When the scout was gone, Coach Langford stepped forward. I met him during a career event at a football training summer camp in Florida, which I'd managed to get a free place on. He must have seen potential because he sought me out, promising he'd be in touch. The next thing I knew, he'd organized for the scout to come to our final game of the season.

"Your star shines bright, you know."

"How'd you figure that one out?" I asked.

"He never cracks a smile."

Looking down at the ground, I stubbed my toe awkwardly into the grass. "Thank you for your help."

When I looked back up, he smiled. "By helping you, I'm helping myself. I expect to see you on my team one day, so don't mess this up. Speaking of not messing things up, you fumbled the ball. I've watched all your old game footage. You never fumble. What happened?"

"My past," I replied quietly.

"You need to bury that shit six feet under, there's no room for it in the NFL. If you're going to do this, you need to be all in." After patting me on the shoulder he then started to walk away. Before he got too far, he threw back over his shoulder, "I've already got a number saved for you. I've never been wrong about a player, don't be the first."

He disappeared into the distance and I let out a sigh. It should have been one of the happiest moments of my life, but instead it was ruined by him, again. I wished it had been simple, that I could have just moved on and left my past behind. But how could I bury something that was still alive?

Following the rest of the team to the locker room, I shuffled over to my locker and opened it. I glanced over my shoulder to make sure the other players were occupied before pulling my phone from out of my bag. Bringing up the number I needed, I quickly typed out a message.

Me: *The figure was at my game.*
Price: *I'll be at your house within the hour. Make sure you're not alone.*

I quickly showered and changed while the rest of the team were still in the room, then shoved my gear into my gym bag. I went in search of Coach Martin and made up some lame excuse about why I needed a ride home. After my stellar performance on the field, he didn't even question helping me.

Mom called out to me from the dining room when I stepped in through the front door. I dropped my bag and found her sitting at the table next to a guy in a suit who looked like he had just graduated from high school. Agent Price.

"Where's Josie?" I asked, a little panicked.

"Freya," said Evan. "How many times do we need to have this conversation? You can't call her Josie any more."

Mom frowned. "She's in her room. How did the game go?"

My rapid breathing settled and I tried to plaster on a smile. "Great, we won."

"So, why is Evan here? Again."

"The figure's back."

She was midway to picking up her water, when her hand jolted, knocking over the glass. She jumped up, cursing to herself as she ran to the kitchen, and returned with a cloth to wipe up the mess.

When she was finished she settled in her seat. Evan cleared his throat and said, "Are you sure you saw him?" His reaction was the same as the last time. He didn't believe me. He thought I was imagining it.

"Of course, I'm fucking sure," I replied, nostrils flaring.

"Ben," my mom scolded.

I was fired up, ready to go in, all guns blazing. But the look she gave me told me to back down, or else. I narrowed my eyes at Evan. "I saw him. It was the same as the other times. One second he was there the next he was gone."

His brow furrowed and he leant back in his chair. "I've checked with the prison each time. It's impossible, unless he can be in two places at once.

Ben ... another agent checked the CCTV footage. There was nothing there."

"Then you'll have to do more digging. He's appearing the same way he did with Mom." I turned to her and pleaded with my eyes. "Tell him how it all happened. How it's happening again."

Looking down at the table, she tangled her fingers together, and under her breath said, "He already knows. But yes, it does sound the same. At the time, I thought I was losing my mind."

Evan closed his eyes and pinched his nose. "This case is going to be the death of me."

Both my mom and I stared at him, mouths open.

Realizing how insensitive his comment was, he quickly opened his eyes and muttered, "Sorry." I watched him stare out of our dining room window, deep in thought until he cleared his throat. "Can I make a suggestion?"

"Yes?" Mom said hesitantly.

"We move you. Different identities. Different location. Again."

My stomach dropped. We knew this was on the cards when the figure began reappearing. It was time to say goodbye to my dream of being in the NFL.

My mom's expression was solemn. It was no doubt a mirror image of my own, especially when she looked at me and asked, "What's wrong?"

"I got the scholarship to Jacksonville University."

She jumped up from her seat, clapping her hands together, before she pulled me into a hug and said, "Baby, that's brilliant!"

"It's not," I replied sadly.

"Why? It's wonderful news! This is what you've been working so hard for."

"How can I go if we're changing our identities?"

Evan held up a hand, and quietly said, "Can I make another suggestion?"

I raised an eyebrow. "Go on."

"Not all witnesses have to be together …"

My mom looked at him with a knowing look, but I wasn't quite sure what he was getting at.

"You've lost me," I said.

"Just your mom and Josie go. It could work."

I frowned. "Why are you so eager for this?"

"Whoever it is and whatever is actually going on, they're focused on you. If we separate you all, you could be a distraction and remove attention from your mom and Josie."

"He'd be hidden in plain sight," said my mom, confirming Evan's thoughts.

I looked between them bewildered. "Are you sure this could work?"

Evan nodded. "Yes, but you'd have to say goodbye to Ben Miller once and for all."

"What do you mean?"

"You have to make the world believe you're someone you're not. You have to stop fighting this. To make people believe you're Michael Becket, you have to wear a mask."

"Like an actual mask?" I asked breaking the seriousness of the moment.

Evan chuckled, then replied, "A metaphorical one. Create a new persona, truly become someone you're not. The media will be there waiting. But they can't dig if they don't know where to find the secrets."

Twenty-Five

Britney

My dress is red. That's the only thing I think as I float in and out of consciousness.

He's torturing me for not giving him what he wants and pain sears through my shoulder where he tore the flesh with his knife. One of many, but this one's the worst. Put me out of my misery already.

The figure left in frustration a while ago and I don't know how long I've been alone. He's trying to break me, but what he doesn't realize is I'm already broken beyond repair. He's chosen the wrong victim.

Even in the heat, I shiver uncontrollably, and I begin to feel lightheaded. Thoughts of how I can escape have been replaced by my wondering how I can put an end to all this. I don't want to be here anymore.

A sinister tune reaches my ears. Humming. The figure steps back into the room, the source of the music now clear.

"Why won't you kill me?" I rasp out.

Just do it, please, make it quick. But I know they won't.

He walks over, tracing a finger lightly around the skin of the wound on my shoulder. The feeling is a sharp contrast to their nails driving in. Internally, I cry in agony, stars fill my vision.

"I'm not finished playing my game."

A whimper falls from my lips and I watch as the figure pulls the gun out again from his pocket, setting it down on the small table. As he ramble's under his breath, I start to slip in and out of consciousness again.

Soon, I won't wake up.

I come back around, and wearily my eyes focus on the window. The light outside isn't as bright, and the white beam has been replaced by a fiery orange glow as the sun starts to set.

That's when I hear it.

I try not to react, but somewhere in the distance, I hear the hum of an engine. I want to cry out, scream for help, but I barely have the energy to speak, as blackness creeps into my vision.

The figure leans in and I feel their breath on my ear, when they say, "Someone else has decided to come and play."

The slam of a car door is the last thing I hear.

***

Becket

The cab pulls up outside the old, red-brick apartment block I lived in as a kid before we were taken in by the Witness Protection Program. Passing money over to the driver, I keep my eyes set on the entrance, never moving them away, just in case. This part of the city has gone from being shady to the kind that people avoid at all costs. Unless they have something to hide.

I step out, desperate to find Britney, and accidentally slam the door shut. I wince. So much for being discreet.

My head falls back as my eyes slowly move up the building, taking in the graffiti, the windows—some broken, some boarded—until they reach the top. Six floors and I'll know if my instincts are right. I don't know what I'll do when I get there, but I have to find Brit.

Before leaving, the cab driver rolls down his window and sticks out his head. "Are you sure you've got the right address?" His eyes move to the front door, with the peeling paintwork and broken padlock.

They're in there I know they are. "One hundred percent," I answer, dismissively.

He doesn't ask any more questions, simply throws the cab into drive, leaving me behind.

I quickly pull my phone out of my pocket and send a message to Evan, giving him the address of where he'll find me. Us. Then, I take a deep breath before stepping through the entryway of the apartment block, back into my old life, back to where this all started and where everything went wrong. My stomach churns as my mind runs through all the possibilities of what I might find.

Moving slowly up the flights of stairs, I'm careful with my footing, stepping around rubbish and broken pieces of furniture that block the way. All the while I create a mental log in my mind, preparing myself for when I need to make a quick exit out of here with Brit. I hope we get to that point.

After climbing a couple of floors, my legs begin to feel heavy, and I rub at my thigh, where every now and again a searing pain shoots through the muscle. I grind my teeth as I try to ignore it and continue

285

pushing higher. I'm five floors up when the pain becomes unbearable. I stop and stand, breathing in and out deeply, trying to get my shit together before I'm faced with my past. Before I find him.

When I get to the top, I struggle to breathe and it has nothing to do with the stairs.

I carry on moving forwards. If I stop, there's a chance fear will take over and that can't happen. My fear is nothing in comparison to what Britney must be feeling and it's that thought alone that has me placing one foot in front of the other. Placing my hands carefully against the slightly open door, I push gently, trying not to make a sound. Please be alive. I sidestep more rubbish and a hole in the floor, setting foot in our old apartment.

I'm halfway along the hallway when I see her in the living area and freeze. The last remains of the sunset burn orange through the boarded-up window, emphasizing the red silk of her dress. A stab of pain fills my chest. Last night it was almost white. My eyes scan over her exposed skin and bile rises in my throat. Her smooth skin is sliced in a pattern. Blood trickles down from each gash. He's turned her into his own work of art. Her matted hair is covering her face, her head slumped down against her chest. I'm sorry, Brit, this is all my fault.

I take a step forward, needing to find out if she's still alive. In my haste, I misjudge my footing and one of the floorboards creaks. The damage is done, that's if the door of the cab didn't already give me away.

With nothing left to lose, I charge towards Britney, collapsing down at her feet.

"Brit," I hiss. "Brit, talk to me."

Running my hands through her hair, tears fall as I take in how damaged and swollen her beautiful face is. My fingers skim over the already purple bruises around her neck, finding their way to just below her jaw, feeling for her pulse. It's weak, barely there. I need to get us out of here and fast. I'm about to start undoing the restraints around her legs when a chill runs down my spine as the clapping starts. Quiet at first, getting louder as footsteps move into the room. Slowly, I turn around.

"You came to play," says the voice from my nightmares.

Through a clenched jaw, I reply, "You wanted me, I'm here."

He doesn't respond.

My eyes skirt to the side, finding a gun on a small table, set up, ready to go. He's baiting me. It's positioned just far enough away I have to leave Britney to get it. He wants me to make a choice. My safety, or hers. He's forgotten—I'm not an eleven-year-old boy anymore. I'm bigger, stronger, faster, and if I'm going down, I'm taking him with me.

A creak close by startles us both. This wasn't part of his plan.

Seizing the moment, I lunge forward. With every ounce of strength I have, I drive my shoulder into his stomach. We both fly through the air. His back slams against the wall behind. I hear the air whoosh out of his body. We both collapse to the ground. It's the opportunity I need. I clamber away, back to the gun. It's almost in reach. But I put too much weight on my bad leg. Buckling under my weight, I fall down. Sliding along the floor, pain threatens to consume me. Stretching out my hand, I manage to grab hold of the gun. Quickly, I roll away. Back towards Brit.

The figure grabs at my ankle. I kick his hand away, trying harder to get to Brit. I'm almost there. A fist collides with my temple and the world tilts. My grip on the gun slackens but I manage to keep hold of it.

287

Hands grab my shoulders from behind. I'm thrown sideways to the ground. The figure climbs over. Pins me to the ground by my throat. It presses down, trying to force the life from my lungs. We're coming to the end of the game.

Blackness creeps in. Only one thing keeps me grounded. The feeling of my hand on the gun. My finger on the trigger. I don't know where I'm aiming. I don't have time to think. I choke for air. With what little strength I have left, I raise my arm.

Right before everything slips away, a deafening bang fills the room. Then, there's nothing.

Twenty-Six

Becket

*B*eep. *Beep. Beep.*

Deja vu. I wonder how many times I'm going to find myself in this position with Britney in my life.

Britney. My eyes shoot open, and I fly forwards, gasping for breath.

"Woah man! Woah woah woah," says Evan. Concerned brown eyes find mine and he places a hand on my shoulder, trying to still me. "It's ok. You're safe. It's ok."

Evan is one of the most closed-off people I know, he never gives an ounce of his feelings away, but right now, he looks weary and broken. I look around the room frantically and it takes a few minutes to accept that I'm no longer in danger. Easing back on the bed, I allow my body to relax and my breathing to settle.

When I'm finally calm, Evan's shoulders slump, defeated. "You had me worried for a moment there."

I look around again, taking in the hospital surroundings. Sunlight glares through the windows, everything looks so clinical. The complete opposite to the last place I remember being. "How long have I been out?" I try to ask, but my voice comes out hoarse. I try to speak more clearly but I can't.

"Don't talk, you'll damage your voice box even more," says Evan.

It all comes back to me. The figure with his hands around my neck, trying to choke the life out of me, trying to put an end to the game we started playing years ago.

But I'm still here.

I remember the bang. The bang when I pressed down on the trigger, not knowing where I was aiming, or if I hit my target. My last ditched attempt to save us both.

I go to speak again, but Evan holds up a hand to stop me. "Let's do it this way." He picks up a piece of paper and a pen from a table off to the side. Of course, he preempted that as soon as I opened my eyes, I would have a million different questions. He passes them over.

I mouth *thank you*. He smiles solemnly.

Something isn't right. Where's Brit? I need to know if she's ok. *Britney?* I write on the paper.

Evan reads it and sighs. "She's in the room next door. She had a spell of consciousness, but it was short."

I frown. Surely, she should have gotten better if she regained consciousness, not worse.

Noticing my frown, Evan explains, "Another agent tried to get a statement before I arrived. He let slip that you'd reported seeing the figure recently."

I know what's coming next.

"It tipped her over the edge, and she lost consciousness again. The doctor said it's her subconscious protecting her from the emotional trauma that, right now, is too much for her to process."

Images of Britney slumped in the chair, covered in blood, creep in and I blink trying to stop them. I can't. I did this to her. I never should have let her in. I can't hear any more about her, not right now, she's alive and that's all that matters.

I pick up the pen again and write, *Did you get him?*

Evan grimaces and glances out the window, telling me everything I need to know. He takes a deep breath before saying, "We found the gun in your hand and found the bullet but that's it. There was a lot of blood at the scene, but there was no trail. It's like he just disappeared."

He's gone?

Evan reads then nods.

I want to scream, but I can't. He's still out there … This game is never going to end. *What now?*

"You need to focus on recovering, as does Britney. We'll need to take statements from you. For now, yours will have to be written, but when your voice recovers, we'll take another."

What about my mom and Josie? What about football?

"Your mom and Josie are fine. He doesn't know where they are. I've upped their security while I'm here. In the meantime, there's a warrant out for his arrest."

I point at the word football, the question he has yet to answer.

"We'll assign you a private detail to be with you at all times, to make sure you're safe. Continue with football, being the focus of the world will keep you safe."

Can I see Britney? I write.

He shakes his head. "No visitors allowed unless it's family, not until she's conscious. She has to be able to give her consent."

We avoid talking about the fact that even when her eyes open, the answer will probably be no.

***

Three days I've been stuck, staring at the same four walls. Apparently being a national treasure means you get extra special care and attention, lucky me. At least I get to stay close to Britney, even though I have yet to see her.

Standing, staring into the bathroom mirror in my en-suite, I inspect the hand marks on my throat. They're the same as the ones my mom had. Their coloring is now a mixture of purple and green. The bruising is starting to heal.

"She's ready for you, Mr. Becket," calls one of the nurses into my room.

I let out a sigh as I follow. After everything Evan told me, I know this isn't going to be a happy reunion. Britney no doubt blames me, and rightly so.

The nurse opens the door to Britney's room, steps in and says, "Mr. Becket is here."

I don't hear a response, but the nurse walks out, offering me a sad smile. I smile back, faking a confidence I don't feel. The room's dark and the curtains have been pulled shut. Evan mentioned she was finding light painful. I suck in a sharp breath when I see her. I want to run over, pull her into my arms and whisper in her hair that she's safe and everything will be ok. But I can't because I don't know if it will.

When my eyes adjust to the light and take her in, rage threatens to consume me. The skin that isn't hidden by her hospital gown reveals a pattern of red slice marks. Her face is still swollen, the bruises have the same coloring as my own. And then ... there's her neck. It has the same marks as mine, as my mom's. We're no longer two of a kind but three. Three survivors of the hands that have ended too many lives.

"B—brit," I say, my voice faltering.

Her eyes stare at her hands, clasped together, resting on the sheets. She doesn't say a word.

"Brit, please, talk to me," I plead.

When she looks up, the familiar sparkle of her eyes has gone—they're empty. She looks at me like she wishes I were dead.

"Don't call me that." She swallows then says quietly, "You knew. You saw the figure."

I nod.

"You knew something was wrong. You knew what that figure meant, and you didn't tell me, didn't warn me. If I'd known I would ha—" she stops in her tracks, choosing not to continue with what she was about to say.

I frown, knowing there's something she's not telling me, but I can't push it, not when she's looking at me like she is.

"You didn't let me prepare," she continues, "or make a choice. You disregarded my safety like it was nothing. You knew about my past—I told you everything, my darkest secrets. But you didn't trust me enough to tell me one of yours, the thing that would have kept me safe." Her throat bobs as she swallows and her voice comes out strangled, "You led me into the hands of a monster."

"I'm sorry, I—I ..." I trail off, not knowing what to say.

"Lost for words? You should be." She swallows and stares at me intently. "Is Michael Becket even your name?"

I shake my head, no. I look at the monitor beside her bed. It bleeps rapidly, informing me how angry she is, just in case I didn't already know.

"Who are you?"

"I don't even know myself anymore," I reply, so quietly I'm not sure if she hears.

"I've been sitting wondering to myself, how someone I loved, and thought loved me back, could do this to me. I understand now that I never should have trusted you, I don't know you at all."

There's nothing I can say, it's the truth. I brought her to Jacksonville to mess with her. I never preempted that another player, with too many cards up his sleeve, was going to join us on the board and mess everything up.

"Get out," she seethes.

They're the same words I said to her when I had my injury and my world felt like it was crumbling down around me. The only difference here—Britney's world hasn't crumbled, its ended. She's got nothing left to give.

I open my mouth to say I'm sorry again, when she screams at the top of her lungs, "Get out!"

Two nurses come rushing into the room. The one who let me in looks at me and calmly says, "You need to leave."

I nod and turn around, my eyes drinking in Britney as I do, wondering if I'll ever see her again.

I get my answer when I'm about to step through the door and she says, "Don't wait for me, there's nothing left to wait for."

Resigned, I walk out, listening out for the click as the door shuts, the sign that this chapter of my life with Britney has come to an end.

***

Britney

"Let me help you."

I hold up a hand, stopping Jess before she tries to place her own on my shoulder. The thought of someone touching me is too much. If she's put out, she doesn't let it show.

Pulling the freshly cut key from my bag, I look at the door to my apartment hesitantly. It's been almost two weeks since I've been here. It will never be long enough. I don't know if I'm ready. My heart pounds in my chest as I slide the key into the lock and turn it. There's nothing there, Britney, relax.

Jess says, "Are you ready to go in?"

I nod, pushing open the door and we both step inside. I walk slowly, my eyes dart around, looking for any sign of danger and my ears prick, listening for sounds out of the ordinary. I can't switch off. I'm on guard, waiting for something to happen. Waiting for the figure to come for me again and wrap their hands around my neck. My throat is dry, and I struggle to swallow, but still, I push myself forward into the living room. An array of different emotions fight to take over. One minute anger, the next sadness, then sheer terror when my eyes settle on the picture of my mom and me. Someone must have replaced the frame.

I flinch when a crashing sound reaches my ears, then the smashing of glass. My eyes find the window—the hooded figure is there. The flash of a knife. The tearing of skin. Blood dripping against silk. An almost deafening bang.

I blink. Everything is still in place, it's all in my head.

I run to the kitchen with Jess closely behind. Leaning over the sink, I empty my stomach with each wave of nausea that hits. I remain there until all I can do is retch. Retching turns into sobs that take over my whole body.

Jess steps in closer, raises a hand carefully, then gently places it on my shoulder. "Shh."

I fall into her arms, tears cascading down my cheeks, finally succumbing to the pain and the fear that might never, ever leave.

We crumble down to the ground together, and Jess rocks me back and forth slowly. All the time saying, "Shh."

Finally, I choke out, "I feel like I can't breathe. I'm suffocating. Each time I close my eyes, he's there."

Jess says quietly, "Let it out. Let it out whenever you need to. Only time can help you heal."

"What if I don't heal?" I ask. "What if I'm too broken?"

"You're not. If you were as weak as you seem to think you are, you wouldn't be here. You might not have justice ... yet. But what you can do, is fight, prove that he didn't kill you or your spirit."

I look around and whimper. "I don't want to be here."

She draws back from me and gives me a smile that doesn't quite reach her eyes. "Then don't be. Come live with me. Pack a bag and let's just go. We'll let the security team know. You don't need to live with reminders each day. You'll torture yourself with fear."

A little while later when I muster up the energy, we stand and go to my room. Jess helps me quickly throw as much clothing as will fit into a bag.

It's when we're leaving that my eyes find the picture of me and my mom on the console table again.

"Do you want to take it?" Jess asks.

"No."

She nods and we walk out of my apartment, leaving the physical reminders of my flawed past behind.

Twenty-Seven

Becket

Two weeks since the fallout. Two weeks since I saw her face. Two weeks since I lost myself when I left Britney in New York.

I did this. Everything is my fault. I don't know what I expected to happen when this whole charade began. Belle doesn't fall for The Beast. She wanted the prince without the flaws. The fairytales lie—there's no such thing as a happily ever after.

"You good?" asks Brad, setting down a tray of food on the table in front of me.

I might have hated leaving Britney behind but I'm glad to be back in Jacksonville, even if we're stuck in a food court with people gawping all around us. Jacko's has the best burgers around and if anything is going to bring me out of my funk, it's the juicy beef patty making my mouth water.

I don't answer Brad's question. I don't have it in me. He knows something went down in New York, he doesn't know what exactly, but he knows it was bad enough for me to close off.

"Hungry?" he asks, raising an eyebrow, watching as I shovel mounds of food into my mouth.

"Starving." I'm midway through taking another bite when I see it. The figure in the black, hooded jacket walking through the food court. I almost choke as I try to swallow. My pulse accelerates and I start to panic.

"Becket what the hell?" shouts Brad as I stand up from the table.

I chase after the figure. I need to know if it's them or not. I reach out my arm, ready to grab their shoulder, but I never make it.

"Let go," I grunt, as Brad tugs me back.

"What are you doing, man?" he stares at me like I've completely lost the plot.

"I have to see if it's him."

"Who are you talking about?" he demands.

Ignoring his question, I step forward. People around us stare and the figure must sense it, because they spin around to see what everyone is looking at. A guy younger than Brad and I throws us a confused look, when he finds he has two of the Jacksonville Jaguars following closely behind.

"Can I help you?" he asks drawing back.

My shoulders slump in defeat. It isn't him. It's all in my head. I can't get him out. It's happening again.

Brad jumps in, answering for me, "Sorry dude, we thought you were one of our other teammates."

The guy shakes his head bewildered and walks away.

Brad mutters under his breath, "Guess he's not a fan of football."

"Can we go?" I ask, my appetite gone. I need to get away from here.

Brad raises an eyebrow. "What happened in New York?"

"It's nothing for you to be concerned about," I reply coldly, looking off into the distance.

"Wrong. I'm your best friend and I have every right to be concerned."

"It was something to do with, Brit, that's all you need to know."

"I told you, man. I knew something like this would happen."

He's wrong, he doesn't know anything.

"Come on, you have to talk to someone about what happened."

He's wrong again. I don't have to talk to anyone. Eleven-year-old me knew better. I don't need friends. I don't need anyone. Only now do I understand the reason why. If I allow people to get close, they will unknowingly become pawns in his game. Like in football, all it takes is one wrong move for everything to come undone, for the game to be lost. I walk away from Brad without a word. He's just another person whose life will be ruined by being a part of mine. The only way to survive is to put the mask back on and push everyone out of my life. For good this time.

***

It's time to play a game.

Gasping for air, my eyes fly open, only to find Coach Langford staring down at me.

"What's this?" I ask, when he throws a scrap of paper on my chest, while I remain sprawled out along the couch.

He takes a few steps back and looks around the room, taking in the empty takeout boxes and clothes haphazardly strewn across the floor and furniture. He frowns when his eyes settle on the bin, overflowing with empty bottles of scotch.

"The number of someone who can help," he replies, his voice rough.

I struggle to sit up, my head pounding from another late night spent with my old best friend: loneliness. "I don't need help."

"Do you remember what I said to you the day you were scouted by Jacksonville University?"

"No," I lie, leaning toward the coffee table and grabbing a cigarette. My whole body relaxes when I take the first drag, nicotine flooding my body, providing the quick fix I need.

His brows draw together as he stares down at me. "I told you I'd never been wrong about a player before ... but I was wrong about you."

"If all you're going to do is stand there and tell me how I'm fucking up my life, you can leave. You'll just be telling me what I already know."

Coach Langford grabs the cigarette from my hand and closes it in his fist. My mouth drops open and I'm about to ask him what he's playing at when he starts to speak again, "I was wrong about you because I thought you had talent we could use."

"Great," I say bitterly, "now you're telling me I have no talent. Wonderful. I thought all I ever had was football, I thought if I ever lost it, I'd have nothing. Now I know I never had anything to begin with. Thanks for that." I sag back into the couch and look up to the ceiling, waiting for him to give up on me and leave.

"Son, I was wrong because you don't have talent, you have a gift."

For a second my heart swells with pride. I can't look at him though, because the walls I've rebuilt are fragile and could fall at any second. There are only so many times I can break until I won't be able to get back up.

"I won't push to know what happened in New York, not yet, but you need to give that number a call."

"What if I don't?" I ask defiantly.

He sighs. "Then you're off the team."

I laugh with wide eyes and I pull at my hair. "Let me get this straight. You're telling me I have a gift but you're going to destroy my future?"

"No, son. I'm trying to save your future."

***

I stare blankly at the woman in front of me in the same way I do each week, feeling absolutely nothing.

"The image in your head, scale it from one to ten."

"Ten."

She thinks I don't notice, but I do. Her brows draw together and her jaw clenches in frustration. It's subtle, but it's there. She thinks I'm a lost cause, just like everyone else. It's been four weeks and we should be making progress. We've made none at all. I'm done, even football isn't worth this, gifted or not.

I stand abruptly from my chair and she asks, "Where are you going?"

"To process this *my* way," I reply, then walk out, without another word.

***

The only thing that fills the empty room is the sound of my hands pounding against a punching bag. Each time exhaustion starts to creep in, the image of the black, hooded figure flashes through my mind and I pound the bag harder. The skin on my knuckles tore hours ago and my fists gleam red. I have to get him out of my head.

"You can't catch a ball without your hands, Becket ..."

I stop before my hand makes contact with the bag again. When I circle around on the spot, I find Coach Langford staring at me.

"How did you find me here?" I ask.

His laugh fills the room. The sound bounces off the exposed bricks that know me better than anyone. These walls have guarded my secrets for years.

"Do you think I'm an idiot? The bruises, you disappearing from time to time. I've known all along."

"Why didn't you stop me?"

"Because at the time, it's what you needed."

"And now?"

His eyes move around the room, searching for answers. "Tell me what happened in New York."

I let out a huff of air and admitting defeat, give him the answer he's been waiting weeks for, "He's back. He got out. He took Britney. Tortured her to get to me."

"Damn it," he mutters, dragging a hand over his face.

What I least expect happens next. Coach Langford pulls his shirt over his head, then walks over to the side of the room and grabs a pair of wraps.

"What are you doing?"

"Helping you to process *your* way. Then you will process *my* way." He steps onto the mat, bouncing his weight between his feet. "I'm him. Hit me."

What the hell does he think he's doing? "No."

"Hit me, Becket."

I shake my head. "No."

"Fine." He walks over to the bag he brought with him and pulls out a black, hooded jacket. Slips it on, zips it up, then pulls up the hood. He spins back around and before I have a chance to register what's happening, he starts to run towards me.

Like in the mall and all the other times, all I see is the black, hooded jacket. I react and charge, tackling him like I would a player on the field. The only difference? I want to destroy him, the figure that tainted my past, destroyed my future. The figure that ruined my life.

We push each other, shoulder to shoulder, then push away and charge again. We hit each other with equal force. We're an equilibrium of strength and at some point, the scale will tip, only one person can win. Coach whips his leg round, colliding with my shins, sending me flying back against the ground. He climbs over and holds me firmly in place with my shoulders. Images of Britney and my mom, *his* hands around their necks, flash through my mind. My fist flies up and cracks Coach across the jaw. He falls back and I dive forward, taking him down, pinning him against the mats.

"Don't let him win," he grunts.

Fighting the darkness, suddenly I can see clearly again. I see Coach, not the figure in the hooded, black jacket. I quickly roll off him and place my head between my knees, gasping for air. When everything settles, we both stand back up, facing each other.

"Tell me what you saw just then."

"Him."

Sadly, he replies, "But it's me. The only thing we have in common is a black jacket. You can't keep letting this haunt you, you have to fight it. Brad told me what happened at the mall. *Please*, see what I'm trying to show you. You have PTSD and left untreated it could become so much worse."

Every part of me aches and exhaustion takes over. "This is where I process. Not in some shrink's office."

"No, son. This is where you hide. What you do here isn't helping, it has to stop. They need you, all of them. Feel the pain of what they've been through and use it to bring you out of that dark hole you've gone down. Because soon, you'll find yourself so deep, you won't be able to crawl back out."

My shoulders slump in defeat and I admit, "I don't know what I'm doing anymore. I don't know how to move on."

Coach walks forward, grabs the back of my neck, and pulls my head forwards. I close my eyes and we stand, foreheads pressed together. It's the closest thing I've had to the comfort and support of a parent in years. When I open my eyes, his are there, the way they always have been, testing me, pushing me, showing me what I'm really made of.

He steps back and says, "Not all death is physical. Don't be held hostage to your past."

A whimper leaves my throat, and just like that, I break in front of the one person I never thought I could be vulnerable with, but maybe should have.

When the pain subsides and I feel like I can breathe again, I swallow and say, "Help me. Tell me what I need to do."

"Fight, Becket. Fight like hell. Don't let him win."

Twenty-Eight

Britney

The familiar smell of coffee hits my nose when I step inside the coffee shop where Evan and I agreed to meet. I look around and find his dark hair, a head above everyone else, tucked away in a corner. He hasn't seen me yet, so I go to the counter and order a coffee first. When I have my order, I make my way to the table where he's sitting.

I watch as he taps away on the screen of his phone. There's no doubting he's hot, in that older, sexy FBI agent kind of way, but my heart doesn't beat for him. It doesn't matter how much time has passed and how much distance there is between us, my heart only beats for one person. A certain NFL asshole.

I clear my throat and he looks up, smiling. "Miss Shaw. It's great to see you again and looking so well."

"Agent Price, please, call me Britney."

He chuckles and gestures to the seat across the table from his. "Well then, please, call me Evan."

"I appreciate that you travelled all this way," I say, sitting down, "but we could have had this conversation over the phone."

He smiles warmly. "I know. I wanted to check you were ok."

He means *he* wanted him to check I was ok.

"I have good days and bad days," I admit.

He nods, knowingly. "That's to be expected. These things aren't easy to come back from."

"You say it like you know." Like I do with Becket, I see something in his eyes, the same thing I see in my own when I look in the mirror. Pain, sadness, experience.

"It comes with the job, seeing the things I do. But less about me, I'm here for you. So, what can I do for you?"

"At the hospital, you offered to tell me a little more about the case. Why?"

"I think you know why. I can't tell you everything, only what is already public knowledge. But I'm assuming you know nothing ..."

"Ok ..." My chest starts to feel tight. I purposely avoid anything that might remind me of what happened. It's too painful.

"Sometimes, knowledge can help with—"

"Closure," I finish.

He gives me a tight smile. "Exactly."

Now I know why he picked the quietest corner, away from the hustle and bustle of people, so we can have this conversation in peace. "Who was it?" I ask.

He doesn't even try to hide his grimace. "The Cat."

I raise an eyebrow. "Seriously? 'The Cat.' Like a pussy cat?"

He chuckles, but his voice is devoid of all emotion when he replies, "The name we give him doesn't come from what he likens himself to be."

A lump forms in my throat and I struggle to swallow, I suddenly know the answer, but still I ask the question, "Then where does it come from?"

"From the game he plays with his victims. He likes to play a game of Cat and Mouse."

307

Everything around me disappears.

"The only time we've ever had a cat in the hotel was when we had mice."
"There was a cat in my room ... I thought someone was being murdered."
"Ew, that means there are mice."

Evan's voice brings me back from the darkness, "Britney?" His face is full of concern.

I shiver despite the heat. My whole body is covered in a sheen of cold sweat.

"Britney?" says Evan, his face full of concern. "We don't have to do this, we can stop."

I shake my head and swallow. "He kept saying it was time to play a game."

Evan glances out of the window before replying, "It's his M.O. It's what he says to all his victims."

"How do you know?"

"Because the child he leaves sitting with the body always tells the officer first on the scene that Mommy lost the game. He always leaves a witness, but never a trace of who he is."

Becket ... his nightmares ... "They were children?" I whisper in horror.

My heart aches for what he's been through and how I treated him when I was in that dark place, I thought I'd never come out of. I blamed the one person I should have sought comfort from, the only person who could understand my pain, because he'd been through the same thing himself. It still doesn't change the fact he didn't trust me enough to tell me something that might have kept me safe.

Evan clears his throat and says, "He was eleven. I can't tell you much more than that I'm afraid. If you want details it has to come from him. It's not my story to tell."

"It's ok. I appreciate you taking the time to come here and tell me what you have. It helps a little."

He leans forward and clasps his hands in front of him on the table. Deep brown eyes bore into mine. "Have you spoken to anyone about what you've been through?"

"No." I look down awkwardly and wrap my hands around my cup.

He slides a card across the table. I keep my gaze set on my coffee while I wait for an explanation.

"She specializes in trauma. She's the best in New York. She could really help you process what you've been through." He pauses, takes a deep breath and continues, "I had to look into your file. I know about your mom and I know what comes with growing up with that kind of parent. This woman also deals with childhood trauma."

My eyes start to water, as I shakily reply, "Thank you."

"There will be some follow-ups in future months. We will keep you up to date on progress if we know or hear anything. Make sure you keep yourself safe." His eyes scour the room and when they find my security detail in the distance, the one Becket outright demanded he pay to always be with me, he settles and looks more at ease. Standing, he smiles down at me. "I have to go, work calls, always. It was great to see you again and to see you looking so much better."

"Thank you."

Before he leaves, he looks down at the card which remains untouched on the table. "Give her a call. She will help make things clearer, help you to process.

She might help you to see you're punishing the wrong person in all of this."

I watch Evan walk out of the coffee shop before I pick up the card. It burns my skin as I pass it between my fingers, wondering to myself whether I'm finally ready to open the box and deal with my past. Whether I'm finally ready to move forward.

***

"How did it go?" asks Jess as she enters the kitchen of our apartment, throwing her bag down on the kitchen worktop.

I look up from my glass of wine with a grimace.

"That bad, huh?"

"It wasn't the best," I admit.

"These things take time. It was your first session. Don't give up yet."

"Evan made it sound like it would be easy," I grumble, picking up my wine glass and taking a long drink.

Jess wanders over to the fridge, pulls out a fresh bottle and fills a glass for herself. She looks over at me expectantly, so I drain what's left in my own and she refills it. Right to the brim. There's a reason we're best friends.

When she's had a sip of her own, she says, "Evan makes it sound easy because he sees these things every day. What you went through isn't normal, it isn't a game."

Blackness creeps in. *It's time to play a game.*

"Shit! I'm so sorry, I didn't mean to say that."

I blink, coming back around, taking in her now ashen face.

"Brit, are you ok?"

"I don't know how to do this. Move on, act like things are normal. They never will be," I admit, staring into the clear liquid in my glass. "What happens next?"

"What would you like to happen next?" asks Jess, visibly righting herself as she comes back around from her mistake. When I don't answer she continues, "You have to want this. If you don't, it won't work. It has to be the right time for you."

I pick up my glass with a shaky hand and swallow the cool liquid down. It provides some relief. I glance back at Jess and nod. I'm ready for her to continue. She's telling me exactly what I need to hear, I just need to actually hear it.

"Somewhere down the line you might be able to get your life back. Is that what you want?"

"Yes," I whisper.

Her face brightens. "What do you want? What's the thing you need most, right at this very moment?"

"Becket," I reply.

"Go over what happened. Take me back to the beginning. You don't have to tell me everything, but maybe we can come up with a plan together."

So, I do. I seek solace in my closest friend, and by telling the story, letting everything out, I'm able to take a step forward.

"It's understandable that you would blame Becket," agrees Jess.

I nod. "It was his fault. If he'd told me what he'd seen, then maybe it wouldn't have happened."

She pauses and bites her lip. "I can see why you'd think that ..."

"I'm sensing a but ..."

"Even if you'd known, it most likely still would have happened."

I frown, not quite sure what she's getting at. "What do you mean?"

311

Quietly, she says, "He's a serial killer, B. It doesn't matter if you knew or not. He still would have found you if he wanted to. Becket isn't responsible for what someone else did."

"But he—"

"Did what he thought was right to protect you and others ... came to your rescue even though it meant putting himself at risk. Admit it, you can't get the answers you want so you're looking for someone to blame."

I narrow my eyes. "That's what you think I'm doing? Placing the blame on someone for the sake of it?"

Hesitantly she answers, "Maybe."

"Why would I blame Becket if it wasn't his fault?"

"Because you know that he loves you. You're lashing out at him because you know you can."

The day in the hospital after Becket's accident passes through my mind. All his misdirected anger towards me for everything that happened. How I stood by him no matter what. I finish, "Because we know that even when the people we love see us at our worst, they'll still be there cheering us on at the sidelines."

What have I done? I don't know how to fix this. There's a lot of water under the bridge, but essentially, I'm punishing Becket for all the wrong things. I've blamed him for something completely out of his control.

I sit pondering to myself for a moment, wondering how I'm supposed to reach out to him when I'm all the way in New York and he's in Jacksonville. *Everything* is against us right now.

Then it hits me. I know what I need to do.

"Where's the fire?" exclaims Jess as I charge to my bedroom.

312

She doesn't have long to figure out what I'm up to, because I rush back out and set my laptop up on the breakfast bar, then take a large drink of wine for courage. Sitting back on my stool, I begin hammering the keyboard, so hard there's a possibility it might break.

"I have something I need to do." After a couple of minutes of typing, I look over at Jess who's standing watching me like a hawk and say, "Quick question: How set in stone is this month's publication?"

She frowns. "It's being approved by the powers that be. Why?"

"How would you like to revisit an old story, one that never made it to print?"

She smirks, beginning to understand where I'm going with this. "I could change a few things around."

I beam at her, an action that feels alien after the past few months. "Great. Could you?"

She doesn't ask any more questions. "I'll go and do it now." Before she leaves, she asks, "Why are you finally writing it?"

I continue typing while I reply, "I'm apologizing with a grand gesture. It's the only way I know how to make him listen."

Twenty-Nine

Becket

There were times in the past when I'd hate Coach Langford's practices. He called them "character building," but there were a few other words I would have used to describe them. Things have changed though. They're still brutal, but they're what keeps me getting up each morning, because it feels like there isn't much else. These past six months there's been nothing. I've shut myself off from the world, afraid that if I let myself feel something, I wouldn't be able to stop. I wouldn't be able to shut the pain out.

Today's big game is my first since the accident. We're in the locker room going through our usual routine, when the door flies open and in stalks my PR rep Shauna. My eyes zone straight in on the magazine in her hand. This can't be good. Not if the last time we were in this kind of scenario is anything to go by.

"Woah, Shauna! If you wanted to catch a glimpse of my beef whistle, all you had to do was ask," hollers Brad.

The rest of the team snicker under their breath. Brad's an idiot, the rest of us know better than to cross her.

"You're disgusting," she snaps back, then throws the magazine down next to me on the bench. "You need to get your head out of your ass and read this." That's all I get before she spins on her heel and stalks out as quick as she came in.

The name of the magazine catches my eye.

Brad shuffles over, with an apprehensive look on his face. "Looks like she might finally have written the article. Coach will be happy. Let's just pray she didn't review your performance in the sack, or we're fucked."

I ignore him. All I can do is stare. As the weeks went by and nothing appeared, I assumed she was never going to write it. I wouldn't have expected her to, not after what happened.

"Are you going to read it or what?" Brad asks nosily, never one for respecting boundaries.

"Not with you hovering over my shoulder like that." I grab the magazine and dart away from him.

He holds up his hands laughing, then winks. "Whatever, man, I'll read about the two she gave your performance later."

Skipping through to the right page, I finally read the heading: *The Becket Behind the Sex Tape.* Not quite what Coach Langford and Shauna had in mind. This was meant to be some huge article, painting me in a different light to the world, not a reminder of my past indiscretions. Maybe I shouldn't read it. If the heading is anything to go by, there's a strong possibility I'm going to want to tear it to shreds. But I can't stop myself, I have to know what she's written.

Our romance was a plane crash. A disaster. It ended as quickly as it began.

315

I always thought one day, I'd meet my dream guy, the one that would sweep me off my feet, whispering sweet nothings in my ear.

What I got? The biggest douchebag in the NFL ... or so I thought.

When I was assigned this article, I was intrigued, along with the rest of the world, to find out who the real Michael Becket was. We live in a society where we're so focused on the Rich and the Famous, that we forget they're normal people, experiencing normal things, normal emotions. Really, all they want is the same thing we do, to be happy.

In a world where you can be anything, be kind. The world has been anything but kind to Michael Becket. People have flaws, people have secrets. He is no exception to that rule. He's one of the most famous football players in the world, and he's as handsome in real life as he is on your screens. Perfectly handsome, perfectly flawed. But his story isn't mine to tell.

What I can say? You should never judge a book by its cover.

That wasn't what I was expecting.

Sitting down on the bench, I rub a hand over my face. I'm not quite sure what it means. Just like she didn't expose all my secrets to the world the first time, she's kept the real me hidden again. She didn't have to. She could have used it as some sort of revenge. But she didn't.

God, I hope it means what I think it does, because I miss her, every second of every day. She told me not to wait. I haven't waited, I've been stuck, absorbed by all things Britney. My feelings haven't changed in the time we've been apart. Without her, none of this—the fame, the fortune, none of it matters.

316

The locker room door flies open again. "Becket!" Coach barks. "My office, now!"

My mind starts racing, trying to figure out what I might have done to piss him off. I come up with nothing, apart from the article. Shoving the magazine in my locker, I close it before walking out of the room.

The sounds of the team singing, "Someone's iiiin trooouuuble," follow me out.

Assholes.

I knock on Coach's office door.

"Come in!" he barks again. He really is in a shitty mood.

"You asked for me Coach?" I say as I step inside.

He looks up from where he's sitting at his desk, his face unreadable. "Actually, I didn't ..."

The door behind me swings shut.

"I did."

I close my eyes. I thought I'd never see her again. Not wanting to waste another second and risk her disappearing out of my life once more, I spin around to check she's really here. "What are you doing here?" I snap, caught off guard. Ok, that didn't come out quite as I intended. "Sorry, it's just the last time I saw you, you told me you never wanted to see me again."

She looks at me uncertainly, those big blue eyes brighter than I remember and says sheepishly, "I thought it would be a surprise. Maybe I should have let you know I was coming?"

I nod, and struggling to speak, reply, "That would have been good." A heads up would have saved me from standing here, gawping like an idiot, unable to figure out what to say.

"Less of the small talk. You have a game in a couple of hours. Becket, you can't screw it up," says Coach Langford, reorganizing some of the papers on his desk, before standing up. "You can talk in here for a bit." He turns to Britney, a smirk on his face. "Please don't make any sex tapes, I don't want my office getting tagged in them."

When he's gone, I stand silently, staring. "To what do I owe this pleasure?"

She frowns. I'm being a bit of a dick towards her, but I don't know what to do. I haven't got a clue why she's here. I don't know how to act. I'm terrified if I open up, let her see how happy I am she's here, she'll throw it back in my face.

"I wanted to speak to you," she replies.

"There are those little things called cellphones. You didn't have to fly all the way here."

"Would you have answered?"

I shrug. "I don't know."

"Exactly."

I'm not sure when it happened, but we're standing toe to toe. I look down, transfixed by the way her chest rises and falls. My heart skips a beat and I feel like I'm about to bring up the contents of my stomach. It's not nerves about the game, it's not even about the article. It's her, this is what she does to me. The walls I put up, she bulldozed down. She makes me nervous, makes me feel things no one ever has, things I didn't think I was capable of feeling, because I thought I was too broken. I thought I didn't deserve anything better.

Having her here in front of me is agony. All I want to do is pull her in and kiss her till our lips are raw. The thought of telling her how I feel is what's most terrifying, but it's what I have to do if I stand a chance of keeping her in my life. "I lied to you ..."

She literally throws her head back and laughs in my face. If it were anyone else, I'd be pissed. But the sound filling the room makes my heart pound and my blood race. "You've lied about a lot."

I shake my head. "I only lied about my name. The rest I just avoided telling you. You got me, Brit, all of me. You got the sides to me that no one's ever seen."

I hear her breath catch in her throat. She wasn't expecting me to be so open, but I'm done hiding things, after all, she now knows *all* of my deepest darkest secrets.

"So, what have you lied about?"

"That night in the alley, after I messed up at the awards. You asked me to fall with you ..." I watch her throat bob when she swallows. "I told you I couldn't and that was a lie. The truth is, Brit. I'd already fallen."

***

Britney

When you love someone, really, truly love someone, you feel what they feel.

To the world, Becket's a closed book. Not to me, not anymore. My heart aches for him because of the things he's been through, the things he's seen. He's carried this burden all these years, sacrificed himself to protect the ones he loves. I meant what I wrote in the article. You never know a person's true story unless they tell you. You should never judge a book by its cover. The Becket the world sees is not the man standing in front of me right now.

"I get why you didn't, but you could have told me," I say, looking up into his eyes.

"I'm sorry."

"For a while I blamed you, I thought it was all your fault. I had my eyes opened to the fact that I was blaming you for something that was out of your control."

He looks down and shifts his weight on his feet. "I never should have gotten involved with you. If I hadn't, this never would have happened."

I place a hand under his chin, lifting it and urging him to look me in the eye. "The thought of never knowing you, never feeling all these things there are between us, scares me more than he does. I've had a shitty life, we both have, but you make it better. You make me want to fight for more."

He leans in and places a gentle kiss on my lips. "I love you, Brit."

"I love you more."

The smirk is back. "How about we go longer than thirty seconds without fighting?"

I laugh again, something I've done more of in the last ten minutes, being around him, than I have in the past six months. It felt like I wasn't capable of doing it without Becket in my life.

"I do have a couple of questions ..."

He nods. "Ask whatever you need to."

So, I ask, and he answers, with me sitting in his lap at Coach Langford's desk. He tells me how everything came about and explains what really happened with the assault case. How he was fighting a battle he never should have had to take part in. How he still is.

The world might not love him, the player with no filter, the NFL's number one asshole. But the reason they don't love him is because they can't see who he really is. The world isn't important though. What matters is us together. Now we know each other's truths, we can finally move forwards, fight our demons, win our battles. Together. We've spent a huge chunk of our lives facing things nobody should ever have to, alone. But now, we have each other.

I wrap my arms tightly around his waist, resting my head against his chest, breathing in his familiar

320

scent. Lavender and birch. At first his heartbeat sounds erratic but then it settles to a slow steady rhythm.

"Did Abby know?" I ask.

He stills. "No. We had the kind of relationship where if there was an issue, we avoided it. We didn't ask questions. It was the way it needed to be. For both of us."

"Ok. Can I ask you one more question?"

"Go on ..."

"What's your real name?"

"Ben Miller."

"Clever," I reply, and his chest vibrates as he chuckles.

"What do I call you?"

"Michael Becket." I lean back and look into his piercing green eyes. "I left Ben Miller behind a long time ago. This is who I am now. I actually have a question myself ..."

"Ask away," I reply. He's answered all of my questions, it's the least I can do. If we're going to move forward, there can be no secrets.

"Why didn't you think you could tell me that you'd been seeing the figure?"

I let out a huff of air before replying. "For the same reason you didn't think you could tell me. To protect you from my past. Sometimes the best way to stay safe is to be oblivious."

Becket nods with understanding. "Who did you think it was?"

I stare straight ahead, not quite able to meet his eye when I tell the next part to the story. "I've spent years trying to pay off my mom's debts and I'd been struggling to keep up with payments. They'd turn up unannounced, I did whatever I could to get money and keep them away. But then I was so absorbed in what was happening with us, when I came to Jacksonville, I forgot I still owed some payments. I thought it was them coming to find me."

"Do I need to be worried?" asks Becket, frowning.

"Not anymore. Neither do I. A couple of months after everything happened, the police came to my apartment ..." Becket's throat bobs as he swallows. "They found *her,* and she paid the price. Her debts aren't mine anymore."

"Is she ..."

"Dead? Yes."

"I'm sorry, Brit."

"Don't be. My mom was dead to me a long time ago. This was merely a technicality. I'm accepting it's ok, that for now I still don't forgive her for everything she did and what she put me through. Maybe one day, but not right now."

Becket struggles to find a reply to the information I've just dumped on him, so I tilt my head and place a small kiss on his lips.

He groans and murmurs against my lips, "I missed you, Brit. I know I can be a prick and I'm not your knight in shining armor. I'm not perfect, but for you, I'll try to be better."

"You're wrong."

He pulls away his brow furrowed. "Why?"

"I don't want perfect. I just want you."

He tugs me back into his chest and places a kiss into my hair. "You're sure about this?"

"Never been surer of anything in my life."

He lifts me with him as he stands up from the chair, then backs me up against the office door. His lips crash down on mine. They're soft. The kiss is anything but. Heat spreads through me and my body hums at how good it is feeling his body against mine again.

322

This is Becket, *my* Becket. He's no longer wearing a mask.

The door rattles in its frame as we kiss frantically, desperate to make up for lost time. A fist hammers against it in response.

"Becket, if you even think about screwing her in my office, consider yourself out of the NFL."

"Sorry, Coach." He groans into my neck, "I want you."

"Later..." I sigh, content but frustrated.

He pulls away and stares me straight in the eyes. "Promise you won't disappear on me?"

"Promise." He kisses me again.

Coach Langford bangs on the door. "Times up, Becket. Get your ass in the locker room with the rest of the team."

Reluctantly, we separate and leave the room.

Later, I watch him on the field. Watch as he sprints ahead with his team and then looks back. His eyes scour thousands of people and then he finds me in the crowd, holds up his hand and waves. I don't know much about what our future holds. Everything is still so uncertain.

But I do know one thing ...

I might have fooled him once, but however long we're together, however long we love each other, I'll do my best never to fool him again.

Thirty

Britney 3 months later

Gentle stroking on my back stirs me from the most peaceful night's sleep I've had in months. Each night since moving in with Becket, the nightmares have lessened. I wish I could say the same for him, but his demons run much deeper than mine. We're a work in progress and we're fighting back, together.

"Mmm. I like waking up like this," I murmur, when he starts to trail kisses along the back of my neck.

"That's good, because I like waking you up like this."

His kisses move down my back, eagerly, but he stops when he reaches my shoulder blade. I feel his breathing quicken. I know if I turn and look back, he will be frowning at one particularly nasty scar, one of the many that serve as harsh reminders of what happened. They remind us that until justice is served, he won't be able to move on, not fully.

"Don't go down that path," I say.

"I don't know what path you're talking about ..."

"Yes. You do. You promised you wouldn't keep doing this to yourself."

The past few months haven't been easy. But never for one minute did I think navigating the aftermath of a traumatic experience as a couple would be.

Playfully he responds, "And why should I keep that promise?"

I roll over and look up at him. "Because you promised that my first day as your fiancée would be a fresh start."

"Oh yeah ... that." He smirks.

I might love him, but he's still an asshole when he wants to be. "Yes ... that. Now, you made a promise and I plan on making sure you keep it."

He begins to lose interest and places a wet kiss on my collarbone, sucking as he strokes my skin with his tongue.

"Want to know a secret?" I ask playfully.

"I don't think I do. I've had enough of secrets."

"I'm going to tell you anyway." I shove him away as he tries to lean in and start kissing my neck again.

"I thought you might."

"I always thought getting older and settling down would be boring. I think you should prove to me I was wrong and show me how fun being engaged can really be." I wiggle my eyebrows at him and without missing a beat, he takes one of my nipples in his mouth, teasing it slowly until my breathing becomes ragged.

When he pulls away, he looks up at me through his lashes, his green eyes have a mischievous glint to them. "I'm not sure I'm the best person for the job. People always referred to me as boring. What do you think?"

His fingertips trail along my skin, down my stomach and slowly south, settling between my legs. When he begins to circle my clit with his fingers, I moan.

"I think you're rather fun," I reply breathlessly, "but I like the world thinking you're boring."

He pulls his hand away. "And why's that?"

"Because it means you're all mine."

"You don't have to worry about that." He moves his body over mine, then slides two fingers inside me, dipping them in and out, hitting the perfect spot. "I'm all yours anyway. I was the moment I first laid eyes on you. I just didn't realize it at the time."

He pulls his fingers out and his mouth finds mine at the same time he slips inside me. His thrusts quickly tip me over the edge, and I fall apart in the best kind of way.

He spends the rest of the morning showing me why my life is worth fighting for. He shows me that in those moments when I gave up the fight and thought I had no reason to live, I was wrong. I have him.

***

We're in the kitchen preparing for dinner in the same way we do every night, when there's a knock at the door. Becket and I both freeze, like we do each time we hear or see anything out of the norm.

I stand with the knife I'm holding hovering in the air, midway through slicing salad. My grip tightens on the handle.

"I'll be right back, don't worry," says Becket, placing a quick kiss on the top of my head.

I nod, but the way his skin has paled shows me he isn't as confident as he's making out. I also don't miss the fact that he doesn't put his knife down—he walks with it in his hand to the front door. We have security teams in place, but things still don't feel any easier.

I hold my breath when I hear the click of the lock, knowing Becket is going to be pushing the handle down and opening the door. Right. About. Now.

"Evan, hi?" I hear him say, his voice floating into the kitchen.

I let go of my knife and it clatters on the marble counter. I drag a shaky hand through my hair. Get it together Brit. He's not here. No one's seen or heard anything for months. He could be dead for all we know. God, I hope he's dead.

"Can I come in?" I hear Evan say. "I have a few things I need to go over."

"Sure."

The door closes and footsteps move through the entryway, getting closer to the kitchen. I'm greeted with the sight of two giants. Evan and Becket together could almost be intimidating if I didn't know them as I do.

"Hi, Evan," I say warmly. "It's great to see you, it's been a while."

"Thankfully," he replies. I know he doesn't mean anything by it.

"We're actually about to sit and eat," says Becket. "Feel free to join us."

Evan looks at me to check it's ok.

I nod. "We always make too much."

"Never enough more like," grunts Becket, the human trash can.

Between the three of us, we set the table. I smile to myself as we do. I never could have predicted I'd be standing in what is now my ginormous kitchen, with one of the most famous NFL players in the world and an FBI agent. It might be an obscure scenario, but despite what it's taken for us to get here, I wouldn't have it any other way.

We're settled at the table and I go to pass Evan the bowl of salad when my engagement ring sparkles in the light.

His eyes widen and he says, "Congratulations."

Becket and I look at each other and grin.

"Nobody knows yet," says Becket. "It only happened last night."

"It's great to see you getting your happy ending. You deserve it. I won't say a word." When we're done eating, Evan pushes his plate away. "That was amazing."

"So, what did you want to clear up with me?" asks Becket.

Evan clears his throat and grimaces. "It was actually Britney I came here to talk to."

I still and Becket frowns.

"Ok?" I say uncertainly.

"It's nothing bad," he says, smiling. "My admin picked up on something in your statement and I have to clear it up. Part of the process. Sorry."

"It's fine, just let me know how I can help."

"It's simple." Evan's phone starts ringing on the table. He looks down at it and mutters, "Sorry." He silences it. "In your statement there was something flagged up. I'm really sorry, Britney, I'm going to have to talk about part of it with you again. Is that, ok?"

I take a deep breath, my confidence wavering ever so slightly. "I'll answer whatever questions you have."

"So, I just need you to confirm something from the beginning, where you recollect first coming around. You used the word *they*. I just need you to confirm that I can change it."

Flashes of those first moments as I regained consciousness, and the voices I heard, flood my mind. I frown. "There's nothing to change."

Evan's brows draw together and he purses his lips. "What do you mean there's nothing to change?"

"The word *they* is right."

He shakes his head. "But you said there was only one person there."

I nod. "The rest of the time, yes. But there wasn't at that point. I heard two voices."

Evan shakes his head again, the line between his brow getting deeper. "You're sure?"

"Yes."

Becket frowns too and we both sit and watch Evan rub a hand across his tightly clenched jaw.

"It doesn't make sense," he says. His phone phone lights up on the table with a message and my eyes move down briefly, reading 'F' as the ID. "Excuse me a moment." He smiles tightly and picks up the phone. As he reads whatever is on the screen he visibly pales. Shaking his head he sets it on the table facedown but it instantly begins ringing. He picks it up and rejects it, only for it to start ringing again. He looks between me and Becket and says, "I'm sorry I'm going to have to take this."

Becket nods and we watch as Evan answers while walking away. He stands in the kitchen, listening intently, then begins pacing back and forth. At the same time the doorbell rings. Becket is too focused on Evan and trying to figure out what's going on to acknowledge it.

"I'll get that," I say. I walk to the front door and open it hesitantly. There's no one there.

I'm about to close it, when something white on the floor catches my attention. A single white lily, resting on top of a small white envelope. Shaking, I bend over to pick it up.

At the same time Evan's voice fills the whole house as he roars, "What do you mean she's gone? Find her!"

"Becket!" I shriek.

He comes charging through the entryway, his eyes bulging. "Brit?"

I look down at the envelope and white lily sitting in my hands.

He walks over and takes the envelope, muttering under his breath, "What the hell is going on?"

I watch as he opens it, frowning when he pulls out a small piece of paper. He reads it, blinks, and then the paper floats to the floor.

"What's wrong?" I ask quietly, not sure I really want to know.

He doesn't get a chance to answer, because Evan races through and looks at Becket. He grabs fists full of his hair, pulling at them. "It's Josie ... she's gone."

My eyes flicker down to the piece of paper on the floor, covered in blood stains. I can just about make out the words:

Fool me once, shame on you.
Fool me twice, shame on me.
Fool me thrice, shame on us both.

Epilogue

Josie

Finishing my shift at the local diner, I step outside, inhaling the warm evening air. If I'd known I was going to be finishing this late, I wouldn't have parked my car away from my usual spot. I know the security detail my brother had assigned to me is close by. They always are. But it still doesn't stop me from looking over my shoulder as I quickly walk along the sidewalk.

It's a relief when my car comes into view. When I get closer, I unlock it. A few steps and my hand is on the handle, about to open the door. I stop. A folded piece of white paper and a single lily underneath the window wiper catches my attention.

Not wanting to hang around outside on my own too long, I pick them up and quickly climb in the car, locking it. Discarding the lily on the passenger seat, my heart races as I slowly open the folded piece of paper. It's probably nothing, I tell myself. Please let it be nothing.

I focus on the chicken scrawl writing. I read it once, blink, then read it again. Then I hold my hand to my mouth trying to stifle a scream.

Freya,
What a beautiful name, it's a shame it's not your own.
Fool me once, shame on you. Fool me twice, shame on me. Fool me thrice, shame on us both.
There won't be a thrice.
Run, Josie, run.
This game is coming to an end and only one person can be the winner.

My heart hammers in my chest. What do I do? I don't want to run, I want to fight back. But I know if I stay I won't be the only one at risk. Becket's spent most of his life protecting us, now it's my turn.

Struggling to swallow over the lump in my throat, I pull out my phone and bring up Evan's number and blinking through the tears type out a message:

I'm sorry.

I hit send then shove the paper in my pocket, discarding the phone on the passenger seat. Before I have a chance to second guess myself, I grab my bag and clamber out of the car, disappearing into the night, quiet as a mouse, leaving Freya behind.

Acknowledgements

They say it takes a village to raise a child. Well, it takes an army to publish a book. For Fool Me Twice, I had the best army I could have asked for and this book wouldn't be what it is without each person involved.

My beta's. What a journey. Thank you for reading the shit version and helping to make it better. Babs – I don't know what I'd do without your expert eye. Kirsten – Your knowledge and understanding of writing has helped me become the writer I am. Kirsty – I'm sorry for sending you dirty sex scenes when you were at work and your honesty and love of books is the reason why I write. Cheryl – Your passion for this book and these characters helped me through some really difficult times and you pushed me to be better. Rachel – I think therapist might be a better title over beta. Your encouragement and support throughout have been invaluable.

A massive thank you to Black Quill editing for spending so much time on the manuscript and helping to make it beautiful. Slowly one manuscript at a time I think we might reduce my comma usage.

Sarah thank you yet again for casting your eagle eye over everything, and just for being my BFF and supporting me on this journey.

Peter and Mum, two of my biggest supporters. The ones who have stuck by and watched when I've worked all hours to get this book finished for the world. You are my inspiration.

My babies, I hope one day you look at what I've achieved and believe that you can do or be anything you want. You just have to believe. Oh, and work really fucking hard.

A special thank you to Bex, to whom this book is dedicated. If you hadn't pushed me, this book would have been its crappy first draft. You helped me to believe that I could write something different. I'm not sure this is quite what you had in mind but hey ho!

Finally, thank you to my readers, your support means the world.

Fool Me Thrice

Run, Josie, Run.
Those were the words he wrote to me and that's
exactly what I did.
I thought I'd gotten away with it, I thought I'd fooled
him thrice.
I should have known better.
This game of Cat and Mouse is coming to an end and
only one person can be the winner.
I'm determined to make sure it's me.

Books by
Lizzie Morton:

Always Series:

Always You
Always Us
Always

Fool Me Series:

Fool Me Once
Fool Me Twice
Fool Me Thrice

Always You

Six years ago Jake Ross, lead guitarist of SCARAB broke my heart. Scrap that, he smashed it into a million unrecognizable pieces and left me to clean up the mess.

Now, I'm back in Brooklyn with one goal: avoid him at all costs. Unfortunately fate has other ideas.

The photography career I worked my ass off for and my hot-shot quarterback boyfriend both become irrelevant. The only thing on my mind is 'what if'.

My wild friends and crazy family agree I should steer clear of him. But when Jake's career becomes entangled with my own, avoidance is impossible. When we're together it's heart-stopping, gut-wrenching, the kind of love that songs are written about.

It was only supposed to be one summer, but I'm left questioning if everything I believed about our past is wrong and what I thought was the end of our journey was only the beginning.

The heart wants it wants, but sometimes in life happily ever afters don't come easily, and ours might prove impossible.

Always Us

How do you mend a broken heart? If anyone has the answer let me know.

It's been two years since I chose to turn my back on the one that got away. I thought I was doing the best for both of us. Instead, I'm fighting to forget what it felt like being in his arms.

Now it's another summer, and this time, I'm surrounded by Rock Gods on Jake's European tour. It's the life most would dream of, but things are never that straight forward and a chance meeting with a stranger leaves me feeling torn.

Just when I think things can't get any worse, I'm faced with one of the biggest decisions I'll ever have to make.

They say the heart wants what it wants, but my heart wants two people at the same time.

Always

My life's about to change and I can't decide if it's for better or worse.

The one person I want, the one I need, doesn't want me back. I'm left wondering if the path I'm about to take, will be one I'll walk alone.

Then the person I least expect gives me exactly what I need. A break from reality. But there's only so long I can hide and when the truth comes out, it's explosive.

I always thought it was fate, that Jake and I would find our way back to each other.

They say what will be, will be. But what if we were never meant to be together?

Printed in Great Britain
by Amazon